PRAISE FOR THE NOVELS OF
# TIM McGUIRE

"*Danger Ridge* belongs on any list of frontier classics."
—Loren D. Estleman

"For those who like action in their Westerns, Tim McGuire's first novel has plenty of it, from start to finish."
—Elmer Kelton

"*Danger Ridge* is one of the best Westerns I've read in years."
—Jack Ballas

"*Nobility* is fast-paced and action-packed. Read it—the Rainmaker will latch right onto you."
—Robert J. Conley

# TEXAS GOLD

## TIM MCGUIRE

BERKLEY BOOKS, NEW YORK

This is a work of fiction. Names, characters, places, and incidents either are the product of the author's imagination or are used fictitiously, and any resemblance to actual persons, living or dead, business establishments, events, or locales is entirely coincidental.

TEXAS GOLD

A Berkley Book / published by arrangement with
the author

PRINTING HISTORY
Berkley edition / August 2004

ISBN: 0-425-19743-3

BERKLEY®
Berkley Books are published by The Berkley Publishing Group, a division of Penguin Group (USA) Inc., 375 Hudson Street, New York, New York 10014. BERKLEY and the "B" design are trademarks belonging to Penguin Group (USA) Inc.

PRINTED IN THE UNITED STATES OF AMERICA

10  9  8  7  6  5  4  3  2  1

For the women who wanted me to write this and forced me to make it more than I intended;

*You all know who you are*

# ACKNOWLEDGMENTS

Many thanks to North Fort Worth Historical Society for their patience with my many questions. A toast of appreciation to the proprietors of the White Elephant Saloon for the education and tour. And as always, special gratitude to the DFW Writers' Workshop for their guidance.

# 1

THERE WASN'T MUCH time left. Once on the boardwalk and in front of the barred windows, a quick wrap of knuckles on the wooden door soon had it opened.

"Back so soon, Les?" Sheriff Norville Tibbits asked while peeking under the cloth cover of the tray. He sniffed the gravy-soaked beef and roasted potatoes. "Seems a shame to waste this on him." Tibbits stepped aside to allow the last meal of the condemned to be served.

Les walked through the office, careful of each step so as not spill any of the meal or reveal all on the tray. Tibbits soon unlocked the barred hallway door. The rattle of keys brought the prisoner out of his bunk.

"Back up, you," ordered the sheriff as he unlocked the cell door. The prisoner complied and sat on the bunk. "This is all you're going to get. Never seen a man who could eat as big a breakfast and now a dinner in such a short time. But don't let it ever be said that the folks in Abilene, Kansas, ain't neighborly when it comes to hanging fellers." He opened the cell door and motioned Les to enter.

The prisoner stared into Les's eyes as the tray was gently placed on the floor. He raised his eyebrows. Les nodded slightly so as not to draw the lawman's attention.

"There you go. You better enjoy it. It'll be sundown before long," said Tibbits as Les stepped from the cell. "I guess I ought to tell Clyde to tie another knot as heavy as you're going to be, Sandy. Wouldn't want there to be no mistakes." He chuckled and locked the door. While standing behind the sheriff, Les knew the time had come and collapsed to the floor.

Tibbits faced around. "What happened to you?"

"My ankle. I must have turned on it wrong."

"Let me see." Tibbits knelt to get a closer look. Each gentle touch of the leg and even the shoe produced a wail of agony. "Can you walk? Or maybe limp a little?"

"No. It hurts awful bad."

"Here, let me help you up," Tibbits held out his hand. Unable to refuse the offer without arousing suspicion, Les gripped the sheriff's hand, but without any effort in the legs, remained on the floor whining in pain despite the big man's tugs.

"Well, then," the sheriff said with concern as he looked to the prisoner and the locked cell door. "I'd carry you to a chair, but my back is likely to give out. I guess I could go get Doc Carter to come over here to have a look at it." He rose stiffly and pointed at the prisoner. "Now you stay away from him as far as you can get," he told Les. "I don't cotton to leavin' children with outlaws, but I guess I got no choice. I'll be back as quick as I can with the doc."

Les nodded. Tibbits scurried out of the hall. The slam of the front door echoed.

"Pretty smart, kid," said Sandy.

Les stood. "We ain't got much time. Hurry up."

Sandy bent over the tray. "Did you bring it?"

"Yeah. Thought Miss Maggie would switch my hide just for touching the bottle."

Sandy lifted the cover. "I don't see it."

"I couldn't bring it out in the open. Look in the coffee cup."

Sandy picked up the cup and after examining it, lifted the lip of the small coffee-filled saucer that rested on the rim. When the prisoner waved his nose over it, Les knew he'd discovered the smell of the whiskey.

"You are a smart kid," said Sandy, swigging the whiskey in one gulp.

"Hurry up. He'll be back any minute. Are you going to tell me or not?"

As Sandy wheezed through his teeth, a smile came across his face. "Been thinking about it. Maybe I ought not tell you for your own good."

Les's heart pounded. "You said this morning, if I was to bring you some whiskey, you'd tell me where there was a heap of gold. Now, I brought you the whiskey. I risked a switching by Miss Maggie when she saw me pouring it, but I told her it was on account you had a bad cough. So she let me take what I gave you. I did my part. Tell me where it is, or . . ."

"Or what? What are you going to do? Tell the sheriff? Hell, you heard him. They're going to string me up in a couple of hours. It don't get much worse than that." Sandy leaned his head back and held the cup straight over his mouth to enjoy the last drops. Once the final drop fell between his gaping jaws, he smacked his lips, savoring the taste. He raised an eyebrow at Les. "I ain't the only one that knows where it's hid. It may not be there no more."

"But you said you were the only one that knew."

"I needed a drink." He huffed out a breath. "Look, I done some pretty lousy things in my days. I even took a man's life over a bad deal of the cards. It's what got me in here. But one thing I ain't done yet is get someone as young as yourself killed. Even if it's still there, there's some tough hombres who would be hunting it too. If they knew you were looking for it, they'd kill you as quick as they would a fly."

"That don't worry me."

"Then it oughta." He looked at the cup. "But you did get me that drink, and I guess I'm beholden to you for that." He looked at Les. "It's in Texas."

"Texas? Where?" asked Les, anxiously looking into the front office.

"About fifty miles south of Fort Worth." Sandy looked to the floor. "It's been there near four years since our *brave* President Davis scampered off toward Mexico with his tail between his legs. Before he could re-spark a new Confederacy, he needed money to rekindle the ideal." Sandy paused to shake the cup over his palm, but the skin remained dry. "So he sent the last shipment of gold bars he had, melted down from the final donations of rings, watch chains, ladies' necklaces, and the sort given to the cause. It weren't much, just a single trunkful. But it's probably worth the effort. I'd say there's at least fifty thousand dollars in that box."

With the one answer yet to be known, the creak of the door seized Les's tongue. A wry smile creased Sandy's lips. Another second and the answer could be given, but Les only got the smile. A deep breath later, the feigned pose of injury was resumed.

"Thank the Lord," Tibbits said, rounding the corner into the hall. "I wouldn't have slept again if anything had happened to that child."

Doc Carter knelt next to Les and touched the ankle and leg.

"Does that hurt?"

"It feels a mite better. Maybe if stand up, I can limp around on it."

Once on two feet, Les lifted the left foot and hopped out of the hall, peering over a shoulder at Sandy leaning against the bars. "You be careful out there, kid," Sandy said.

"Hush your mouth," Tibbits ordered. "The fool don't even have a right mind. Been blabbing nothing but nonsense since he's been in here."

Once out of the hall, Les limped into the chair. "Are you still going to hang him, Sheriff?"

Tibbits removed his pocket watch. "Not for another hour at least. But don't let that trouble you. You worry about that leg of yours."

Doc Carter held the ankle with both palms. "Don't seem like it's broke. I think you'll be fine as long as you keep weight off it for a couple of days."

He helped Les from the chair, allowing his shoulder to be used as a crutch until they left the sheriff's office. Out on the boardwalk, Les squinted at the western sun. Although the walk to the boardinghouse was an easy one, the lie would have to continue through the traffic and across the street. He guided Les through the maze of shoulders and legs to the front of Miss Maggie's boardinghouse. A polite nod to the doc, and Les turned the knob.

"I thank you for your help."

"Sure you can make it inside?"

"Oh, yes, I'm sure."

The doc released his hold on the arm. "You get right up to bed. Rest that leg."

"I will, sir." A twist of the knob, and with three hops around the door it was quietly shut. A sigh later, both feet were firmly on the wooden floor.

"Les? Is that you?" asked Miss Maggie from the parlor.

"Yes'um. It is."

"Did that filth of a man drink the liquor first?" she asked with folded arms. Les nodded. "I shouldn't have let you take it to him. Cough or no, a man should have a clear head when about to meet his maker." Her pious tone changed as she stared at Les. "You all right? You look a little pale yourself."

"I'm fine. It's just that I wish they weren't going to hang him. I've kind of took a liking to him."

Miss Maggie came near and wrapped a comforting arm around Les. "Don't fret over that awful man. If it weren't the Lord's will to be kind to fellow Christians, even those that lie, steal, and kill, then I'd never let you go over there. Don't let him play any of the devil's tricks with your mind. He's a low-down scoundrel deserving of what's coming to him." She squeezed a little more. "There now. It will be over very soon. Then we can all get back to doing what we were before all this."

Les cringed inside at her words. Although a small bond had grown, Sandy Wallace was going to hang and nothing would stop it. The secret to a life without sweeping, mopping, and washing would be gone with him. With head down, the young one nodded and left the loving arms of Miss Maggie. Up the stairs and into the first room on the right, Les found the confines that had been the only sanctuary since arriving eight years ago.

Memories came to mind, none of them fond. Barely able to be recalled, the visions of a place called New York consisted of tall roofs, men in tall hats with angry stares, the bonneted ladies turning their eyes away and shaking their heads. If you didn't have a ma or pa, you had to become used to it.

Snow piles were stacked against the walls of buildings to keep the streets clear. It didn't warm up until spring, wrapping a frigid grip on the halls and the rooms. The two constant memories of the East were shivering and the hunger.

The long cold journey to the West lasted for what seemed half a lifetime. When the train finally stopped, more men and women stared at them in the same way too, but not for the same reason. These people looked for kids of their own to raise. Some were chosen to replace ones dead of disease. Others, especially boys, were picked like livestock to work the soil and help on farms.

Les was lucky. Miss Maggie's bright and warm smile looked like a candle in the night. Upon laying eyes on it, Les headed to it like a moth. However, there were chores waiting. At first, it wasn't bad, but as life passed by the front windows and down the street to the saloons, sweeping floors lost its appeal. Miss Maggie didn't let saddle tramps or trail hands in the house, so it was always a wonder what went on at the far side of the tracks.

Loud voices below woke Les from the dream. A glance to the window showed the dusk light against the hotel's tired gray boards. A rush to the sill revealed the mob gathering in the street for the spectacle. It wouldn't be fitting to view from so far, so Les snuck down the stairs. The aroma of pot roast filled the parlor. Miss Maggie's supper was prompt at six o'clock, but the table wasn't set. There could be time.

Out the front door, Les knifed through the crowd. Men with small children on their shoulders made sure the lesson of what happened to the lawless would be seen. Most of the women gathered off to the side in an attempt to see without being seen. Some likely would argue the event not suitable for ladies to observe. Les had reached the front ring of spectators encircling the gallows. A slow look upward showed the condemned already on the platform.

Sheriff Tibbits came to the front and removed a paper from his vest pocket along with his spectacles. Once he propped the rims on his nose, he held the paper near the lantern hung from one of the posts.

"Sanford Howard Wallace, you have been found guilty of the cold-blooded murder of Jacob Tyson on March fourth of this year, by a jury of your peers, and have been sentenced by said jury to be hung by the neck until dead on this day, August fifteenth, in the year of our lord 1869. I, as a duly sworn law officer of the county, am hereby to comply with the order of the circuit court and carry out the sentence. Have you any last words?"

The silence of Sandy's stare hushed the crowd. Once all was quiet, he dipped his eyes for only a moment while grunting his throat clear. "I'm truly sorry for what I done. If I hadn't been drunk, I don't think I would have done it, even though the man I killed pulled four straight flushes and everybody knows that ain't possible. Still, I shouldn't have shot a bullet in him for every flush he pulled. That wasn't right of me, and I'm thankful he didn't have no kin here to mourn him. My only other regret is leaving my own kin behind in Arkansas to come to this place, which is too far for them to come and mourn me. That's all I wish I could have at this time." He turned to Tibbits and nodded.

The sheriff approached with a black sack. His usual giddy manner over the notion of the act absent, he stretched the opening and lifted it above the prisoner's head. "I don't want that," Sandy said.

"Hell, it ain't for you to say. There's women and kids down there. We can't have your tongue popping out."

Sandy looked down, his stare penetrating into Les. "The house of San Ramon. Find it." He blinked only twice, his eyes darting to the crowd and seeming to fix on one spot. "And you better hurry."

That said, Tibbits pushed the hood over Sandy's head, then motioned to the black-coated executioner. "Clyde, you heard him. Let's make this quick." The man quickly slipped the noose around Sandy's neck while Reverend Baker opened his Bible. A slight nudge in the back had Sandy move forward a half step.

"The Lord is my shepherd. I shall not want."

Tibbits nodded and the lever was thrown. Half of the platform swung down. The body dropped just as the sack of flour had in the morning. With the sudden halt, a loud snap pierced the air, quickly followed by the ripple of groans and the sounds of awe of the crowd. The body dangled at the rope's end, slightly swaying side to side, the legs twitching until finally coming to a stop like a spun spoke of a wheel. After the sentence had been served in full, Tibbits extended his hand to the black-coated man. "Nice job as always, Clyde."

With the show over, the crowd dispersed, some with looks of regret for coming, others with unsatisfied disappointment. Les, having witnessed death for the first time, inhaled deeply, replacing the air the horrible sight had stolen, and returned to the boardinghouse. The table was now set and supper would soon be served. Just as in the afternoon, the same slow climb up the stairs led to the safety of the first room on the right. Miss Maggie always inspected for clean hands at her table, so Les went to the basin. While pouring the water, the mirror on the wall reflected a different image. With concentration, a figure appeared in the glass that wasn't in the room.

Sandy's last words were haunting. If he had truly

thought the idea dangerous, then why would he have stared so long and uttered the location? And his final warning to hurry couldn't be ignored. Texas was full of cowhands, or so it had been said by everyone. Two days prior, a herd of longhorns had been led down the street to the pens on the other side of the tracks. If one was to make the journey, the simplest way would be to return with those drovers. However, they might not accept the company of a weakling.

Grabbing hair and extending it out to the shoulder, Les folded it until it rested above the ear. A glance at the smooth cheeks convinced Les that they needed smudges of dirt to appear more like those of someone used to the life on the frontier. However, the biggest problem remained in the bottom of the mirror. An arm pressed against the chest wouldn't conceal the change to adolescence.

Miss Maggie's shrill voice broke through the daydream. "Les? Leslie Mavis Turnbow, you get down here right now. You are late for my supper, young lady."

# 2

THE FOGHORN OF the *Robert E. Lee* sounded the hour of nine. The night waters of the Mississippi were calm enough not to spill a drop of Rance Cash's Kentucky bourbon. He took his eyes off the glass to concentrate on his opponents. What began as a gentlemanly game of cards between six players dwindled to three in a contest of wills.

To the left sat Bertrum Lackey, trader of cotton and corn and formerly of slaves along the river. At more than fifty years of age, his experience in business made him a wealthy man. Two years prior to the division of North and South, the rumor said that Lackey sold his entire stock in all commodities and gone abroad to avoid the coming hardship and confiscation of his assets for the cause. Wise investments in the companies making arms for the both sides made for an inventory of cash. Once civility returned after the Civil War, so did he resume the life of a Southerner. Life had taught him not to choose sides unless he would come out ahead in the end.

Across the table sat a more formidable opponent. Colton Schuyler was one who played for pride. If the stakes were matchsticks rather than a thousand dollars, his grimace wouldn't change. His background was shrouded in legend blacker than his slick hair and goatee. Some thought he a professional gambler, starting with the mining camps in the East. As he gained a reputation as unbeatable at poker, he drew challengers from those risking near fortunes just for the honor of playing. Others said he was a gunman. One who killed for hire, normally employed by men seeking a higher station and either needing rivals eliminated or witnesses to their past silenced. He hated to lose, and especially to a kid not yet thirty years old.

The garter-sleeved dealer finished the shuffle and placed the deck in the center of the table. "It is now Mr. Schuyler's choice of play."

Schuyler cut the deck all the while staring Rance in the eye. His voice was calm and cold. "Five cards. Stud poker."

Rance nodded, flashing a bit of his smile in salutation of the choice so as not to show any apprehension. Schuyler remained stern-faced. Rance knew there was little doubt about the reason. Newcomers to any new territory weren't welcome to stay. All that was desired from them was to leave their money on the way out. It was no different at a card table. Since joining the game, Rance had collected almost twelve hundred dollars more than when he arrived, mostly from the players long departed. He was even with Schuyler and just ahead of Lackey. However, there was a question of pride, a tension in the air as to who owned these hunting grounds.

Rance was just passing through and wanted no part of overthrowing a king. Nevertheless, Schuyler had a reputation to maintain. If he didn't emerge as the clear winner, then maybe fewer players would journey so far to play him when the *Robert E. Lee* returned to New Orleans. It was evident Schuyler meant to break Rance on this hand, in one play, and he chose the one game capable of doing it.

The dealer flung a single card facedown to each man in rotation to the left. A bevy of spectators, men in tailored coats and top hats, women in long gowns, crowded the table with eager interest. Some players broken from previous action watched for a lesson for their next game. The ladies on their arms appeared more attentive to who would claim all the winnings, no doubt hoping to become that lucky soul's new companion.

With each player's hole card in place, the dealer flipped the three of diamonds to Lackey. Next, he slid the jack of clubs to Schuyler. Last, he tossed the three of hearts to Rance, who curled the edge of his hole card just enough to see the ten of diamonds.

"Mr. Schuyler, you have the option," the dealer announced.

Schuyler looked at his hole card and picked up two green chips and placed them in the center of the table. "I'll open at two hundred dollars."

Rance casually threw two green chips into the pot. "I'll call." Lackey did the same without hesitation. The dealer dealt each player a third card. Schuyler drew the four of spades, Rance the five of clubs, Lackey the two of diamonds. The dealer looked to Rance.

"Mr. Cash, you're high with five."

A quick glance was all that was needed to sum up the play. Lackey had the best hand with a possible straight flush. Schuyler held cards in different suits with no straight possible. It was the frustration and attraction to the game all playing at once.

Rance concluded his evaluation just as a young brunette in curled locks and an off-the-shoulder dress leaned closer for a better view of the game, providing him with an eyeful of her cleavage. Whether by accident or plan, he was allowed to see just enough to keep him looking, perhaps leading him to a greater disaster, too intrigued by what he saw and desiring to gaze upon what was as yet out of sight. Indeed, it was a man's game in all respects.

"Mr. Cash?" the dealer repeated. "It is to you."

His attention to the game resumed, he picked up a yellow chip. "Five hundred." A mild sound of awe went

through the crowd. Rance reached in his coat and removed
a cheroot, rolling the end between his lips. As he saw
Lackey call the bet, he couldn't help notice the brunette
noticing him. He bit off the tip of the smoke. She rolled her
tongue along her upper lip, then winked. When he struck a
match against his heel to light the end, she fanned air in
front of her face and moaned.

"I'll see five hundred. And raise one thousand."

Schuyler's voice turned Rance's head in time to see a
black chip thrown into the pot. He took a puff to give him
time to survey the table. The hands were the same, but to
get another card and stay in the game, it would cost him
one of his remaining three black chips. Yet to turn tail and
leave the game wouldn't gain him any respect, and would
leave hard-earned winnings behind. He grinned, accepting
this spider's invitation into the web.

"I'll see your thousand." He matched glares with
Schuyler, doing his best not to show fear, although his
heart was pumping enough blood through his veins to turn
his cheeks as red as a rose. The play had reached a point
where there was no backing off.

Lackey paused before tossing a black chip into the pot.
"Seems you boys have more than what you're showing."
He turned to Rance. "If I didn't know better, I'd think you
two were trying to set me up like one of those cattle drivers
in those cow towns in the West."

While the dealer distributed a fourth card to all, Rance
watched as he considered Lackey's remark. The four of
hearts slid in front of Rance, the queen of spades to
Lackey, and the nine of diamonds to Schuyler. The dealer
pointed his finger at Lackey.

With the arrival of the spade, Lackey's possible flush
and straight were gone. Now the only hope was to build
pairs or three of a kind. Schuyler's hand kept getting worse
with three different cards in three suits. Yet it didn't appear
to deter his steely expression. Rance blinked at his own
hand. His had more potential, but lacked what he needed in
the hole.

"Let's make it interesting. I'll raise five hundred," said Lackey as he nudged a yellow chip to the pot.

Rance recognized the play. "I'm curious, what did you mean about the cow towns of the West?" He sipped the liquor while waiting for his answer from Lackey and watching Schuyler.

"Every summer, Texas cattlemen drive their herds to the railheads now in Kansas. Most of the men are really boys, away from their homes for the first time with more money than they ever had in all their lives."

"I'll see the five hundred," Schuyler announced without paying attention to the conversation. "And raise another thousand."

Rance drew on the cigar for time. It was now fifteen hundred dollars to him. Not wanting to show concern for the high stakes, he glanced at Lackey. "And so?"

At first puzzled at Rance's question while faced with such a major decision, Lackey continued. "Well, once those boys find themselves surrounded by so many venues to spend their wages, be it the numerous saloons, several haberdasheries in order to shed their soiled clothes for new ones, and of course the innumerable brothels to. . ." He paused while scanning the surrounding ladies of social distinction. "Well, let us say that they're restless while waiting for a bed to open up, so to speak."

Rance grinned at the inference. Wanting to hear more, he placed the cheroot in an ashtray, then picked up two black chips. "I'll call the fifteen hundred and raise five hundred." The move was in part to test Lackey's resolve to stay in the game. If the Southerner had a competitive hand, two thousand dollars more was not too much to scare him off, but if he didn't have another card of value, he wasn't one to bluff his way through the play. The other part was simple. Schuyler needed to be shown he couldn't bluff either.

Lackey smirked. "I'm afraid I've always prided myself on exploiting sound ventures. I must admit, this is not one of them. I'll fold." He leaned back in his chair with what could be perceived as relief from the contest and beguiled attraction as to the outcome.

Rance didn't want to allow all the attention to rest with the game. "So, these cowboys, what is it they do to bide their time?"

"I'll call," Schuyler said, matching the bet.

While the dealer snapped out the cards, Rance rolled his wrist to keep Lackey to the subject.

"They find a friendly game of dice, or faro, or—"

The jack of spades joined Schuyler's hand. The deuce of clubs came to Rance. "Go on," he said while contemplating his options. It was better to seem distracted while Schuyler checked his hole card. With only twin jacks the hand was little threat. While Rance concentrated on Lackey's yarn, he kept an eye on Schuyler's fumbling with the facedown card.

"Or they find a poker game. Normally the first time they ever played. But with three months pay burning holes in their pockets while waiting to get upstairs, they drink up the courage to take a chance."

Rance chuckled. "The first time, huh?" He picked up his cigar and noticed the end had gone cold. "But they still play?" he asked while reaching in his vest pocket for a match with his right fore and middle finger. He passed the match to his left hand with a fluid motion to check his own hole card with his right, shielding the card with his aligned fingers. Confident he now held an upper hand, he listened to Lackey and struck the match.

"Oh, my, yes. And play until they lose everything. Some do have tempers, and almost all carry pistols, but if a careful player can balance all that, then he'll have thirty drunk cowboys with a hundred dollars apiece in their pocket every week for the entire summer. They even let you deal the cards."

Rance again chuckled, until Schuyler bet. "I'll bet eight hundred and fifty dollars."

It didn't escape Rance's notice that that was all the

chips Rance had in front of him. It wasn't sporting if one
player simply bet more than his opponents. Schuyler had
ample chips to do so, but it was a manly dare to challenge
another player to bet his all. However, Rance was prepared
for the risk. He shoved the remaining chips to the center.
"Call."

Schuyler flipped his hole card with a sheepish grin.
"Three jacks."

Rance stared at the jack of hearts, which matched the
other two. The three of a kind didn't surprise him, and
whether the third was always there or recently installed
once the second showed up it really didn't matter. It was
there now. Rance took another long puff, then put the cigar
in the ashtray and with his right hand revealed his ace in
the hole.

"Five clubs, four hearts, three hearts, two clubs, and an-
chored by ace of spades. Straight." Applause from the
spectators greeted the play. With the superior hand, Rance
strained to withhold his own sheepish grin as Schuyler's
disappeared as fast as snowball in a bonfire. Without gloat-
ing, Rance smiled at the result while encircling his arms
around the pot and dragging it in front of him. Matching
colors, he quickly stacked the chips and counted the take.

"Eleven thousand three hundred," he said as he shoved
the stacks to the amazed dealer. "Not too many large bills,
please." Rance turned to Lackey. "So you say this goes on
for the whole summer?"

Lackey nodded. "Of course, and is likely to as long as
the trains continue to haul cattle. However, I must say, I
don't know why you would want to travel to such a desolate place as Kansas. There's nothing there but dust and Indians. Seems to me you're doing just fine here surrounded
by the luxury of the *Robert E. Lee.*"

As the dealer slapped the stacks of greenbacks on the
table, Rance picked them up and swigged the rest of his
drink while thinking of the fortune in his hand, and reflect-
ing on the fortunate need for a match in his vest to light his
cigar. "Sometimes you've got to stay ahead of your luck."

Schuyler slowly and deliberately drew a Remington pistol from a holster inside his coat and aimed it at Rance. Shrieks from the surrounding women pierced the air as their men receded quickly from the table. All three players and the dealer remained seated. The slick-haired pistoleer faced the dealer. "Count the cards."

The dealer forced his trembling fingers to turn over Lackey's hole card to find the eight of clubs.

"I see your reputation is earned," Rance said to Schuyler, who nodded.

"We'll see about yours, Mr. Cash."

"Colton, there's no need for gunplay," Lackey said.

"Shut up. It's my money I'm worried about. You can recover yours in what manner you wish. There's no way he had that hand."

Rance casually sat while watching the dealer retrieve Lackey's cards. "Well, there's only one way to know," said Rance, scooping up the cards in front of him and handing them to the dealer. He settled back in his chair, brushing his right hand over the pocket where his own pepperbox pistol was hidden. However, with a barrel trained at his head, it was a fool's play to try and beat Schuyler with a gun. Wits were a better weapon. "I find it curious, Mr. Schuyler," he started as the dealer dealt the cards in four neat columns according to suit. "How are you certain I couldn't have had the hand?"

The question hung in the air as the dealer finished his count. "Fifty-two cards. All of them are here."

The announcement opened Schuyler's eyes wide. "The ten of diamonds?" The dealer pulled the card from the column and held it up for all to see.

"There's only one way for you to be so certain about which cards I had, Mr. Schuyler." Rance stopped short of accusing him of marking cards, but the point was made for even the simplest mind. And the gunman knew it, but he didn't lower his pistol.

"I don't know how you did it, Mr. Cash. But I'm going to make certain you won't do it again. Not on this boat. Not

on this river. I want you off this boat at the next port. If not
by your own means, then by mine. You follow what I'm
saying?"

Rance rose from the chair, slowly tucking the cash in
his coat pocket. He extended his hand to Lackey, who accepted it. "It was a pleasure to meet your acquaintance, sir.
I wish I could say that about all those at the table. In light
of the present animosity, I'll speak to the captain to pro-
cure a boat for the shore." He tipped his hat to the ladies,
thumbed a one-hundred-dollar bill to the dealer, and left
the gambling parlor.

Once on the portico, he strode on the way to his cabin.
Unable to resist, he pulled the wad of winnings from his
pocket and thumbed through the bills. Never had he held
such a fortune.

"Mr. Cash?" a feminine voice called. He froze for an instant, then slowly faced around to see the curled-haired
brunette standing alone thirty feet behind. She scurried to
come next to his side. "I wanted to tell you how much I admire your skills at cards."

He tipped his hat. "Why, thank you, ma'am."

"Miss," she uttered quickly. "Miss Rosemary Tuggle.
From Pittsburgh."

Swayed by her attractive features, he flashed his gleam.
"I'm so very glad to meet you, Miss Tuggle." After the
two stood on the wooden deck staring at each other for
nearly a minute, Rance felt compelled to speak. "Can I be
of service?"

She fanned her face. "Since you asked, yes, but I wish to
be in more discreet surroundings. Is your cabin nearby?"

It was normally an indecent proposal, but Rance was
too intrigued to refuse and politely held his arm out, which
she took. Not a word was said the short distance around the
corner and up the small flight of stairs to his cabin door. He
unlocked the door and opened it, extending his palm for
the lady to enter. He followed her in, and shut the door behind him.

"Now, what can I do for you?"

She faced about to him, gently but firmly placing both her lace-knit gloves to his cheeks, and kissed him in more than a sisterly manner on the lips. "I want you to take me. Now and forever, where you go."

"Miss Tuggle," he replied with some shock. "Pardon me, but what about the man you were with in the parlor?"

She kissed him again. "He's of no matter to me. Did you look at him? He doesn't have the . . ." She darted her eyes down to Rance's trousers. "Distinguishing presence of a man like you."

He gladly accepted another of her kisses, realizing the presence she was truly enamored with was likely the money in his pocket rather than any of his anatomy. He put his hands on her shoulders to stop her kisses. "Miss Tuggle. I am in great admiration of your beauty. But I am going west. A flower as delicate as yourself would find the harsh conditions unbearable. I'm afraid when I travel, I do so alone."

She leaned close, kissed his lips once more, then whispered to his ear in a breathy voice, "I will do anything you ask." She took a step back, slid the dress from her shoulders, and pushed it to the floor. The bodice and petticoat thinly veiled the contours of her femininity.

He sighed at the temptation. It was an impossible offer to accept, but one hard to ignore. However, since the night was young, he decided to play the hand as dealt and removed his coat, taking her into his firm embrace. During their kiss, it struck him that when the stakes were high, it was better to bluff to stay in the game. If the risk became too great, he could always fold later.

Les found it hard to keep her mind on the dishes in the scrub bucket. Although Miss Maggie's supper was enjoyed by Mr. Horace Willingham, who bought cattle for people in Pennsylvania, and Mrs. Tyrone F. Harman and her daughter Penelope, who waited for the train west to join Mr. Harman on the new rail line in California, Les found the meal less than tasty. Her appetite had been lost with the snap of Sandy Wallace's neck.

Nearly six weeks of her life had been spent tending to the hunger of the now-dead murderer. Sandy never seemed the criminal type, not as far as Les determined. It was her first experience witnessing the behavior of condemned men, and as far she could tell, Sandy had seemed a Christian remorseful for his crime.

However sad for old Sandy, what kept her attention from cleaning the dishes to the usual sparkle were his last words to her. Texas was a far-off place for a girl of sixteen. Even Penelope traveled with the safety of her mother on a warm train, and she confessed to being near eighteen. Les couldn't wait two years, nor did she have a mother to escort her. Miss Maggie had grown roots in this town, and would only scold a sermon full of reasons why the notion was so foolish.

Still, there was no getting it out of her head. With fifty thousand dollars she wouldn't have to scrub one more dish. She could buy fancy clothes like those of Hannah Pinkel, who always made it a point to be late for Sunday service just to stroll down the aisle in front of the congregation to show off her latest dress from someplace north called Chicago.

"Les?" Miss Maggie's voice could send a greater shiver through the skin than a winter's morning. "Did you put out the fresh linen in Mr. Willingham's room?"

"Yes'um." Les kept her nose to swiping the dishes as fast as her arm could move in the fearful realization that all but one were still in the bucket an hour after supper.

"Remember to sweep out the hallway."

"Already done it." Another plate came dripping from the bucket.

"Well, good. Then after you're done, it'll be time for you to get to bed."

Les took in a long breath. "Yes'um."

"What's wrong, dear? You still aren't fretting over that terrible man, are you?" Les felt a hand on her shoulder encouraging her to turn, but stayed firm in her stance so as not to show only three plates in the stack.

"No. I'm just a little tired. That's all."

"Well, now," Miss Maggie said, wrapping a consoling arm around Les's shoulder. "Why don't you go get into bed. I can do the rest of these."

With eyes wide in panic, Les huddled her shoulders around the bucket in attempt to shield it from Miss Maggie. "No. Really, I'm fine."

The arm fell away. "Young lady, I want to get to bed sometime tonight too. At the rate you're cleaning those plates, you'll be here until sunrise, and I'm not leaving a child alone downstairs. Now here, give me the rag and you get your little body under the covers and get a good night's rest."

Discouraged at the discovery, Les reluctantly surrendered the rag and apron and turned for the stairs. When she went by the front door, she paused in thought of what it would take to step through it without plans of returning. A heavy sigh later, she relented to the reality of how unlikely that was to occur. Again up the stairs and into the first room on the right, she fell back onto the bed.

The stars sparkled through the window in the clear night sky. Visions of Texas cascaded in her mind. All she'd ever heard of the place was how big it was. There were always tales the cowhands told of how it took a month to ride from one border to another. If it were true, the rest of the summer would be needed just to get to the boundary line, and the whole winter to find the house of Ramon that Sandy had mentioned. And where was it? She exhaled a long breath at the frustration of not knowing.

Still, it would be a wonderful place to see. Green grass rolling over hills to the very edge of the horizon. Pastures filled with cattle fat from grazing all spring. By the time they would be driven to market, a hefty price of forty dollars a head could be fetched for the entire herd. Then there would be a house. A glorious house painted white with three floors. Four or maybe five pillars standing across the front porch supported the spacious balcony above where children played.

She would be sitting on the swing in a white dress watching her husband arrive in a single-horse surrey. He would be in his Sunday best, wearing a tall hat like Mr. Conrad Pinkel wore, and a vest shimmering in gold. He would jump from the surrey and skip through the white gate as he made his way to the house. He would charge up the ten steps to sweep her into his arms. Around and around he would spin her, sunlight glaring into her eyes, then blue sky. The more she spun, the more dazed she became.

Les woke shaking her head. Taking a firm grip of the mattress, she found herself under the covers still wearing the blouse and skirt. Yet her dream was so real she still felt a mite dizzy.

Her attention was drawn to the window. It was no use trying to put her mind to other concerns so as to get back to sleep. She threw off the blanket and went to it. Lanterns on the street glimmered in the distance. The first thing she had to know was where exactly was Texas and how could she get there. The answer was on the far side of the tracks.

She went to her dresser, brushed her hair, swept the wrinkles from the skirt and blouse, tied on her shoes, and crept from her room into the hall. The house below was dark. The old boards creaked with every step. As she placed each foot, Les sucked in and held her breath, certain Miss Maggie would come from the back of the house with a candle wondering why someone would be walking about so late in the night.

At the top of the stairs, she dipped her foot and placed her weight on it. A mouse squeak was the only result. Les was confident she was the only soul to have heard it. She peered at the remaining nineteen steps into the darkness, all with their own individual noises they made when stepped on. If one was to dance on them, a tune rivaling piano music could be played.

With her eyes still on the steps, she contemplated how and where she needed to place each foot so as to make the least noise. She doubted it possible, even if she were to place her toes over the sturdy front edge of the step. During her thoughts, her eyes drifted to the banister.

When she'd first arrived at this house, it had caught her attention immediately. While younger, she'd enjoyed mastering the technique needed to slide to the very end. However, she was younger then, with not as much body to carry. But with all the factors in mind, it now appeared the sole choice to get to the bottom as quietly as possible.

Inching over on the top step, she took a firm grip of the rail. Inhaling deep, she placed the other hand around the polished oak, then eased her left leg over the top. Three aching pops sounded from the wood. Les clutched the rail and squinted tightly, sure that Miss Maggie would discover her. There would be questions. She needed to have answers. Why was she up here? This late at night? Dressed as if planning on leaving the house? Not a single excuse entered her mind. As she struggled to find one, even something to blame for her being here, several seconds passed. No lights from the back of the house. As if by a miracle, Miss Maggie hadn't awakened.

Les took it as a sign she wasn't to be deterred. She eased her grip on the rail and slid a few inches. Confident she could make it out of the house, she released all pressure. With legs lifted, but still squeezing her thighs, she whisked down the long slick rail. Stopped by the sculpted knob end, she dismounted by swinging her right leg as if on a horse. On her toes, she crept to the front door.

She nudged the lever up to unlock the latch and wrapped her hand around the large knob. Gently she turned it until the loud crack of the bolt moving boomed through the house. There was no time to wait and count how many people in the house came to see the reason for the noise. A tug had the door ajar, and Les swiftly slipped through the opening.

Careful not to step on the equally noisy planks on the raised boardwalk, she caught a glimpse of the light that shone through the sheriff's office window. Even if she didn't make a peep, it was risky for a young girl to travel along the center of town. No matter her business, it would arouse curiosity, if not demand that an adult take her back to Miss Maggie for being alone outside at such an hour.

She went into the alley next to the boardinghouse and entered the brushy field. With the high grass to conceal her, she trudged over clumps of dirt and rocks. Swatting stems from her path, she finally crossed the train tracks.

Laughter rose from the string of buildings. As she crept to the fence at the rear of the third house in the row, Les bobbed her head up, down, and side to side in order to see inside. Unable to sight anyone from the distance, she approached the window. As she did, the person she sought walked past her view.

Les went to the window, still careful not to be seen in case one of the town's prominent citizens might happen to be inside. In an apple-red robe, the lady who called herself Shenandoah sat on a stool in front of a vanity table and wall mirror rolling a black stocking while her legs were crossed at the knee.

Les tapped on the glass. The lady at first seemed startled, then came to the window and pulled back the bolt on the frame and opened it. "Chester Franks, is that you out there? Go back to your wife."

"No, ma'am," Les whispered. "It's me." She stepped into the light.

"Honey, what are you doing out here?"

"I have an awful problem and I thought maybe you could help me with it."

"Why, sure. What do you need from me?"

Les didn't feel comfortable in the back alley. The numerous drunks lying on the dirt and against the wall appeared too sober for her to tell her story. "Can I come in there?"

With a puzzled face, Shenandoah stuck her head out from the window and peered both left and right. "Well, I guess it'll be all right. Make sure no one sees you." She extended a hand, and Les took it while lifting her shoe to the bottom sill. "If anyone sees you and tells that mother of yours, she'll come barging in here and pull out every root from my head for letting you in here."

With the tug, Les hopped, thrusting her weight forward. She landed half in and half out. Shenandoah stepped back just as a mule would fight reins, but the girl couldn't get more than her hips up and through the window. Finally, the lady snared a grip of the girl's skirt and resumed her step back until Les spilt onto the floor. Just as quickly, Shenandoah slammed the window shut and drew the shade.

"Now, honey, what is it I can do for you?"

Rising from the floor, Les first brushed her clothes of dust. Unsure how to begin, she took a moment to look at the tall woman with her coal-black hair all spun in a weave atop her head. "Well, it's going to sound strange what I need to ask you."

"Well, go ahead, girl. I figured it had to be something you needed awful bad. It ain't like I get many visitors through my back window. Least, not young girls."

Heart pounding, Les took a deep breath, mostly in an attempt to steady her quivering chin. "We're friends, aren't we?"

The question brought a chuckle to Shenandoah. "I would duly hope so. Why?" She eyed Les's skirt. "Is this about something only girls need know about?"

Confused by the reply, Les shook her head. "I don't think so. But I didn't think it was something I could tell Miss Maggie about."

A smile came over the lady's face. "Sounds like it has to do with men." She went back over to the stool. Les watched her, taking the time to think of the right words. Shenandoah resumed rolling the stocking. Once it was in a round net, she drew the sheer fabric over her foot and with small tugs at the top and bottom, she slowly unfurled the black stocking past the knee stopping at her thigh.

Still without the proper words in mind, Les blurted out what she had to say. "I need to get to Texas."

"Texas?" The surprise was written by the lady's raised brow. "What in the world for?"

Unable to think of a convincing answer, Les decided it was time to get everything off her mind. "Do you know about the man Sheriff Tibbits hung this evening?"

"Sandy Wallace?" Her answer came with a single shake of her head. "You could say that I got to know him one night as well as a woman could know a man. What's he got to do with you?"

"He told me where there was some gold stored in Texas just before they dropped him from the platform."

Shenandoah cackled. "Honey," she said with a tone of motherly affection. "You ought not take anything that man was saying for the truth. He was just having some fun with you."

"No. He told me the place, right before. I saw the look on his face." With an expression of fond doubt still etched in the lady's eyes, Les stared back. "I know it sounds awful foolish. But there was something the way he said it. I don't think it's a lie. Why would a man about to get hung tell me a lie?"

"Because it's just like a man to give misery to everyone he can. Especially if he ain't going to be around to face up to the trouble it caused. Take it from me, it's the way they're made."

Although that might have been true, it wasn't what Les wanted to hear. "I thought you would help me." She turned for the window with shoulders drooped. When she grabbed the latch, she got the response she had desired.

"What do you want me to do, honey?"

# 3

LES FACED THE lady with new heart. "Do you know anyone going to Texas?"

The lady scoffed. "Sugar, I've been entertaining men from Texas for the last three years. I'd think by now I got to know every man in the saddle from the place."

The sly grin on Shenandoah's face gave Les the idea she might have gained an ally. "Do you think you could talk one of them into taking me there?"

The grin firmly in place, the lady shook her head. "Not a chance in Hades. If I were to get one of these drovers to take a young girl all alone to Texas, the folks in this town would run me out on a rail in tar and feathers. And I'd agree with them. What kind of woman do you think I am?"

"But you wouldn't be sending me all alone. I would be with who you sent me with. You would know them."

The lady cackled. "Oh, I know them all right. You wouldn't get far before they have you doing all the cooking and washing. And that would be if you were in luck. Those boys may be Bible-toting churchgoers when they're at their home, but you get them on that long trail and it won't take no time before they're going to want to show you their

long tails between their legs. Young girl or no. Know what
I mean?"

"Tails? What do you mean tails?"

The lady took a stance with fists punched against the
hips like that of Miss Maggie when she was convinced Les
knew better. "Don't you tell me a girl of your age don't
know what makes men different than us girls."

An instant passed before Les recalled what her foster
mother first told her about men. "They do what they do because they don't know any better?"

Another cackle and a confirming nod. "Couldn't have
said that better." The nod gradually turned to a head shake.
"But I'm still not of a mind to help send you off to your
death. No, not a girl with a bunch of drovers."

This idea had troubled Les too. Even if she snuck from
the house and attempted the journey on her own, there
would be men sent to bring her back to Miss Maggie. She
didn't know which she feared most, the unknown perils of
the trip or the certain punishment. Being the lone girl
among strange men wouldn't allow for any comfort. As the
lady stood in front of the mirror and adjusted her blouse to
fit at the front, Les thought of when she'd last stood in
front of a mirror.

"What if I didn't go as a girl?"

In the reflection, Les saw Shenandoah's eyes lock in
place, but not on her own image. Slowly, the lady turned
around. "What are you saying?"

"If I wasn't to look like a girl. If I was to dress like a
man. I could change my looks so as to fool them."

Fists went on hips again. "You are bound and determined to do this, aren't you? No matter how foolhardy. You
think those drovers wouldn't spot you as a girl right off?"

Although the question had come to mind, and exactly
how she was to act in the proper manner remained to be answered, the excitement bubbled in her blood and tingled
every nerve. "Yes, ma'am. I think I can. I know I can," she
said with a confident nod. During long moments of looking the lady in the eye, the difficulty of winning Shenan-

doah's agreement went from pushing a boulder to sweeping pebbles from a rug.

"I suppose you could be made to look like a boy. A very young one at that," the lady muttered.

Les couldn't hold back the grin growing across her face. "Yes, ma'am. I could."

The lady's lips curled. "I guess I better help you make it there. I'd hate to admit to folks that I was party to it and you didn't make it there."

Gleeful, Les charged and hugged the lady. "Thank you. Thank you."

"Don't be thanking me just yet. I ain't done nothing."

"No. But you will. I know you will."

Shenandoah peered down at Les with the doubting face of a parent. At last, she gripped Les's shoulders and arched her brow. "Let's see who's here." She turned for the door. Opening it only enough to peer with a single eye into the outer parlor, the lady surveyed the customers in the company of her workers. Les squatted in order to peek too.

Dim lantern light projecting on the red velvet drapes gave the room a scarlet glow. Just three men sat in chairs, each with a woman perched on their lap. While two couples remained difficult to see in the dark, the last pair were in clear view. Arlene, a girl not more than five years older than Les, rubbed the chest of her guest while he wrapped arms around her waist. The cowboy's face was partly concealed by Arlene's blond hair, pinned-up save for a few strands that drooped from each side. Her blue shimmy sparkled in the light. Both she and the young cowboy had wide grins. When Les bobbed to one side for a better view, she caught the attention of Shenandoah.

"Hide your eyes, child. This isn't something you ought to be seeing." The lady opened the door slightly wider as if to step into the parlor. Les couldn't help notice that a near-silent hum from Shenandoah had Arlene glance toward the door. It took only a few seconds before the young blond girl left the lap of her guest and entered the office.

"Howdy, Les. Why are you here?" Arlene said with the

same courtesy as if they'd met on the boardwalk on Sunday morning. Les replied with a smile. Arlene looked at her boss with raised eyebrows, the blue eyes surrounded by thick black lashes lit up from her sun-scorched face.

"She is needing a favor from us," Shenandoah answered. "Who is that man?"

"I don't know for sure. He said his name is Monty. One of the cowboys from the drive that came in day before yesterday."

The lady cast an eye at Les, then at Arlene. "Have you invited him to . . . to . . ."

"Not yet," Arlene responded with a smirk. "I was getting to know him when I saw you."

"Well," the lady said with that sly grin, "I want you to be especially friendly to this one. We may need something from him."

"Like what?"

"Oh, just things that will come off naturally. I need you to find out certain things about him. For beginners, where's he from?"

"Oh," Arlene replied with the same casual voice. "Someplace in Texas. He told me he leaves in the morning with two others to go back." A hint of a smile creased her lips. "He said he wanted something to remember to take back with him."

"Oh, we'll give him something." Shenandoah went to her vanity. "But first, I think we're going to need to give him something to make him more agreeable to stay a little longer." She opened a side drawer and removed a small vial. "When you offer him a drink, pour no more than half into the liquor." She handed Arlene the small bottle. "If you give it to him early enough, you may not have to use your wares."

"I don't want to kill him. He ain't half bad to look at."

"This won't. It's laudanum. A little opium with alcohol. Doc Carter gave it to me for the aches I've been having. It will take away every ache he's ever had. Plus make him sleep better. Once you're sure he's out for a while, bring all he's wearing in here."

"Where are you hurting?" asked Les.

"You never mind about that. It's a hazard of this vocation I don't want you to suffer."

"I've taken that," Arlene said. "It tastes awful. He'll know it as soon as he smells it."

Shenandoah raised her brow. "You may be right." She fumbled through the drawer once more and brought out a small pillbox. "Here, give him this."

Arlene picked up the pillbox and popped open the lid. "What is it?"

"They call it chloral. I got it from the Chinese from the south of town. You can't taste nor smell it. Works faster than the opium. You give only one pill to him, he'll be out faster than you can blow out a candle." She looked at Les. "You pay no notice to any of this I'm saying." The lady turned her attention to Arlene. "You better get back to him before he leaves to find someone else to cure his lonesome. And learn who all he's riding with." She waved the blond girl from the room. Arlene turned to go, first wrapping one pill in her palm before she casually crept into the parlor.

Shenandoah put on her shawl. "There's a few things we're going to be needing," she said walking to the door. "Only one place I know to get them. Now, you stay in this room, do you hear me? If I catch you out there, I'll take a switch to you myself, then march you back to Maggie this night. Understand?"

Les nodded so hard and fast her neck felt sore. The lady slipped out the door and closed it behind her. Alone, Les smiled at the excitement buzzing on her skin. An idea all her own took shape before her very eyes. The happiness swirled in her head. But an instant's thought about what she was leaving behind dampened the thrill.

Most all the memories she carried were of this town, and not more than a handful were moments she cared to recall. Miss Maggie had been a good mother, but too often the maternal worry got in the way of Les discovering what was just beyond the front door. Les figured that as a near-adult woman, she owed herself the opportunity to find out, and with a heap of money, she could go to all the places talked about by the guests at the dinner table.

A man's giddy hoot brought her from the daydream. Never one to ignore what she couldn't see, Les went to the door and opened it ever so slowly. Cautious to heed Shenandoah's warning, she took care not to put a foot into the parlor.

Arlene had found the cowboy's lap once more, and it appeared he was the one laughing. The blond girl continued her rubbing of his chest and face while talking so softly Les couldn't hear any words. A moment later Arlene leaned into the cowboy's ear. After a few utterances, she kissed his cheek. His eyes opened wide and his lips settled to a contented smile. She rose from his lap and took him by the hand bringing him out of the chair as if she was leading a puppy dog.

As they approached, Les's heart pumped so fast it flushed her face. She closed the door. When she heard the thud of another door closing, she reopened it, but didn't see Arlene or the cowboy. However, light from beneath an adjacent door signaled their whereabouts. When there was more movement from the other parlor guests, Les quickly shut the door.

More laughter through the wall where the mirror hung brought Les's curiosity to a boil. It reminded her when she was younger and knew where Miss Maggie hid the gifts for Christmas. Something so close, yet its whereabouts unknown, was too much of a temptation. She put an ear to the wall, but only muffled voices were heard. She moved to another spot, and a few words of conversation could be made out. She moved again, and a few more words were understood. Each success took her closer to the mirror.

Finally, she noticed the sound was best from behind it. A quick observation of how it hung revealed hinges on one side. While she realized this likely wasn't something allowed, she decided that if she only took a peek, she could set the mirror right before Shenandoah returned. Les tugged gently on the edge, and the mirror swung open like a door revealing a small hole no bigger than a penny. She squinted one eye and gazed into the hole.

The small room was lit by a single lantern with the wick turned nearly all the way down. A bed for only one was all that could be seen. The cowboy fell back onto the mattress like he'd been pushed there. He wiped his mouth with his sleeve, appearing to have just swallowed a drink with a few drips still dangling from his stubbled chin. When he leaned forward to sit on the edge, Les could see he didn't look more than a few years older than she, and was probably the same age as Arlene.

The blond girl came into view. The first item removed was the cowboy's dust-stained hat, which Arlene flung behind her. Next, the girl began unbuttoning the young man's shirt with his smiling permission. When she struggled with a few of the buttons, he helped her manage all of them through the slots and pulled the shirt from his chest.

She bent from sight. A small grimace broke over the cowboy's face and the rustle of his pants could be heard. He bent down out of Les's view, and returned holding a single boot, which he tossed aside. Arlene now stood with the other boot in hand, and did the same.

With still-happy grins, the two nuzzled noses. The blond girl kissed his cheek again, stood straight, and peeled the thin straps of the shimmy from her shoulders. The blue shimmering garment fell to the floor.

Les felt her eyes widen and her face flush to a tingle. Able to see only Arlene's bare back, she saw the young man's face dip from sight while Arlene ran her fingers through his tangled hair. Now, the blond girl let out a giggle and pushed the cowboy back, falling on top of him and out of Les's sight.

On the tip of her toes, Les strained to see where they had gone and what they were doing, then heard the creak of the door to the parlor. Instantly, she pulled the mirror back into its proper place and picked up a figurine of a clown from the vanity before Shenandoah was fully in the room.

"What are you doing in here, honey?" the lady asked holding a sack.

"Oh." Les paused to think. "Just taking notice of all the things you have to look at in here."

A low groan vibrated through the wall, followed by a constant rhythmic thump. The lady peered at Les. "Don't pay any attention to that."

"No, ma'am. I wasn't."

The lady took a deep breath. "Well, let's see what I have for you." She went to her vanity, opened the sack, and removed a rusted tin can full of mud.

"What is that for?" asked Les.

"You."

"Me?" she answered with shock.

The lady nodded and was about to speak, but the increasing groans made her hesitate for the moment. "This here is what every man claiming to be from Texas has on his face." She took Les by the hand and led her to the chair in front of the vanity. While staring at her image, Les saw the lady scoop the mud, patting it in both hands. Once it was in the shape of a flapjack, she smeared thin coats on Les's cheeks. Both of them concentrated on the reflection as each stroke brought black and brown smears. "We've got to cover up all that peach fuzz."

The mirror shook with louder thumps sending ripples through the glass like the surface of a pond. The shaking made Les's face a hard target for Shenandoah to track with the smudges. She consistently brushed some mud into Les's hair. Frustrated, the lady gripped all the hair in one hand while smearing mud on the cheeks with the other. Les concentrated on her own face, recalling the same daydream when she'd held back the hair.

"That'll do for the time." Shenandoah looked at Les through the mirror. "We need to do something with this too," she said, holding the hair in a tail. Still with a firm grip, she reached into the vanity drawer and drew scissors. "I ain't no barber."

As she took the first cut, more furious thuds pounded into the room. Shenandoah again appeared frustrated. Her hand jerked each time she tried to set the scissors to cut. "I'll wait. Shouldn't be long." The thumping slowed, but the jolt through wall was felt through the floor. The final three thumps each took longer than the one before, until the loudest of groans sounded like someone was in the worst of agony. As the groan faded, peace settled through the wall and room. "Sounds like our cowboy is done."

The lady snipped off a handful of hair from the side of Les's head. Years of undisturbed growth fell from Les's scalp in sheets. It made her ill, so she closed her eyes. She felt the tugs of hair and heard the clap of the scissors. The scissors encircled her head with one snap after another, with extra time spent at the nape.

"There, that looks like a young cowhand."

The lady's proud announcement had Les open an eye. The sight of the new look forced open the other. What had once been a head of long hair brushed twice a day had been reduced to uneven clumps resembling most of the men at the boardinghouse upon waking from a restless sleep to hurry for breakfast. She put her palm to the erect strands at the top, which were the same length as the cowlick at the back. Too polite to cry in front of the lady, she wasn't sure whether she looked like a young drover, but she knew she no longer looked like a girl.

"It'll be better with a hat on," the lady assured her.

Les nodded to agree, but inside prayed it was true. A brief knock at the door signaled Arlene's entrance. Back in her shimmy, Arlene hugged a bundle of clothes to her chest with one hand, and struggled to shut the door with both boots clasped in the other. "Here they are." Her happy expression quickly soured after a few seconds of gawking at Les. Arlene's mouth fell agape. "Oh, dear. What happened? Have you got lice? Don't come near me if you do."

"No, she doesn't," Shenandoah said with disgust at the

notion. It took an instant for Arlene to realize the haircut had been done by her boss. The sour face turned bittersweet. "Oh. I see now. Yes, you . . . do . . . look . . . look . . . you . . . look."

Les knew how Arlene felt. "It'll be better with the hat on."

Arlene snapped her fingers, dug through the bundle, and produced the dark brown hat with dust caked on the wide brim. "Of course it will." She planted it on Les, and all three viewed the new appearance through the reflection in the mirror. "You're a handsome one, dear."

"Just one more item to be settled," the lady said as she knelt and put her hand in the sack, then craned her neck at Arlene. "Is he sleeping?"

"Like a baby. Never known one not to after. Probably didn't need what you gave me. But I gave it to him anyway."

"Just as well. He'll be out until noon tomorrow." Shenandoah stood and held out her palm. Arlene's face went sour again. The blond girl dug into the pants pocket and slapped a stack of ten silver dollars into the lady's hand. The lady cut the stack at three coins.

"You know, with him in my bed, I can't do any business," Arlene said.

After a moment's pause, Shenandoah snarled, then cut the stack in half, taking the five coins and tucking them into her cleavage. Arlene snatched the remaining five, and did the same. The lady, still with a displeased face, met Les's eyes through the mirror. "Take off your blouse, honey."

The order startled Les after what she'd just witnessed. She feared for a moment the lady thought coins were hidden in her top. "There ain't nothing there."

"Well," said Shenandoah. "There's too much there now to catch a man's notice." Les hesitated. Never had she undressed in front of anyone to the bare skin, not even Miss Maggie. "Come on, girl. It ain't like this will be our first time."

With reluctance, Les slowly complied, threading the buttons through the holes until all of them fell free. Shenandoah and Arlene helped slip the blouse from the shoulders. Les froze. All she could do was stare into the mirror as the other women slid the straps of the slip from her shoulders. She'd seen other women nearly naked, and couldn't help notice how she wasn't as filled out as they were.

"That's a nice little pair, dear. You could make some money here with those. There's a lot of old men that pay extra for the younger girls."

"Hush," Shenandoah said to Arlene while draping a bedsheet over the front of Les. "She's got better plans than to stay here. Got something worth more waiting on her." The lady finished with a wink Les saw in the mirror. "Going to have to wrap strips around them tight enough to get you flat as a boy, though. You better find what you're looking for soon, honey. Another six months and there won't be no hiding these."

The lady reached to the candy dish on the vanity for several peppermints and gave them to Les, then drew a pair of scissors from the top of the vanity. "Here. Suck on them. Take the rest with you. You'll need the energy for that long trip. Besides, for right now, they'll keep you from screaming when we tie these on you."

# 4

BY THE BREAK of dawn, Rance had put on his shirt, coat, and trousers. With hat on head and boots in hand, he silently gave Miss Rosemary Tuggle from Pittsburgh one last glance as she slept snuggled in the sheets of his bed, then left the cabin. He stepped into the boots and went upstairs toward the pilot house. With the captain of the *Robert E. Lee* still asleep, Rance was able to influence the night pilot, with the help of an ample bribe, to steer the paddle wheeler toward the nearest shore.

He returned to the lower deck and paid a steward to row him to the bank in a dinghy. They arrived along a pier, where Rance debarked with a tip of his cap to the riverboat. It was a short distance from the pier to the center of town. The sun had climbed over the eastern horizon when he made his way to various shops that lined the streets. The proprietors all appeared at the same time to unlock their stores, but there was a particular business he sought. From one boardwalk to the next, he walked the small hamlet until he spotted the sign that stopped him. TAILOR was painted on the window. A peek inside showed only darkness. While he waited, he took casual notice of a posted political bill. ELECT JOSIAH HANKS FOR CONGRESS.

"Been waiting long?" The question turned him back to the front door. A hunched elder gentleman with a thinning scalp unlocked the latch.

"Not at all." Rance entered the shop, admiring the rolls of fine fabric while the old man lit a lamp. "What's the name of this town?"

"St. Mary's Landing, Missouri. What can I do for you, young fellow?" Rance removed his coat, withdrawing the gun and the folded currency. "That's an old pepperbox, isn't it? Haven't seen one of those in years."

Rance grinned. "Yes, it is."

"Thirty-caliber?"

"Thirty-one." Rance looked pleased at his choice of the pistol with six rotating barrels. Although advised against purchasing the tricky weapon by the gunsmith in New Orleans, he was fond of its looks with the hammer on top of the nipple row. It was a gambler's gun.

"What do you want, mister?"

Reminded of the purpose of his visit, he opened the coat. "Is it possible to sew something into the lining?"

The tailor shrugged. "I guess so. What do you have in mind?"

Rance smiled as he unfolded the bills. "Oh, let's say about ten thousand dollars."

A sharp jolt to the sole of the boots snapped Les from her sleep. Reflex raised her gloved hand to shield her eyes from the morning brilliance. She squinted above her fingers and just under the hat's brim at the figure hovering above. As the shadow gradually faded, a young man's face emerged with a broad smile. With eyes now wide open, she saw his brown hat cinched by a cord under his chin, and his sky-blue shirt with pale suspenders. Dusty boots poked from beneath faded chaps, tied to each leg, which met at the waist. The only part uncovered was the light gray shade of his trousers in the middle.

"You a drover?"

Stuck for an answer, she arched her brow and sank her

head back against the saddle in attempt to feign not hearing the question. Witnessing drunks in the street after all-night stupors, she hoped blinking would give her the look of a seasoned trail hand suffering from a severe bender.

"What's the trouble? Suck on a bottle too long?" The youthful smile widened. He turned the grin over his shoulder, then quickly put it back at her. "How come you're wearing Monty's duds? Where is he anyway?"

Les got to her feet, bumping her head against the corral rail. The pain wasn't a helpful distraction. The questions came too fast, and she didn't feel any comfort at a broad-shouldered cowboy with a pistol tucked in his belt standing over her. After wiping the dust from her behind and pants legs, she still didn't come up with a suitable reply she would believe. She wasn't sure about him. "I won them."

"Won them?" The puzzlement on his face proved her wrong and sent her heart racing. "Won them at what? Playing cards?"

The guess seemed an ample excuse. She nodded.

"I never known Monty to play cards. Especially when he's drinking. Claimed he lost a month's pay when couldn't tell what hand he had. Said he swore off it."

When she stood before Miss Maggie after being caught in a lie, Les always came up with a better one even if it didn't convince. However, she was lost in the constant friendly smile of the cowboy. It confused her. If he knew she was lying, why did he keep looking at her in such a kind manner? Awakening from the instant daydream, she offered the first reason in her head. "Maybe it was dice? He must have been more drunk than he thought."

A second passed, then another. The cowboy started a slow nod, which quickened when he scratched his chin. "That does sound like Monty."

"Let's find him and get."

The gruff voice came from the left. Les focused on a taller man wearing a checkered shirt and shiny tanned leather vest. Weathered chaps wrapped around brown dun-

garees with a pistol snugged in a holster high on the right
hip. His hat brim curled slightly on the sides and had no
strap. Grizzled hair was sprinkled in the brown like the hair
of a middle-aged father, but his reddened face was marked
by a stiff jaw and not the hint of a smile.

The younger one only shook his head once. "Might as
well look in the cathouses. Best bet as any." He began the
march toward the row of houses across the tracks.

"You won't find him there," she said. The young cowboy stopped, and she knew the question before he asked it.

"How's that?"

The lying trade was heaps tougher than with Miss Maggie. Usually when things didn't make sense, Les could
stare down her adoptive mother until a shake of the head
indicated her surrender to a childhood fib. These men
didn't seem amused. Instead of trying to fib down an entirely new path, she thought that a side road to the truth
might actually be believed. "Well, you probably will find
him. But he ain't coming with you."

The young one faced the older only a moment, then
turned his warm grin back at her. "And why is that?"

Again, pressure for another excuse gave her a feeling of
drawing water from an empty well. Honesty appeared the
only clear road to reason. Nevertheless, if it was the whole
truth, she'd be staked to this town the rest of her life, not to
mention switched on her bare behind until bloody by Miss
Maggie, who was likely to rise from her bed at any moment. Something had to be said to keep the cowboy's eyes
out of hers. If he kept beaming at her, she was likely to
start bawling from guilt.

"All right. I guess I ought to tell you what really is the
story." Both men showed no reaction. "I'm coming with
you due to Monty quit you. He told me last night this was
his last drive, and paid me five dollars to show up here in
his stead and tell you so he could get the first night's sleep
he'd known in three months."

Once more the young one looked to the older drover.
Neither appeared persuaded. It was the best she could

come up with in such a short time and if they called her on it, she was out of ideas. After the younger man looked at her and back at the old one several times, she knew they weren't sold. She'd have to confess.

"Sounds like Monty," they both announced in unison.

"Hell, let's leave him," the old one said. "More money for just the two of us. It's getting near seven and we ain't made an inch out of this day. We don't have time to find him, much less roust him from some whore's bed and talk him into coming." When the older man faced about, so did the young one. Suddenly, Les stood alone watching both of them walk to their saddled horses.

Fear gripped her throat. Her stomach churned worse than when caught in the lie. The chance she'd seen hours ago to leave Abilene was stepping into the stirrup. Attempts to speak only came as muted grunts. Without the courage to talk them into taking her along, instinct took over her legs. Step by step, she edged closer to them as they climbed into their saddles and steered their horses to the gated pen. When they brought the horses full about, Les had strayed in the way.

The young one reined in. "Something else he told you to tell us?"

Although not sure which were the right words to use, she said the only sincere thing she could think of. "I thought I was coming with you."

It took just an instant before both men snickered as if hearing a joke. "What's your name?"

"Les."

"Les what?"

The first answer in her head was Turnbow. It was Miss Maggie's name, and despite seldom referred to by the family name by folks in town, it was the truth. Yet a half an instant later, the idea scared her. Should these men realize the truth, they might try to track down Miss Maggie in order not to leave a child in the street. "Wallace," she answered, thinking of Sandy's last name. He wasn't using it anymore.

"Wallace?" the old drover repeated as if inquiring. She wasn't sure if he'd attended the hanging the night before, or had taken note of the condemned, but it was too late to change the story. No one could be unsure of their family name. Les just nodded. She'd said enough.

The young one beamed once more. "Well, Les, I'm Jody Barnes. Pleased to meet you. But we're heading back to Ellis County in Texas to the ranch of Mr. J.S. Cooper. Now, that's over five hundred miles from here over the worst ground God ever made. Something tells me you never done this type of work before."

Les peeked down at her shirt.

"I didn't think so. I'm sorry, but this ain't no trip for no tinhorn kid."

At first disappointed at their attitude, she took heart he didn't say "girl." She stood her ground. "But I can cook. And I can ride. And I can, I can, I can—"

"You can what?" the old one grumped. "You can get in the way? You can get yourself killed?"

Jody chuckled again at the crack. "Maybe next year. We'll have another drive then. You wait on us to come back."

For some that might have been a good enough answer. "I can't wait another year. I was planning on leaving now."

"And why is that?"

The simplest answer was the honest one. "Because I want to go to Texas. I want to see what it's like. See if it's all that these men claim it is."

Jody leaned forward in his saddle. "That the sole reason?" His eyes penetrated into hers as if knowing there was more.

"I got no one here to stay for," she added. She peeked over her shoulder across the tracks. Although she'd lied at least nine times a day most of her life, that lie pained her more than any before. She resumed a pleading gaze at Jody, who only straightened in the saddle.

For a moment he looked to the cloudless sky, but quickly turned his doubtful face to her. "How old are you?"

"Sixteen."

"Sixteen? Damn, when I was sixteen I had done filled out the front of my britches. I'd guess you ain't gone through the change, have you?"

"What change?"

The question brought sly grins to both of their faces. Les couldn't allow them to use it as an excuse. "How old are *you*?" she asked.

"Old enough," Jody confidently answered. "We ain't talking about if I can make the trip. I believe it was falling on you." They both nudged their horses to amble around her, but Les stepped in their path. She had a last card to play: dicker and beg.

"If you let me go with you, I'll cook every meal. I won't complain or commence to whining, I'll-I'll do whatever it is you fellows don't like doing. And I'll do it for nothing. No pay."

Their slow glances at each other gave her confidence she'd pricked a nerve. Back and forth she peered into both faces for a sign her offer was accepted. Jody was the first to look at her.

"You got a horse?"

Her breath eased, but the question brought equal excitement and concern. She peeked initially at the saddle, then at the pen full of horses.

"Grab your saddle and pick you out one," said Jody with some cheer in his voice. As if she was shot from a gun, Les ran to the corral rail and gripped the saddle horn. The weight stopped her the same as pulling a stump from the ground. Not wanting to appear a weakling girl, she put both hands to it and twisted her shoulders around to carry it and the blanket on her back. She strained to keep her knees from buckling at each slow step. Both drovers sat atop their horses without any sign of helping her through the struggle. Once at the gate, she slipped the rope knot from the post and slowly entered the horses' domain. Even they cast doubtful eyes at her.

Slogging through the loose dirt and dung, she ap-

proached a tall gelding. When she neared, it slowly moved
from her path as if making a polite gesture. A brown sorrel
stood nearby, but it scampered from her clumsy stride.
Whenever she took a step toward another, Les was met
with the same skittish reaction. If she was to capture a
horse on her own, the morning would be lost. She felt the
pressure from the unseen cowboys at her back, no doubt
enjoying her failure, but she knew they would tire from her
delay and might call off the deal.

Just as the herd separated like water that had been
splashed, a black-and-white paint stood firm at the far end
of the corral. With her arms tingling from the constant
weight, Les remembered the peppermint in her pocket and
Shenandoah telling her it would give her energy. Needing a
rest, she let the saddle slip from her side and slam into the
muck. Her own head dizzy, she reached in her pocket and
pulled out a single nugget of the candy. Like a shout to dinner, the paint's ears perked forward and it slowly took cautious steps toward Les.

Recognizing a sweet tooth, she pulled another peppermint from her pocket and offered it to the paint with a flat
palm. Its lips picked it cleanly like fingers. The opportunity
to make a friend couldn't be lost. Patting the neck, she
spread the blanket across its back without a revolt. She
knew she would have only one chance at getting the saddle
on the animal, so as her enthusiasm flushed her cheeks, she
gripped both ends and with one grunting yelp lifted and
tossed the saddle across its back. The paint merely turned
to look as if unimpressed by Les's achievement. To keep
the horse as a friend, Les gave it another nugget. She knelt
under the girth to retrieve both ends of the cinch. Accustomed to threading clasps on corsets, she slipped the far
end through the metal hoops, and not wanting to pull too
tight so as to spook the paint, she gradually pulled it until
she felt it was tight enough. The bridle was an easier matter. The paint took to it with another nugget, but at this rate,
she would run out of the candy before she would leave
town.

"Better give her a punch," Jody said.

"What?" The idea seemed cruel. "I'm not going to punch her."

"Then you'll fall right on your butt. She's sucked in air to stretch the cinch. As soon as you put a foot up, that saddle is going to slide right off."

Reluctant and fearful he was right, Les balled a fist and prepared a blow to the paint's girth before she closed her eyes. She swung hard. Her fist bounced off the hide like a dirt clod against a brick wall. When Les opened her eyes, the bulge around the horse's stomach shrank and she heard what sounded like a belch from the mare.

She pulled the cinch once more, and found there was slack to take up. This time she didn't leave space for the animal's comfort. Although she didn't want to hurt the horse, she also didn't want to get hurt herself. After the saddle seemed secure, she tugged the horn and it didn't move. The mare didn't seem to mind.

Again she patted the neck of her new friend and walked to the left side. When she lifted her foot, she found the stirrup hung chest high. With her foot sliding inside the huge boot, she slapped the heel to bring the toe of the boot as far forward as possible. The tip barely protruded through the stirrup. Without thinking further, she pulled against the saddle and closed her eyes. After several squirming moments, she found herself atop the paint, only she lay across the saddle like those she seen the sheriff bring in dead. Les scooted her bottom so as to sit astride.

With a cleansing breath, she took silent pride in the success of saddling her first horse. Both men didn't appear congratulatory. With a spurless nudge, the paint went forward to the gate. Jody's smile didn't waver, but it didn't seem genuine.

"You sure you want to do this?"

When Jody asked, she wanted to answer quickly, but she also thought of what could lay ahead. If she needed that long just to saddle her horse, what more might she be asked to do and how long would it take her? Still, there was a fortune with a future that went along with all that was demanded. She was sure. "Yes. Yes, I do."

"All right," Jody replied with a single nod. He turned his horse and waved for her to follow. At the door to the livery stood two mules with sacks and bundles strapped to their backs.

"Where are all the cows?" she asked.

Jody gawked at her, again peeking over his shoulder at the older one for a single instant. "We don't take any cows back to Texas. That's why we brought them here. We're taking the remuda back." He pointed to the mules. "This be your duty. You keep just ahead of us with them. We'll eat dinner in about six hours." He freed the reins with a single yank and held them out for her.

Orders understood, she took the mules' reins one-handed while gripping the paint's with the other hand. Sluggish at first, the mules followed the lead. Les guided the paint past the last corral post. When she went by the first house next to the railroad tracks, she peeked at Shenandoah's room. Although she knew better, she couldn't help think the lady was smiling down on her. If not for her help, Les wouldn't be crossing the iron rails at that very moment. There would always be a debt owed, and one day, Les promised herself to repay it.

While other familiar houses came and went without much fear of being noticed, Les cast an eye to the front porch she had swept all her life as she approached from the left. She snugged the hat firmly to hide her face. It wouldn't be more than minutes from now that Miss Maggie would be climbing those stairs to wake her. She could always hear those heavy feet on the creaky steps. That memory wouldn't be missed. Neither would the constant harping over how dirty the basins were, or whether enough wood had been cut for the stove.

Once the house was at her back, she peeked over her

shoulder. Both drovers had all the horses out of the pen and weren't more than a hundred feet behind. There wasn't time to dawdle over memories. Les swiped her eyes and nose with her sleeve and grunted her throat clear.

# 5

A SHARP JOLT to the sole of the boots snapped Rance from his sleep. Still squinting from the morning's brilliance through the passenger car windows, he nudged the black stiff brim off his brow with a single finger. He focused on the hovering figure of an attractive lady in a pale white gown, wearing a hat of ruffled fabric with lace and holding a parasol.

"You clumsy lout!"

Not yet fully aware of the circumstances, he was puzzled by the insult. He did notice her Southern accent, and the scowl that showed her temper matched her fire-red hair.

"How dare you leave your filthy boots in the aisle as if this were some tramp house."

Rance peeked at his black coat and vest covering his white shirt with string tie. A quick glance about the car revealed him to be one of the best-attired men.

She angled her head over her shoulder. "Burt, teach this vagabond the proper manners when aboard my train."

A burly fellow of at least six feet, with a full trimmed beard and wearing a neat dark tweed coat, stepped next to the woman. "Yes, Mrs. Schaefer." He opened the coat and drew a cudgel from his belt. "Come with me, you," he said, snatching a handful of Rance's collar. The woman scampered from view as Burt yanked Rance from the seat and into the aisle.

"Wait, friend," Rance coughed out. "I think we need to talk." He didn't have time to reach for the pepperbox inside his coat. The big man swung the club, but the thick wood barrel slapped against Rance's palm. Distracted by saving his head from being cracked like an egg, Rance felt an elbow slam into his jaw, throwing his hat off. His knees buckled from the blow.

Once Rance was on the floor, Burt dragged him like a sack of potatoes toward the door. Rance tried to get to his feet, but the pace of the slide kept him from gaining balance. The rush of air blew the brown hair from his face. Just as he got to his feet, he went head-first onto the outer landing.

Gravel and wooden ties speeding by under the coupling came into view. Rance grabbed the iron handrail and stopped Burt's tug from launching him from the rumbling train. The big man again swung the cudgel. Rance leaned back, dodging its swath. The polished oak blackjack crashed on the wrought iron and splintered in two. The handle now had a sharp edge like a dagger.

"Now just hold up there—Burt, is it? Why don't we talk this over like the gentlemen that we are. You can go and tell the lady you did your job. I'll go back and sit with the conductor and she'll never know the difference. How 'bout it? Deal?"

The burly man had a gleam in his eye showing he preferred a better solution. "How 'bout I just cut your heart out and show it to her."

Rance shook his head. "No. That I don't like."

Burt lunged with the jagged point first. Reflex pushed Rance back prone on the landing. The big man stumbled onto him from the sway of the train. Rance grabbed the wooden knife inches away from his belly. If Burt got to his knees, the substantial weight would plunge the point into Rance's chest.

When Burt put one knee to the landing, the gap between his legs made an easy target. Rance rammed a knee into the big man's crotch. The force crumpled Burt forward. Rance seized the chance to keep Burt's momentum forward by ramming the same knee into the burly fellow's sizable behind, sending him further forward.

A frightened scream followed. The second smack was intended just to get the huge body off his chest, but when Rance twisted about, Burt wasn't in sight. Rance crawled to the edge in enough time to spot the bodyguard rolling down the side of the embankment.

Rance sucked in breath and exhaled slowly. Only inches were between him and the same trip Burt was now making. One hand on the handrail, he pulled himself to his feet and peeked back inside the car for any further employees of Mrs. Schaefer. The passengers wore shocked faces as he entered, closed the door, and retrieved his hat. He wasn't sure if the reaction was due to the violence of the fight or the fact he was the one returning to his seat.

A handkerchief of the same pattern as the lady's gown lay on the wooden bench. He picked it up, and the scent of lilac wafted by his nose. With muscles and bones aching, he gave thought to resting on the bench, but couldn't ignore the handkerchief or decide if it was a coincidence or an invitation. He followed the scent to the back of the car, traversed both landings into the next car, walked through it to the rear door, and went outside.

Unlike the rest of the train, the stained oak door before him had a brass handle. He was certain it would be locked, but his gambling nature had him at least give it a turn. The latch slipped open and the door creaked as it slowly swung inside. He carefully entered and shut the door. The Pullman car was adorned with fine cherry furniture, and satin green drapes were pulled open with a half-drawn shade.

"Who is it?" asked the voice from behind a dressing partition. It belonged to the same woman in the aisle but the welcoming tone was new.

"Ransom B. Cash, Mrs. Schaefer. I'm sorry to intrude,

but I wanted to apologize in person for the incident earlier. Now, it seems I have something that belongs to you. I felt duty-bound to return it."

The gown already hung over the top edge of the partition. A corset quickly was flung on top of it. Seconds after came a camisole, then petticoats flipped atop another section. Rance took a deep breath. It didn't seem likely this was the same woman who'd ordered him thrown from the train. He was always a betting man, and the odds favored a pair of barrels of a shotgun about to round the corner of the partition.

He was wrong, and had never been so thankful. Dressed in a silk purple robe, the woman emerged from behind the dressing partition, the strawberry hair hanging loose on her fair-skinned shoulders. Difficult not to notice through the sheer garment, the only pair that pointed at him weren't from a shotgun. He let out his breath while admiring articles about Mrs. Schaefer more private than her car.

"I'm happy it is you to return it, Mr. Cash."

"Well," Rance said, clearing his throat, "you'll pardon me for saying this, but it didn't seem that way a few minutes ago."

"Oh, that," she replied with a slight giggle. "I really didn't want you removed from the train. That Burt, he misunderstood what I had in mind." She approached him, her eyes darting from boots to hat. "I wanted something else." With a delicate touch, she slipped the handkerchief through his fingers. She gently put it to her nose and inhaled the fragrance. "Delightful, don't you think?"

Rance nodded, a bit afraid of a quick mood change.

She put her palm to his chest while the other hand spread the robe from her bosom. "I bathe in it. It is all over my body." She leaned closer to his face and whispered, "Wouldn't you like to sniff for yourself?"

As her lips came within inches of his, the options for the next few minutes ran through his mind. Accustomed to the company of women in intimate settings, normally he initiated such interludes. Her advances brought his desires

pounding through his veins. This woman's blood was at a
boil too. If he were to pass on the opportunity, it might trigger an explosion of wrath that would surely get him
scorched. Since the next train station wasn't for hours, he
chose to spend them enjoying the ride.

"Who am I to refuse the offer from a lady." He dipped
his head to her chest and suckled. Her moaned exhale signaled consent. Encouraged by her flinging the hat away
and her fingers' rough brush through his hair, he increased
the intensity of the loving assault. With spirited vigor, he
slid his hands inside her robe and ran them down her ribs
and behind her back. The action was met with her firm
clutch of his hair and yanking his lips to hers.

"I knew you were an interesting man when I first laid
eyes on you, Mr. Cash," she gasped between kisses, rubbing her cheeks against his two-day stubble. "I love a hairy
man's face. I know I'm with a man. It makes me feel more
of a woman."

"My friends call me Rance."

"I saw you fight through the door window. So valiant.
Do you know what it does to the inside of a woman when
she sees a valiant man? A brave man? A virile man?"

"No, Mrs. Schaefer," he replied with lips and nose con-
torted against her. "What does it do?"

She flipped the robe off the shoulders and did the same
to his coat. The weight of the pepperbox drew her notice to
its butt. "A dangerous man too. Any more weapons you
have hidden?" Rance coyly raised his eyebrows for her to
seek the answer.

A pull of the tie loosened the knot from the collar. After
fumbling to unthread the top button, she parted the shirt in
a frenzy, popping the links off one by one. She kissed his
bare neck, then multiple times on his chest and twice at his
abdomen. With the force of any saloon bouncer, she
pushed him in an armless chair against the wall and began
unfastening his belt.

"I want you to know I am a lady," she said while on her
knees. "I am raised from fine stock, the Cordells of South

Carolina. However, I am one that needs the social accompaniment of my peers, conversation of my friends, and enticing suggestions made by other gentlemen. You understand, don't you? Here I am a bird in a cage. I've been imprisoned on this train for nearly a month traveling to the forsaken desert of Utah to see silly men make speeches and pound spikes in the ground. My husband is Hiram Schaefer, president of the Eastern Pacific Railway. Do you know him?" Rance shook his head instantly, not wanting to slow her from removing his trousers. "He is a very kind man, and I am a happily married woman. But he is twenty-five years my senior. I don't think he realizes what fires burn inside a young female as myself." With his trouser waist loose from under his backside, she yanked the trousers to the floor. "He views the conjugal relations between man and wife like fine champagne, something enjoyed only on special occasions." She gazed fondly at his full attention. "I see them more like water. A daily necessity." Matters in hand, she sank astride onto his lap.

The union met with equal hums of mutual satisfaction. The rock of the train on the tracks provided a rhythm for the roll of her hips. He grabbed her behind to steady her position. Back and forth she rode, her eyes closed, mouth agape while leaning back, huffing with each thrust.

Unsure why or how he'd fallen into such a pleasurable fortune, he pondered the situation despite his lack of interest in the question. He needed to keep his mind busy or otherwise disappoint Mrs. Schaefer. Since a young man, he'd been blessed with a friendly face to ladies. Not one for school, he'd avoided books and learned his lessons on life in the gambling halls, one always a week's travel from the next. Discovering the allure of money on the kind affections of the fairer gender, he'd mastered the varied games of chance with cards and dice to assure certain finishes in his favor. Winning was seldom the same risk as that his opponents might notice his technique at gaining a better hand or roll. As he perfected his technique, he used his winnings, took pride in his appearance and the success it exemplified.

However, it occurred to him at that moment that the woman heaving her primal passions upon his waist possessed more wealth than he could ever provide. Perhaps her attraction to him was due to his youth and charm. As her huffs climbed to wails of ecstasy, he surmised his only part in this tryst was being available at the time to quench a young woman's heated hunger. A rap at the door chased away his wandering perpendance.

"Miriam, are you in there?"

The deep male voice distracted Rance's virility. Mrs. Schaefer no doubt sensed the change. "Just a minute, Hiram," she called, then leaned forward to Rance's ear panting, "If you stop, I'll yell rape."

The threat didn't help to maintain an amorous state of mind. To forestall her threat, he pawed her breasts to arouse his masculinity. The action affected her as well. She quickened her pace, which heightened her cries.

"Miriam. Open this door. Are you all right? My dear, should I call for the doctor? You sound in distress."

With strong deliberate strokes, she grabbed Rance's nape with the strength of a blacksmith and replied to her husband, "I'm coming." Without interruption, she reached above to grab the brake cord strung throughout the cars. With a loud grunt, she yanked it. An instant passed before the entire car's momentum, including all the cherry furniture and the red-haired beauty herself, slammed against him. He was unable to keep his mind clear, and the warmth rushing over him triggered his release. Her pace and the train slowed as gradually as a boat moving to port.

Miriam Schaefer pulled Rance's lips to hers and planted a loving kiss on his mouth. "Ransom B. Cash, it was a divine delight meeting you."

"It was my pleasure, Mrs. Schaefer."

More pounding on the door boomed through the car. With a sly grin, the young bride of the rail tycoon rose from his lap and retrieved her robe along with his hat and coat. "You must leave now. My husband is a very jealous man."

Rance pulled up his trousers. "You don't say?"

She nodded, slipped into the sheer robe, and found another of considerable heavier fabric from the partition. "He once caught me and an old suitor of mine in our house. Poor Rodney. After Hiram's men were done with him, he was prevented from fathering any children for his new wife."

The news hastened Rance's securing of his trousers. There was no time to repair the shirt. Furious impacts to the door followed. Like a fox in the coop with the farmer at the wire, Rance searched about for an escape. His eyes fixed on the half-drawn shade. He flipped the shade out of his way and slipped free both latches. The window slid open with a thud. With one leg through to the outside, he turned to her.

"Do you have a horse?"

"In the front animal car. A beautiful white gelding."

At first he was pleased to learn of a mount for escape, but the delight faded upon realizing even her horse had been castrated. Rance left through the window without a good-bye. He only had time to run to the front of the train while the rest of the Eastern Pacific Railway crew searched for him in Miriam Schaefer's private car.

# 6

WITH A SORE right arm, Les tugged the reins of the slow mules. Peeking over her shoulder, she saw the remuda with dust flying less than a quarter mile behind. It had come time to admit this was a fool venture.

All the plans that swirled in her head didn't include a dry throat, the sun burning on her bare neck, two stubborn mules, and a tender bottom worn sore from less than a half day in the saddle. If she weren't pretending to be a boy and could just be a girl again for five minutes, she'd let herself cry. The pounding of hooves on the ground stopped her from considering the idea.

First glancing over the right shoulder, then the left, she spotted Jody approaching with his horse at a trot. "You got trouble?" he asked slowing his horse next to the paint.

"No," she replied in as innocent tone as she thought believable.

His pleasant smile appeared as he tilted his hat back. "Well, you should be about three or four miles ahead with dinner on the fire by now."

"I should?" She shook her head, realizing such a naive question wouldn't help her cause to convince *she* was a *he*.

"I mean, yeah, I should. But these ornery mules you stuck me with don't like to move very fast."

"So, smack them on their butts. They'll get to moving. Hell, we're getting mighty hungry. You don't want to get ole Smith riled at you on the first day 'cause his belly is aching and you ain't got the food ready."

Les peeked behind again. "Is that him? Smith? That's his name?"

"Yes, sir." The words startled her, but she shook them off as he continued. "The only name I know to call him by. No Sam or Charlie, just Smith. And he'll hiss like a rattler if you ask him about it. A man that keeps all his own inside. That he is. A rough son of the devil he can be when things don't go the way he sees. So if I be you, I'd put some want-to at the rear of these critters and get up ahead and start a fire."

"Is he the boss?"

"No. Mr. Frank J. Pearl is the trail boss. But he left the first night to get back to his spread. Most of the boys left after the second night and some others are still there."

"Yeah," Les said, thinking of how she'd gotten this far. "I know."

"Oh, I forgot. Seems you already met Monty. But there's still some other fellows stuck in beds somewhere, if they're lucky. Heck, I saw four or five of them on a saloon floor."

"So, how come all those cowboys come up there and only you two are taking back the horses?" Les was a little afraid she'd asked a question she should have known the answer to, but took the risk just to keep talking. She was enjoying that smile.

"Well, Jorge and Monty normally run the remuda. But Jorge, he took off as soon as he got his pay. Said he had some pretty little señorita waiting on him back near San Antone that wasn't going to wait any longer. And you know what happened to Monty. Smith and I are outriders mostly. But Mr. Pearl asked us to help Monty get these saddle ponies home on account Mr. J.S. Cooper didn't want to sell off a perfectly good herd of horses he'd have to replace next year. Said he'd pay us an extra ten dollars. And I could use the money."

Les listened to every word, but still didn't hear an answer. "But why just two? Or three if you count me."

Jody huffed a laugh. "Steers ain't like horses. Them longhorns, they'll wander in every which direction if you don't drive them straight, looking for a patch of grass or clover to graze. Or they'll get snagged in trees, stuck in a mud hole, traipse through cactus and the like. Sometimes you're sure them horns start at one end and go right through that skull of theirs to the other end leaving no room for brains. Now, horses are a different animal. They don't like being on their own. You move a few of them and the rest chase behind. Almost like there was something special the leader was after and they didn't want to miss out. If they was people, it'd be like going to a barn dance to meet the prettiest girls in the county and you didn't want to be left with the one that ain't never been behind that barn. You know what I mean?" He raised his brow and nodded. "I know you ain't that young not to have the urge in your drawers."

Les felt her eyes widen. She sat in the saddle stuck for an answer. She didn't know exactly what urge he meant, and wasn't yet used to the drawers she wore. As he nodded with a sly smile, she mirrored it in hopes he wouldn't ask further.

"About the only thing you got to worry about with horses on an open range is wild mustangs. If a stallion smells any of these mares coming into season, he'll likely charge this herd, flashing his tail to attract them to join his harem. Can cause a stampede if he's willing to fight for them. Then he cuts mares and fillies out and they follow. And he studs them so as to spread his line."

A shout from behind turned both their heads. Smith waved his arm. "Well," Jody said, "seems I need get back. You, little man, need to get your fanny up ahead and get to sizzling bacon." He reined around and swatted each mule on the rear, sending both scampering ahead of the paint. Les kicked the horse's flanks and it responded. Instead of dragging the mules behind, she strained to keep her grip on the reins while staying in the saddle as all three animals went at a gallop over a hill.

For what seemed like an hour, but couldn't been more than five minutes, Les regained control of the three and got them to a calm trot. A look back showed she rode over a hill and into a small valley out of sight of any dust the remuda could put in the air. With Jody's warning to get the midday meal ready in a hurry, she pulled back on the mules' and paint's reins. Sliding from the saddle, she know there was no time to rub the aches from her back and rump. She limped with a tingle in her legs to one of the bundles, and threw the first flap open where she had listened to the clang of metal for the entire ride. Iron rods and pans were packed precisely to fit. She was hesitant to disturb the cooking tools for fear she'd never get them back the same way, but the time beating away in her mind had her yank each utensil out one by one.

She slid the poles into the slotted hooks of the spit. Proud she accomplished so much in small time, she next looked for matches. The second bundle held only sacks of flour and cornmeal. When she went to the other side, she stumbled on a stone and lost her balance into the rear of the mule.

Just as when Jody had swatted it, the mule bolted. In an instant, the only thing to grasp while on her knees was the tail. Face-first through the dirt, Les hung on for dear life while avoiding hooves flung at her head from left and right. With the other hand, she took another handful of hair thinking she'd get a better grip. The mule reared and kicked.

Hind legs flew with a fury. Les was thrown in the air, then slammed to the ground. Each time breath pumped from her lungs worse than five of Miss Maggie's slaps to cure a cough. The mule stopped kicking, either from fatigue or the weight on its tail. Les didn't care which, grateful the animal had ceased its tantrum.

Too weak to rise from the ground and not wanting to lessen her grip a bit, Les lay as if frozen. Her constant drag on the tail had tired the animal enough that it squatted on one flank, barely sparing her head the brunt of its body, yet keeping her pinned underneath.

Thoughts of thirst and starvation filled her mind, as she thought she was doomed to stay in the position the rest of her life. About the time she was ready to take a bite into a leg, gambling that the act might get her stomped or set the mule charging over the prairie once more, she heard the beat of hooves again.

"Hey, kid, you alive?" came the familiar call of Jody. With only a view of the mule's smelly hide, she listened to his horse slow and the increasing closeness of his voice. "Can you hear me? Say something. You alive?"

Sure she'd lost any pride or respect, she decided relief from the bottom of the mule's rear was worth the embarrassment. "Yeah, I am alive. Wouldn't mind getting up."

The crush of dust under Jody's boots went to the front of the mule. Within seconds, he shouted and the animal rose from her shoulder. Bright sunshine was never so welcome. She swiped the dust from her face as he knelt by her side. Once she cleared the grime from her eyes, she looked at that smile.

"I never seen a fellow so green."

She knew it wasn't a compliment, but took no offense. She deserved it, and wondered how many more failures she'd face before she got to Texas. "Thank you." The words came out before she knew. At first fearful such courtesy wouldn't be the nature of a man or even a boy, she saw a genuine acceptance etch his face.

"Don't mention it. I know what it's like to be a first-timer." He stood, his figure hovering above the same as that morning. She couldn't help but stare, even though she figured it wasn't natural for one man to do so to another. He held out a hand, and for an instant she let the pretense slip, allowing a grin to crease her face. She took his hand and he tugged her to her feet. Standing within an inch of his chest, she shook the inner tingle away and recalled how manly she was to act.

"Obliged at the help. Guess I still got a thing to know about these stink-filled varmints."

Jody laughed. "That be true." He sighed, all the while looking at her. She peeked at his gaze, wondering what next she would be told. For a second she imagined he had noticed too much. She peeked at her front. The collar was still buttoned at the top. No sign of the sheet bandaging her bosom showed, but he kept staring. Frantic, she searched for a word that would divert his eyes from her. He spoke first.

"Likely my mistake for pushing this on you so fast. Tell you what, this was to be my part, the cooking. I'll set this up this time. You watch careful. I'll not volunteer again."

She nodded as he went to the bundles on the mules. As he did, a distant call came from over the hill. Just as dust rose, a single horse crested the hill, quickly followed by two, then five more. The remuda had arrived, and Les knew there was likely more scolding to come from the crusty Smith.

As she watched the herd assembled within a short distance, the old wrangler circling them to a neat pack, the smell of smoke turned her around. Jody had erected the spit, flames licking the pan full of bacon from beneath. Smith rode from the herd at a half gallop, reining in to the point of jerking his mount's head nearly from the body. He slid from the saddle and walked with a purpose to Jody, who knelt by the fire. After only a glare directed at her, the old cowboy turned his attention to the young one. She thought it best to keep clear of him. If it were an option, she would have run to hide in the middle of the remuda.

"Is this how it's going to be? You wet-nursing the kid while I'm by myself to keep them straight?"

Jody stood without absorbing any of Smith's foul mood.

"I told him that I was only going to do this once. He was watching me careful so as to get the hang of it for next time."

Les felt hollow inside. She hadn't noticed the lesson, but to admit so would build a hotter flame than the one under the bacon. "I'm sorry, Mr. Smith. It was my doing that kept him from helping you." He turned his craggy face at her. Never knowing exactly what a bullet to the gut felt like, she thought surely this must be close to next as bad. "I'm sorry for slowing you up. I won't do so anymore."

Smith kept dead aim at her soul through her eyes, and at least a thousand words passed through her mind until finally he said just a few. "Seen a bellyful like you. Boys thinking they're men. Let me tell you once and get this out. You ain't no man. Ain't sure you make much of a boy neither. We got thirty days to get back to Texas and back home to tend to our own business. Ten dollars ain't much of a bounty for it, so the quicker we get there the less money we lose. I don't know why you wanted to come for. Don't know what you think is waiting on you. Texas is full of the same. Kids thinking they're men looking for a man's job. If I wasn't sure you'd get lost and get yourself killed, I'd cut you loose and send you back to your ma and pa and tell them they ain't done raising you. But since I can't, you'd better get a heap better starting now. If I'm just one day late due to you, I'll skin you myself and make a belt. You hear me? You better watch and listen all you can. Stop thinking you're a man. 'Cause you ain't."

Les nodded as best she could. Most of her body was seized in fright, but she did manage an answer. "Yes, sir. Can't argue with that. Not a word."

Done with the tongue-lashing, he went and sat by the fire. "Better save the coffee," he said to Jody. "We've lost enough time today."

Unsure why, she couldn't keep herself from joining them. As she watched the grease bubble and pop, her mind kept repeating what Smith said over and over. Even though there wasn't much to see, she kept a keen eye on every

move Jody made in hopes of absorbing knowledge. While
the meat turned from pink to brown, none of the three
spoke.

As the uneasy silence persisted and the level of boiling
fat rose to submerge the bacon, Jody put down the stirring
fork and sank his hand into a canvas sack. Out came a biscuit. He cut it in two, stabbed a piece of bacon, and
clamped it between the halves. The first one went to Smith,
whose attention seemed mostly focused on the ground yet
to cover.

Jody cut another biscuit, slid the bacon into it, and
handed it to Les. The bread wasn't the same soft dough
Miss Maggie prided herself on during breakfast. Les en-
dured the sting of the hot drippings on her wrist and took a
bite. She'd eaten softer apples. Finally able to tear a single
piece off, the bread cracking like wood splintering, she
spent most of her time chewing while the two men had
downed their entire biscuits and were splitting another
each. Jody peeked at her and smirked at her struggle to
swallow.

Finished with their seconds, they slugged down gulps of
water and rose. "Dinner is over," Jody told her, pointing at
the spit. "I'll leave you to strike this." Both men swiped
their sleeves across their mouths and went to secure the
saddle cinches. Les sat, yet to finish the remainder of the
biscuit, and despite the hunger didn't mind putting it down.

As she stood, the rub of the cloth wrap around her ribs
felt as hot as the bacon grease. She sucked in air and
paused for only a second, knowing a whine would be
heard. Finally on two feet, she sized up the task of taking
the spit apart. Good sense told her the first thing was to
squelch the fire and let the iron cool.

She picked up one of the canteens, took off the cap, and
poured a stream into the coals. The sizzle sent a cloud of
steam into the air. While she was watching the flames disappear, the canteen was torn from her grip with the force
of gale.

Smith stood in front of her, his chest at her nose. His

face was redder than the hot coals, his eyes wide with the hate of a snake piercing into hers. "You dopey?" he yelled, lifting the back of a hand at her. She cowered at the sign of a slap. Despite her squinted view, she saw him ease the hand to the side, but his angry face didn't slacken. "You don't drown fires. You smother them." He raked dirt with his heel over the steaming coals. Swipe by swipe, the steam dispersed until there was no sign a fire had ever been started. "When your throat is as dry as that dust, you remember you spent your share of water on the fire." He capped the canteen and tossed it to the ground. His steely stare poked through her eyes, cutting into her soul. He shook his head in disgust and stepped away.

Only then able to take in air, she watched him walk to his horse, reciting her best prayer to stop her arms from shaking.

# 7

LEVI CURRY SWUNG the ax dead center into the barrel-width stump. The edge slammed into the rotted elm only an inch. Exhausted by the morning's work and frustrated by the lack of progress to clear the obstruction from the prospective cotton field, he released the wooden handle and arched his aching back. "Damn this."

Eli couldn't stop his swing, and struck his brother's ax with his own, cracking his own handle. "Look what you done. What's the problem?"

With a finger pointed at the stump, Levi growled like a dog shielding a bone. "How long we be at this? Two weeks?"

"More like two months if you count when we started. But it ain't like we be at it ever' day."

Still stretching the pain from his lumbar, the older of the two scanned the field of high grass and shook his head. "Ever since Ma passed, we've been working this worthless patch of dirt and ain't seen a way to gain four bits profit. And we ain't likely to neither, with all the tax these carpet-baggers are taking. Goddamn Yankees."

"What'd you expect? They been here over four years taking what ain't theirs. If we'd won the war, likely we'd be in the North taking their money instead of they being in Arkansas taking ours." Eli tossed the broken tool aside, pulled the tobacco pouch from his coat, and rolled a smoke. "Didn't ever look like there was much prospect of being here. But even if Ma didn't will the place, I can't say I know of a different place we'd be." He struck the match against his muddy heel and lit the paper.

Levi felt the grin crease his face. "I do."

Like staring into the mirror, his brother shared the same sly face. "Can't do nothing about that yet."

"No, but the time is nearing. Our new *President* Grant, the butchering bastard, has asked for peace. I'd like to give him peace. A *piece* of lead between his eyes."

"Talk like that ain't going to do no good." Eli took a drag and gave Levi the smoke. "Things ain't never going to be like they was." He picked up Levi's ax and resumed taking swings into the stump. While watching his brother toil at the remains of a tree older than both of them and more than twice as stubborn, Levi took to heart what his brother said.

The days of running through this once-furrowed field didn't seem like they belonged to him anymore. His pa behind a plow pulled by a team of mules, reins draped over his neck, barking like a hound at his sons' play of hurling clumps of sod at each other. They knew how long they had to play before their father stopped the mules to take a strap to them. At the time it was the worst fright to see the old man at a march with a belt in hand. Whether it was ignoring his call to quit playing or shirking a single chore, even an innocent act of disrespect to an elder, the result was always the same. As a deacon, his favorite sermon concerned spoiling children by sparing the rod, which he recited while lashing the leather against their bare backs. Although the red marks faded away from the flesh, the sting never did.

When the call came to defend the rights of sovereign states, the old man volunteered himself and his sons. With the life of a farmer gladly abandoned, despite their mother's tears, it became an even greater delight to kill bluebellies. Steadying a musket at a man at first was no worse than at a turkey, until the prey returned fire. During retreat at Pea Ridge, Levi found his wounded brother and buried his pa. With lead flying as thick as a nest of hornets, soldiering lost its flavor.

Since he and his brother were sons of the South, fellow Southerners provided what could be spared for the cause. Once their kindness played out, raids on those that had food and supplies whether from North or South kept them alive. When Sherman left from Chattanooga and burned all he passed on the way to the sea, what could be salvaged wasn't worth much. The trick was to stay ahead of the advancing blue uniforms and loot in name of Union before the Yankees.

Only fate put them at the head of the Confederacy's escape. Clandestine columns of riders and wagons threaded through the lines, evading the enemy and their own pickets on the way west. Raised at the foot of the Ouachitas, the brothers had knowledge of the land that proved valuable. With healthy provisions, they led the way for the dream of President Davis to regroup in Texas.

If not for the capture of the South's leader in Georgia, the treasury would have been spent to establish a new order in Mexico or even South America. Instead, with Davis a prisoner of General Grant, a chosen few were given the task to hide the gold of the South in Texas so as to not have it confiscated by the Army of the United States.

Eli's growl drew attention. "The edge is so blunted," he said, shaking the ax to get it loose from the stump, "it ain't cutting nothing, just slamming into it."

Levi huffed a laugh and slapped his brother's shoulder. "You know, we aren't planters. Don't know why we thought to give it a try in the first place. We'd only be working for to pay the taxes. I was just thinking, there's got to be something in town more in our line, hear."

"I ain't of mind to argue." Eli twisted his shoulders. The

two walked to their house, each favoring sore joints from the morning's labor.

The sun-bathed streets of Arkadelphia were clogged with wagons of cotton steered toward the river for transport. The Currys rode through the traffic. Levi reined in his horse, paused, then guided it to the side. Eli followed his brother.

"Did you see them wagons?"

"Yeah. So?" Eli answered while tethering the reins to a pillar.

"What say we go to the Exchange House and see if they need a pair of guards to ride over all that white money."

Eli shrugged and held an agreeable grin. "Can't find nothing wrong with that." The two made their way through the maze of shoulders on the boardwalk, passing four alleys, finally arriving at the three-story building where traders on the top floor bought, sold, and bartered fortunes on the sweat of the common man.

They entered and made their way to the rows of the freshly ginned crops stacked in wrapped bundles. In the far corner, a staircase built from the wall led to the upper floors. Although not the work of breaking up a stump, the heavy air, thick with the lint, made the journey up the stairs enough to break a sweat. Levi removed his hat upon reaching the third floor. A glance behind showed the same sweat on Eli's forehead.

Desks littered the space, all manned with stiff-collared white-shirt clerks scrawling numbers on lined paper. They weren't here to see any of those, but only one man. Franklin Turner ran the operation and was the single soul to approve such a hire as the Currys sought.

Hats in hand, the two edged closer to the rear desk surrounded by its polished oak railing. Another clerk stood at the front of the desk concealing the man in the chair. With whatever needed decision made and signature blotted, the clerk stepped aside, revealing the rotund, dapper-dressed, and thin-haired owner of the exchange sucking on a thumb-sized stogie.

Turner's brow raised. "Well, look what the south wind blew in. I think that must be the Curry boys."

Levi smiled in respect. "Yessir, Mr. Turner. It be us."

"Come in, come in. Have a seat." The brothers accepted the invitation. Levi sat in a chair next to Eli, amazed at Turner's hospitality. "What can I do for you boys?"

Nervous from not knowing what words to use, Levi cleared his throat and blurted out what they wanted. "We're looking for jobs as guards for your stock traveling to the river port, Mr. Turner. We done that kind of work before. I know we're good at it." The wisp of confidence building inside him, bolstered by Eli's supporting nod, faded into the thick air at Turner's stern stare.

"Oh, this isn't a social call. You boys are just a couple of vagrants wanting something to do that doesn't take much effort." Turner shook his head. "Can't help you. No. This is a business. Not a charity house. I already have trained men doing that job that have been with me for years. Now, I have work to do myself. You boys know how to get out."

Weak from the rebuke, Levi didn't have the strength to rise from the chair. A bit disconcerted after the initial courtesy, he scrambled for ideas. "Mr. Turner, sir. There isn't anything to do you need doing? You know us. We're sons of Arkansas. Strong and able to work. We fought for the ways of the South, to keep businessmen such as yourself in the ways and manner you're accustomed. We can be teamsters or loaders."

Turner leaned back in his chair and unstuck the cigar from his teeth. "What do you want from me?" he said with the voice of a man in surrender. "I don't have jobs to hand out like pennies to the poor. This is business. I have expenses to make up, debts to pay, taxes on everything I do." His upper lip curled. "If you boys had won the war, maybe matters would be different, but that isn't the case."

Out of ideas and with what little pride he had nearly gone, Levi nodded to Eli for them to leave. Slowly, they stood, Levi not wanting to say more for fear there would be a fee charged for Turner's time. As he turned, the owner's low tone stopped them at the railing.

"I thought you boys had some land."

"That is a fact, sir," Levi said, peering back over a shoulder at Turner. "But the soil hadn't been worked so long, it takes a heap of work to see it planted."

Turner nodded once. "Might be someone offer to buy it."

Levi looked at his brother. Eli's surprised gaze had him scratch the edge of his mustache. "I guess we could listen. We were talking this morning about selling it. But you know it is prime land. Fifty-three acres with a creek running through the center."

"Well, I'm sure you could get a fair price. I'll spread the word you're putting it up for sale. May have one of these Northern fellows wanting to find a home to make here."

The remark kept Levi firm on his feet. He grabbed Eli's sleeve to keep from leaving. "What's that you say? Northern fellows?" The idea of selling the place their mother spent her last years on, where she was now buried, to a stinking Northerner boiled his gut. He forced a beaming smile. "I ain't sure I know what you're saying."

Turner had his brow arched like a man staring at a child who should have known better than to keep out of the rain. "You know the Federals are leaving. Both here and Texas. After all, little action happened here compared to the states in the East."

Levi hadn't heard the news, and stopped listening upon utterance of the single word. "Texas?" As Turner continued, Levi looked at his brother. Words wouldn't have told what each other was thinking any better. The opportunity was obvious. After a few seconds passed, Turner's voice filtered into his ear.

". . . not completely, but it will happen soon."

"What?" Levi said, shaking his head. "I beg your pardon, Mr. Turner. I didn't get all you said."

Turner closed his mouth, appearing irritated at their lack of attention. "I said that since Texas has sworn loyalty to the Union and promised the vote to the Negroes, some troopers in some parts have withdrawn, although not completely, but that will happen soon."

It sounded like a verse from the Bible, almost too good to be true. Levi faced his brother, recognizing the same disbelief that must have been etched on his own face. After a moment, he looked at the old fat man. "That's good to know, Mr. Turner. We'll keep it in mind." Levi waved his hat in a gesture of parting, then nodded his head at his brother to leave. They scampered down the stairs and through the warehouse like children on Christmas morn.

Once on the boardwalk, Levi was stopped by the sunlight. He quickly put on his hat to shield his eyes from the brilliance, hoping he'd not awakened from a daydream. Eli joined him on the boardwalk.

"Brother, you thinking what I'm thinking?" asked Eli.

Levi gave him a confident smile. "We got to get to Texas." They walked down the boardwalk, through the maze of shoulders and between the alleys to the next boardwalk.

"What about the farm?"

"To hell with the farm. Besides, it'll be there when we get back." From shade to sunshine, they strode toward their horses. "We're going to need some supplies for the trip." Levi darted off the boardwalk with his brother in tow, dodging the traffic of riders and wagons. Once across the street, he went to the general store. He stopped at the front door and waited for Eli. "How much money do you have?"

Eli dug in his pocket, drew out forty cents in coins, and held them out in his palm. "That's the last of what I got. What about you?"

"You got more than me." Levi turned for the door. "Let me do all the talking." He went into the store and walked beside the shelves of canned fruit and flour sacks. Picks, shovels, and brooms hung from hooks on the wall. An aproned clerk stood behind the counter. "Howdy, neighbor," said Levi.

The clerk nodded warily.

"Look here, me and my brother are going to be traveling to Texas. And we're needing proper supplies for the trip." As he spoke, Levi's eyes drifted behind the clerk to the rack of rifles lined in a row on the wall. "And what we're needing is a stake of beans, coffee, bacon, some flour, some of them fruit cans, just to get us there."

The clerk shook his head. "Ain't no credit buys here. All of it is Yankee silver or gold paid at the time of purchase."

The refusal initially curled Levi's lip, but he fought off the scowl and forced a pleasant smile. "I understand. So many destitutes since the war." He leaned closer. "But, neighbor, I have an offer for you." With only a peek at his brother loitering near the front door, Levi stared the clerk in the eye and whispered, "How would you like to own fifty-three acres of prime farmland?"

The clerk stepped back with a confused face. "What would I do with fifty-three acres?"

"You farm it. Grow tobacco, cotton, beets, or you pay someone to do it for you and split the profit." The clerk at first looked doubtful, so Levi increased his smile. "Hell, you get one of these slaves that ain't got a home no more and let them work it. Once the crop comes in, you run him off the land and keep all the profit yourself."

"I'm not in the landlord business, nor am I a farmer."

"You don't have to be. They'll do all the work."

With a shaking finger, the clerk leaned closer. "Why don't *you* want to get rich with this plan?"

The question was a good one. Levi dipped his eyes to the floor. "There's painful memories for us living there. Our ma and pa both lived and passed while on the place. The memories hurt too much to think about. We can't live there with them."

"Sweet Jesus." Eli's loud proclamation turned both men's attention from the counter toward him. The younger brother held a newspaper close to his face, then turned it toward Levi. "You ought to see this."

Levi clenched his jaw, angered at the interruption, but he curled his lips up into a smile and faced the clerk. "Excuse me for just a minute. Consider my offer." Casually, he walked to his brother with his best attempt to control his temper. "What the hell you want?" he muttered angrily so as not to be heard by the clerk.

Eli showed him the paper. "Sandy Wallace is dead."

The news instantly changed his mood to disbelief. "What are you saying? *The* Sandy Wallace?"

"The same. The one we rode with from Georgia to Texas, brother." Eli huffed a giddy laugh. "The one we buried that gold with in—"

"Hush," Levi barked, then glanced behind to see the clerk scribbling on a pad. Then he looked at the story that detailed his friend's demise. "Says here he was hung for murder in Kansas."

"That's what I'm telling you," Eli whispered back. "This is a sign from above. From Jesus himself, telling us it is our time. With the Yankees leaving Texas, and now with Sandy dead."

It was hard to deny. Visions of a fortune in gold waiting to be hauled off drifted into Levi's head. But before he fully enjoyed all the benefits of his easy life to come, the rude face of reality slammed into his mind. His own face went cold as he turned to his brother. "What about Marcus? Marcus Broussard?"

Eli's eyes widened. "You think he's still alive?"

"Who knows," Levi said with a shrug. "He was from Texas. He could have dug it up and taken it all himself by now."

"But that weren't the deal. We all agreed to wait until the Yankees left before we'd split it up. That way there'd be no Federals interfering with us."

"You think that matters a damn? Look at us. I ain't trusting that any of us would be waiting on the others. Now, Sandy's dead. Maybe he took it. Marcus Broussard lives there. Randolph Smiley may be out of prison by now. Hell, Jeff Davis himself may have plans to snoop around for it. If it's still there, we need to go get it now." It took only a moment to get an agreeing nod from his brother.

Once confident of their plan, Levi returned to the counter where the clerk still scribbled on the pad. "How 'bout it, neighbor?"

"Don't know," was the answer. "It don't seem right. Fifty-three acres of farmland should come to well over two hundred dollars. Seems mighty cheap for some sacks of flour and some peaches."

Levi's smile returned at the clerk's concern. "That's why I only offer it to *you*. Hear, you stake us to all of that." His eyes once again drifted to the rifle rack. "And a pair of them Spencer rifles with a box of cartridges apiece, and neighbor, I'll hand over the deed today."

After the six-mile afternoon, the remuda stopped for night camp. Les returned to the fire with tin bowls. With one knee next to the spit, she stirred the ladle through the beans and salt pork and raised it out of the pot to slop in the bowls. The steaming mix was her first attempt at cooking. She looked for approval.

Jody took the bowl, taking turns shaking each hand off the hot bowl. He drew a biscuit from the canvas sack, dabbing it into the beans, then sucking on the bread. Smith simply took his from the ground and held it without a hint of pain. Likely his calloused hands were the reason.

With the men eating without complaints, she took it as a compliment and served herself. With a dip of the spoon into the beans, she stuck it in her mouth. Fire singed her tongue. She blew while keeping the food in her mouth. Embarrassed by the smirks on their faces, she swallowed. Her throat burned like a hot iron stoked by a blacksmith. With her mouth clear, she gasped for cool air and coughed up the remnants.

"Little hot, ain't it," said Jody, enjoying her distress. "That's why it's better to let it simmer down a mite." He tossed her a biscuit and she did the same as he had. "All in all, it ain't bad." He turned to Smith.

"It's food."

The scorching mouthful gradually sunk down inside,

feeling as if it was setting flames with each inch. For relief, she reached for a coffee tin and poured it full. Never before allowed to drink the brew, she meant to sip at the edge, but she needed liquid relief and instead slurped too much. Hot coffee swirled in her already scalded mouth. She attempted to spit some back in the tin, but while doing so inhaled a drop or two. Gagging for breath, she coughed out coffee mixed with bean broth to the dirt, then heaved in air, repeating the convulsion until able to maintain stable breathing. She wiped the tears from her eyes with her sleeve, and saw Jody in the throes of a hearty guffaw.

"Let me ask you, Les. Where you from? I know it ain't from anywhere out here. Most fellows know by the age of ten not to gulp down coffee."

She took a moment, not wanting to say too much. She'd showed more ignorance than she wanted and needed to limit the mistake. The first thought was of the train to the West. "From the East."

"Figures," Smith grunted.

"Where'bouts?" asked Jody. He spooned in a mouthful of beans. While he ate, she again waited for an answer to come to mind. "A place called New York City. I don't remember much about it. It was a long time ago."

He swallowed the beans with a slight twinge in his eye. "Long time ago? What you doing out here?" He bit off half the biscuit.

Les realized the questions wouldn't stop until she satisfied his curiosity. The first thought was to expand the lie. But considering her lack of success in convincing them about what she knew, the idea of fibbing about working in the livery or mercantile would lead to further lies she wouldn't know the answers to, bringing a need for more lies. Pondering the effects of the truth, she decided it would be believed and not reveal her most important secret. "I worked at Miss Maggie Turnbow's boardinghouse. Sweeping and washing the plates and the linen."

"Sweeping and washing? Sounds like a girl's job."

Her heart beat faster. She must have said too much. The

choice wasn't hers where she ended up, and besides, it was work and she felt angry that he made it sound like an easy duty. "I did what I was told. Didn't matter to me at the time. It kept me eating."

Jody nodded. "I can side with that. I done chores for my folks when I was little." He stuffed the rest of the biscuit in his mouth, pushing his cheeks as wide as a prairie dog's. "She your ma? This Maggie lady?"

Just as she knelt close enough for the fire's heat to sting her face, she felt the questions were nearing another danger. Smith leaned toward the pot and refilled his bowl and took another biscuit. Both of them sat staring at her. She grunted. It had come time for the whole truth.

"I was put on a train of orphans when I was very young and sent out West." With the rest of her story still stuck in her throat, she noticed Jody had stopped chewing. A glance at Smith showed his spoon frozen in place in front of his mouth.

"So, you don't have a ma or pa. Like regular kids," Jody said, his constant smile faded for the first time. Her mild nod made him shake his head. "Must have been hard. A boy as yourself sent to a far-off place with no folks."

Les, sensing for once the truth had satisfied them both, kept nodding and only opened her lips to sip the cooler coffee.

"That's a shame. I feel poorly for funning you on not knowing your business. You not having a ma or pa, can't say I could expect you to know."

Les kept nodding, realizing no more need be said. The two men helped themselves to most of the pot. She dealt herself a little more, stabbing the biscuit into the beans to soften the hard bread. Once she swabbed the dish clean, she set it on the ground, her restless stomach having also been satisfied.

The two men finished in a short time. Her coffee tin half empty, she topped it off, allowing time for it to cool. While waiting, she rewarded herself with a deep breath for the hard day, and gathered the courage to ask her own set of questions. Before she could mold the words, Jody slipped a harmonica from his pocket and tooted the dust clear of it with the full scale of notes. Not wanting to interrupt, she held back from speaking, and settled on the ground intrigued to listen.

Jody glanced only at Smith. "What say for a serenade?" The old wrangler kept his eyes toward the twilight. Not discouraged, Jody put the instrument to his lips and dual tinny tones vibrated into the night. In a low pitch at first, a tune emerged, the notes rising and falling, sometimes at a roll, then just as quick changing to climbing steps of stairs.

He cupped a hand around the end, waving his fingers, giving the tune a muffled wobbly sound. As she watched, Les could imagine the notes as he formed them with each motion. While he played, her eyes drifted to Smith. Almost as if the music soothed his gruff manner, he took a pipe and pouch from his vest and crammed tobacco into the bowl. Just as he completed the task, Jody softened his tune to silence.

"You're good with that," Les said.

Jody modestly nodded twice. "Been playing for a long spell. My pa taught me when I was small and I just kept at it. Comes in handy when you're out riding. Away from home."

His mention of home provided a chance to learn more. She couldn't resist. If ever she was to ask, this was it. She dipped her eyes to the dirt so to not seem too interested. "Where's home?"

"Oh, I'm from a little place just west of San Antone. My folks have a spread there, raising hogs and chickens." He stopped as if something got caught in his throat. "They're still there. But I'm not." He finished with a quick grin, but it faded just as quick.

Les let it pass, unsure if something pained him about his past. She knew what it meant to think of something that wasn't pleasant to recall. However, her curiosity wasn't satisfied.

Jody, his smile returned, continued and looked at Smith,

who took a flaming twig and sucked fire into the pipe to ignite the tobacco. "Joined this outfit two years past. Told them I wanted to see things I ain't never seen nor likely would if I stayed where I was. So I joined up. They put me on drag and I ate dust for three months." He looked to Les and winked. "Don't know what you missed. Maybe next year you'll get the chance. Anyway, I stayed with the drive all the way to Abilene. I got my pay, near ninety dollars, and I seen the elephant for the first time. Knew then this is what I want to do."

Les shook her head, confused by what he said, but she didn't want to ask and face further embarrassment. Instead, she peeked at Smith, who puffed one cloud of smoke after another spiraling into the cool night air. His hat, still drawn tight, hid his eyes in shadow. The same stern jaw she'd seen for the entire day remained. She never knew what was on his mind, but by his nature it must never be pleasant.

Another tune pierced the silence. Jody blew long slow notes, four in a low tone, the fifth slightly higher, and the rest between the range. As he repeated the melody, it seemed to attract the interest of Smith. If Les guessed right, the song seemed to have a pleasing effect.

Jody played on, stretching the notes, wagging his hands in front of the instrument. The longer it went on, the more slack there was in Smith's jaw. Finally, slowing the same melody, Jody held a high note and finished with two lower ones.

Smith tapped the pipe against a log. "I'll take the first watch," he said in the softest voice Les had heard from him the entire day she'd known him. She watched as he took his saddle and in no particular hurry headed toward his horse.

# 8

THE SCENT OF burning wood led Rance through the dark. He crept to a clump of trees and bobbed his head to see through the branches in hopes to spot who was camped. Unable to get a good look, he stepped one long stride at a time to the right. He needed to know.

If it appeared trackers were on his trail, he needed to retreat back to the white gelding and keep riding. If it were friendly folks, he needed a meal. While he was moving further to the right, his attention remained fixed on the fire in the center. There was no one in sight. As relief eased the tension in his chest, the cold pinch of steel poked at his cheek.

"Hold it right there or I'll scatter your ears in different counties, mister."

Rance stiffened. He scraped his cheeks when edging his face around to see the double barrels of a shotgun. He forced a smile. "Listen, friend, I'm not who you think. It wasn't me, whatever it is you think I did."

"You ain't the one prowling around here in the bushes?"

"Oh, that." Rance cautiously moved enough to have his nose between the dual muzzles. "I was just attracted by the light. Thought I would see if I had new neighbors."

"Neighbors? You just parade yourself into the light where I can get a good look at you."

With the shotgun now at his back, Rance was pushed to the center of the camp. The large wagon with the white canopy sat at the edge of the light. An adult lady crept from the shadows with the same fright etched on her face as the small boy just ahead of her apron.

"Right there's good." Rance stopped when the holder of the shotgun stepped in front. The hat with a huge brim covered most of his features, but the thick mustache stretched to the ends of his jaw. "Now, you tell who you are and what you're doing out there."

Unsure if he should give his true name for fear it might spread to unfriendly ears, he remembered another. "My name is Hanks." The muzzles pushed up Rance's chin, but not high enough that he didn't notice a young woman with angelic features emerge from the dark clutching the Holy Bible to her chest. "Reverend Josiah Hanks."

"Reverend?" The prod of the muzzles slackened. "You're a reverend?"

"So help me," Rance said holding up his right hand. The shotgun slowly left the point of his chin. He inhaled for the first time in several minutes.

"My apology. Didn't know who it was out there."

"No apology needed, friend." Rance's eyes drifted back to the young beauty. "With women and children to protect, you can't be too careful."

"Strange, though, I never seen a parson dressed in such fancy duds."

The shotgun's aim remained casually at Rance's chest. "Given by those of my flock," Rance said. He wrinkled his nose. "Is that the delightful aroma of a woman's cooking?"

"Yes," came from near the wagon. Rance peered past the inquisitor with the scattergun to see the older lady step away from the wagon. "Could I offer you some, Reverend Hanks?"

Quick to display the gleam that had gained him many an advantage, Rance sidestepped the shotgun and walked toward the fire. A kettle hung over the flame. The lady took the ladle and scooped it full of stew, delivering it into a bowl. She handed it to Rance with a welcoming smile.

He tipped his hat, then took the bowl from her. "Thank you, ma'am. I'm truly grateful for the hospitality." While he dipped the spoon in the potatoes and meat, his eyes drifted to the beauty with the Bible. The older lady walked in front of him, obscuring the view.

"Where are they?"

The question interrupted his concentration. "Who?" he answered while slightly distracted.

"Your flock. Where are the people of your congregation?"

A detail he hadn't considered. He quickly stuffed another spoonful into his mouth. As he savored the tasty broth, he contemplated suitable excuses. The truth was not one, although the more he thought, certain parts could serve as proper background. He swallowed, grunting the last of the stew from his throat. Again, he flashed his gleam.

"I left those folks near St. Mary's Landing on the Mississippi." Surprise curled the brow of the man and woman. "Don't be alarmed. It was actually the will of those people that sent me on my way." The surprise turned to bewilderment. In his own mind, he didn't understand. Needing more time, he stuffed another spoonful into his mouth. Mutterings from the two adults signaled their mood was changing from a friendly nature to one of suspicion. Even without a certain message in mind, and still he had to say something to quell the concern.

"You see, I'd done all I could for those folks." He shook his head and pointed his finger to the ground. "It was their suggestion that I embark out on my own"—he hesitated— "alone, and spread my preaching to a whole new lot. I've been traveling ever since. That is how I came to you folks, here."

The man rubbed his chin. "Awful strange. Never heard of a congregation wanting their parson to leave. Normally they follow him to new places."

"They didn't want to be selfish." Rance thought it a good response until he thought of a reason why it made sense. He relied on his smile to give him time. "You see, they got to know the ways of the Lord just as good as I did. In fact, one of them thought he knew the ways better than me. It got to a point where if I were to stay, then he and I just wouldn't have been getting along. So I thought it best for all concerned to set about on my own way. As soon as possible."

"How noble of you," said the lady. "For you to think of the best interest of them rather than yourself."

Rance took another bite while trying to maintain as humble a face as he could muster. Once he swallowed, he thought it time to learn about this new flock. "What about you people? I don't recall your name."

"Forgive us, Reverend. I'm Abigail Fuller. This is my husband Thomas," she said, pointing to the man with the shotgun. She led the boy to the front with her palm to the back of his neck. "This is our son, Horton." She stepped aside and held out an extended arm. The young beauty stepped into the glow of the fire, the light beaming against her high cheeks, lighting the long hair streaming over her shoulders, and setting a twinkle in her hazel eyes. "And this is our niece Ruth."

Rance couldn't keep his eyes from her. His heart pounded. He'd seen many a striking woman, mostly in the confines of a bedroom. However, this girl looked like she'd walked off the canvas of a painting and the artist was purity. Realizing he stood with his mouth agape, he shook his head and removed his hat. "What a beautiful"—he paused to remove the word *creature* from his tongue—"family. What a beautiful family. You must be very proud, Mrs. Fuller. And Mr. Fuller too, of course."

The man stood, the shotgun now with the stock to the ground, without as friendly a manner as his wife. After a moment, the side of his lip curled and he showed an open palm to the ground. "I guess we might as well sit."

"Well, why don't we," Rance said, always keeping his

smile in place as he sat on a log. Mrs. Fuller retrieved a
stool from the wagon. The boy put the seat of his pants on
the dirt. Ruth knelt with her skirt under both knees. As
Rance kept his eyes on her, her uncle sat at the other end of
the log. The jar of the weight jolted Rance in more than
one way. "Where do you folks hail from?"

"We're from Franklin County in Tennessee." The cheer
in Abigail Fuller's voice faded as quick as her grin. "We
had a small place there."

Sensing that their memory of home wasn't a pleasant
one, Rance turned the subject to the present. "What brings
you out here?"

"We're going to New Mexico," said Mr. Fuller, who
helped himself to the stew. "Following the Santa Fe Trail."

"New Mexico? Seems like a far-off place for you."

Rance's remark was met with lowered brow from Fuller.
"Why you say that?"

"Well . . ." Rance hesitated, anxious not to offend. "It
just seems to be such a desolate land to travel to when you
come from such a fine state as that of Tennessee." The
compliment wasn't taken with the spirit intended. Mrs.
Fuller's eyes dipped to the fire. Her husband seemed to
take an extended time chewing on the stew. Horton sat con-
tent to eat his meal. A glance at Ruth showed her eyes fixed
on Rance.

A quick glimpse at the adults showed neither noticed
their niece's attentive focus. Not one to blush, Rance did
break away from her eye contact, partly in fear of being
caught, but more because of the uneasy feeling his words
had given the Fullers. There was no doubt more to this
family's story. As a man of the cloth, he would be duty-
bound to seek the truth and heal the wound inside both of
them. It took a second to remind himself of his true calling.
It was one thing to pretend to be someone he wasn't. It was
another to act it. Not to good folk. Not to these people.

"That was mighty fine food, Mrs. Fuller. You are one
good cook. I am beholden to you for your kindness." The

lady raised her head and grinned. Rance turned his attention to Thomas. "What line are you in, Mr. Fuller?"

"I'm a carpenter by trade." The answer finished with a nod.

"A carpenter. Now there is an honorable profession. Just as the man above. I'll bet you can build a house that would stand for a hundred years all by yourself."

Despite the appreciative smirk, Thomas shook his head and sighed. "Truth said, there weren't much hiring to build. Most of the work done near our home was all brought in by the Northerners. I took to raising corn and beets just to pay my debts until farming took all the money I could raise. There wasn't nothing to live on."

The somber mood resumed, and Rance felt uneasy at the family's plight. Not needing further complications to his plans, he thought it best to leave them with their worries and not add to his own. Still, it was proper to be cordial. If he ran like a spooked cat, their suspicions could be raised enough to alert the next law they came across. It would be better to part on neighborly terms.

"Well, I'm sure this is all in the plans of the man above. It is a test. All the trouble you've had in the past is just his way of steering you where it is he wants you to go." Lost in his own point, he scrambled to tie his rambling words into some inspiration. "You see"—he hesitated, shaking his finger to the night's sky, waiting for the next words to enter his head—"his plan is for you is to . . . need. That's it, I'm sure. You have to have 'want.' That is what is guiding your path. Just as it says in the holy book." The finger now pointed at Ruth and the Bible. "Those that thou shall not want . . . then. . . . won't get nothing. So, it's for the best that you continue wanting and he will see that you get it." He stuffed the last of the stew in his mouth as quick as possible.

Confused as to the theme of his first sermon, he swirled the stew in his mouth while watching the four in front of him twitch lips and brows while pondering his words. All of them appeared as confused as he. Rance peeked over his shoulder for the fastest route back to the gelding for a hasty escape. The sound of Abigail's voice made him cringe. He was sure she was about to chide him for his false ministry.

"That was by far the most . . . intriguing message I think I have ever heard."

Rance stopped squinting and opened both eyes with relief when Thomas nodded and looked at him with a mild smile.

"I have to say, it does make sense," said Thomas. "But does it really say that in the Bible?"

Rance again held up his right hand. "As my witness. Of course, I did put what it says into common language for you people who may not get the true meaning among all those fancy *thous* and *thines*."

"Why do you suppose it would say that kind of thing?" asked Thomas. "About putting people through all that it does."

Rance put his palm to his chest. "Who am I to question the Divine."

"Yes. That's right, Thomas." Abigail turned her fond face to Rance. "Reverend Hanks, would you like more stew?"

"That's very kind of you, ma'am. But I don't want to impose on you fine folks anymore. I'll just be getting on my way."

"You're leaving?" Mrs. Fuller's shock froze Rance as he stood. "You mean you can't stay and travel with us? You said yourself you had no one to return to. Why don't you join us? You could come to New Mexico with us. I'm sure a man of your knowledge of the Gospel is a rare thing there."

"Oh, I'm sure you're right about that," Rance said, his eyes drifting to the lovely Ruth, admiring her unspoiled radiance and her womanhood blossoming beneath her lace-collared blouse. "I really shouldn't."

"Nonsense," Abigail said, rising with her welcoming

smile as when he'd first arrived. "You can sleep with Mr. Fuller under the wagon. I'll make a place for you."

Before he could decline, the woman had started for the wagon. At first he was reluctant, but the more he thought about the prospect of traveling with this family, the better the idea seemed. If trackers were following, they might well ignore a covered wagon, providing he rode close enough to it not to be noticed from far away. The added benefit of meals cooked by a woman was another enticement.

Ruth rose and gave him a passing glance as she went to join her aunt. She had not uttered a single word, yet he was sure she had an interest in him as he had in her. As if in a trance, he watched her walk to the wagon.

Thomas handed him a blanket. "Hope you don't mind me snoring, Parson."

# 9

THE WARMTH OF the dawning sun didn't help Les shake the sleep from her face. A breakfast of last night's left-over beans wasn't sitting well while swaying in the saddle. Even the paint and the pack mules weren't awake, as shown by her having to nudge them along after every ten steps. It seemed all concerned could have used an hour or maybe a day more sleep.

She glanced behind and found the remuda as always not very far behind. As she twisted, her lower back reminded her how long she'd been in the saddle. Worse, her bottom felt like it had been worn to the bone. Maybe if she had drunk more coffee her bones wouldn't feel so sore, or her muscles so weak. She actually was developing a taste for the stuff, or maybe just a tolerance. Either way, the next camp, she'd make a point to slurp more of the bitter, tongue-burning java.

The view ahead distracted her attention from the fatigue. Low dark clouds moved to the east, while higher clouds with the look of butter skipped over a slice of bread glowed like hot iron on a blacksmith's anvil. An occasional gust of cool air slapped at her cheek and opened her eyes.

A distant ridge stood in silhouette against the near-white light behind it and the dimness overhead.

Yells and hoots came from behind. Les twisted about in the saddle. Jody and Smith rode at a gallop, flanking each side of the herd. The horses moved as one, like a giant swarm of bees with no firm edge on any one side. Confused as to the reason, Les pulled up on the reins as the herd passed to her left.

Jody steered away from the mass at an angle toward her. "We're going to run them. Get them past this rain." He kicked his mount to take his position at the herd's forward flank. As she watched him gallop off, a raindrop hit her nose. When she looked up, lightning streaked through the cloud. The hair on her neck rose stiff. Fearful of lightning since a child, she kicked the paint. It was all it needed to bolt in pursuit of the herd. The sudden jolt yanked the reins to the mules from her hands.

With a death grip on the horn, she stayed in the saddle as the paint charged over the uneven ground. The cool air slapped her face, blowing her eyes wide open. Rocked back and forth by the horse's gait, she pulled herself to lean forward in a crouch while putting her weight in the stirrups. A glance behind showed the slower mules at a run too, but falling behind the speed of the paint.

She faced forward. Dust from so many hooves pounding the dirt rose from the plain. She didn't worry about losing sight of the remuda, for her horse was bound and determined to join the group. Another drop struck her back, then another, then four. Like a wave, rain pelted the grass. A sheet of gray shrouded the dust, the remuda, and all in front from view. In an instant, water dripped off the front of the hat brim and into her eyes as if poured over her head from a bucket. Her vision blurred, she hoped she'd guessed right about the paint's instinct because she couldn't tell which way she was riding.

As fast as the rain arrived, it passed like a drape being drawn open, allowing bright sunlight into view. Once able

to let one hand off the horn, she swiped her sleeve across
her face to clear her eyes. There was no dust. No horses.

Before she had a chance to look to the side, she felt the
ground give way under her. Her body seized every muscle,
her eyes squinted from the shock. The jolt of solid ground
slammed her into the saddle. A second later she realized
the paint had leapt from a ridge and down a slope. Again,
she clung to the horn for dear life.

As the horse strode down the incline, Les's head constantly whipping back like it was on the end of a string, she
could see the large dark blotch through her watering eyes.
After several more times of being tossed about in the saddle, the paint finally reached level ground. Hopeful what
she'd seen wasn't a mistake, she found her prayers answered when she recognized the shape of the remuda.

She resumed the crouch and let her horse have rein to
run, anxious herself to catch the herd. The paint's stride
made it feel like she was flying. The freshly washed air
splashed against her cheeks, rippling her sleeves, sinking
beneath her shirt to chill every inch of bare skin found.
Never had she gone so fast. Even her bottom didn't mind
the rapid undulation caused by the horse's gallop.

As she approached, Jody rode alongside the tightly
grouped herd. The paint's greater speed allowed Les to
gradually pass. She glanced to the side, watching the un-
saddled ponies glide almost effortlessly across the prairie,
shoulders and backs flexing and stretching in fluid motion,
manes swaying like flags, nostrils flared to fuel the fire
propelling them. With her blood racing through her own
veins just as fast, she let out a yell.

As she hooted as loud and as long as her lungs held air,
she barely heard Jody's call as he rode next to her.
"Where's the mules?" The excitement was still flowing,
and reality took several seconds before it dropped like a
stone to the pit of her stomach. She pulled back on the
reins, but the paint shook the bit, not wanting to stop, until
finally its gait slowed to a lope. Les turned it to face about.
The mules stood on the slope. Both grazed on the grass of

the hill. Her heart racing from the ride and the scare, Les sat relieved that all the supplies for the ride to Texas weren't headed back to Abilene. With a glance over her shoulder, she saw the remuda slowed to a gentle advance. She took a deep breath and blew it out.

As the morning seeped away, the trip had resumed its normal pace. Jody and Smith had pushed the horses to the east to avoid driving them up a rocky precipice. Les, on the other hand, saw it as a way to gain the time lost chasing the stubborn mules, which hadn't wanted to leave the tender yellow grass.

She nudged the paint through the small brush, tugging at the mules' reins to keep them close behind through the thorny bushes. When she reached the base of the hill, she stared at the top. It was not very high, but the incline was sharp. Without confidence to maintain balance in the saddle and hold the two sets of reins, she dismounted and tied the mules' reins to the horn, taking the paint's and trudging on foot up the hill.

The first few steps were taken with ease. Once she was halfway, she leaned forward just to remain standing. The ornery animals were no help. Every time she gained ground, their reluctance stopped her momentum and her boots slipped on the small stones and pebbles layering the slope. Les dug in her heels and marched backward using the paint's weight as a counterbalance to keep from falling back on the rocks. One slow step after another, she gauged her success by the view of the plain below. The yellowing grass stretched to the horizon. Despite the morning's small and fast storm, the lack of constant rainfall had dried the land to mostly dust. The only green was from trees with tall tops, which dotted the plain for as far as the eye could see.

With a fresh breeze to her back, she twisted around to claim the top of the hill. Beneath her was a different scene. Green grass swayed from the breeze. Trees bunched together in groves around a creek full with water flowing so fast she could see the white ripples lapping over one another. The familiar call of Jody's voice to the herd carried into her ear.

To the distant left, the remuda filtered through the trees and into the wide grass expanse. Les gazed with her mouth open. Her eyes drifted south. Only blue sky went to the very end with nary a cloud, black or white. She felt as if she'd walked through a different door. If this was Texas, it was all that was said about it.

She got to her feet and walked the animals over the hill with greater ease. It made sense they were more agreeable headed down a slope rather than up. Once at the bottom, she mounted the paint and within minutes rejoined the herd.

As she came near, Smith rode toward her. He pulled up and came alongside. "Where you been?" As always, there was no smile.

"I had trouble getting them over that hill."

"You should have followed us." He pointed to a break in the trees where two large boulders overhung the creek. "We'll make camp at that spot. Get a fire started."

She nodded at the order, but there was a question she had to ask. "Are we close to Texas?"

Smith yanked back on the reins. "Texas? Hell, we ain't even out of Kansas. You think after three days we cover five hundred miles?" He finished with a shake of his head and a kick to his horse.

She watched him ride back to the remuda, asking herself why she would ask him such a question. Whenever she was by herself with the old man, her gut twisted in knots. Maybe it was just the pinch of the sheet strips wound around her ribs. Either way, she resolved not to ask or even talk to him if she could help it for the rest of the trip.

Despite the slow pace, she made it to the boulders and drew the cooking tools from the packs. With only three tries, she set aflame undergrowth she'd gathered and the fallen twigs that littered the ground under the trees. The two men had long since settled the herd in a small clearing surrounded by the trees. As she stirred the beans in the pot, she noticed the men talking out of her earshot. Convinced the conversation involved her and the stupid questions she asked, she tried to keep her mind on the food.

Not long after, Jody's friendly approach through the grass brought her head up. He looked into the pot and crinkled his nose. "Smells like I got time for a bath."

"Yeah, it will take a while for the beans to heat up—" The notion of what he said hit her like a hammer to the head. Slowly she looked at him. Jody already had the chaps off and began pulling one boot. Les sat stunned. "You mean, you're going to take one now?"

Jody nodded. "That was the idea." He pointed to the pot. "You should too. Be a half hour before them beans are any good to eat."

Once again, she found her lungs squeezed for air. She put her head down to the pot, hiding her eyes from his smile. "No, I got to stir them up or they'll burn on the bottom."

"Suit yourself."

As she twirled the ladle, she heard the rustle of clothes over her shoulder. To the front, Smith walked to one of the boulders. First he looked at Les, who didn't like looking at him and kept her eyes darting back to the pot. Then, his glare went over her shoulder.

"That's a good idea. Think I'll join you, son."

Her eyes widened. Now, she would have two men in bare skin parading around her. She huddled closer to the pot for fear of catching a glimpse of one or both. From the corner of her vision, she saw Smith strip his chaps from his legs. She stirred faster. Then he yanked off his boots and unbuttoned his shirt. When he put his hands to his belt, she ducked her head to the right.

There Jody strutted to the creek, his bare backside in clear sight. Even though she knew it was a sin to look, she couldn't keep from it. The skin of his back, arms, legs, and butt was a pale white all the way to his neck, where it turned red as a rooster's comb. She watched him walk into the stream. The current lapped at his waist, then his ribs, and finally his shoulders.

The jangle of a belt buckle turned her attention to the right. Smith, gray hair spattered about his chest, had shed his pants and just begun his walk to the water. Although it was the same view, it didn't hold the same fascination as with Jody, and so she found it easier to avert her attention. A moment more spent whirling beans, and it was safe to peer at the two men up to their necks in the creek.

Les took a deep breath. Slowly letting it out, she tried to relax after having narrowly escaped an embarrassing moment, or so she thought.

"Hey, Les," Jody called. "Throw us a soap."

Hesitant at first, she thought of declining, feigning to be too busy. However, after another second, she concluded the delay would only force Jody to climb out of the water after the soap. She rose and went to the packs. She flipped open the flap and searched through the sacks of cornmeal, flour, bacon, coffee, and many sacks of beans to find a brown-paper-wrapped bar. Les slipped the string off a corner and peeled the soap from the paper. She went to the edge of the shore. Jody stood, his hips barely above the surface. He trudged through the water, more of his waist revealed with every step closer. Again nervous, she tossed the soap into the water. The swift current instantly swept the floating bar down the stream.

"Damnit," he said as he tried to walk after it, then swam in a last effort to catch it. Too embarrassed to watch more, she returned to the pot. "What are you thinking, boy?" Jody chided. "Nearly lost the only soap we got."

She didn't reply, too scared to utter any words for fear whatever she'd say would make matters worse. As minutes passed, she heard the thrash of the men in the water, but she stared at the beans. As the brown sauce bubbled, she still stirred while wondering how long she had before they found her out. All the warnings from Shenandoah came back to mind. The more she remembered the lady's words of caution for a girl traveling with men, the more it made her shiver. The image of Smith's whispers to Jody shook the ladle enough to bring the bacon to the top. To them it was no game.

She heard both of them climb out of the creek and complain of the cold while praising the refreshment of the bath. Although they weren't shy about walking about in nakedness, she managed not to peek. Little time went past until they had put on the same dirty drawers, shirts, and pants.

Jody came next to her to kneel by the fire. "Smells like I was right," he said while angling his nose over the pot. He grabbed a bowl and ladled himself a portion. His bright grin beamed even more with his wet hair combed back behind the ears. She had a hard time not staring at that face, but when she sensed him notice, she darted her eyes to Smith. The old wrangler buttoned his shirt. "You should take a dip yourself," Jody said.

"Then the beans would have burned," Les answered, turning back to Jody.

"Sounds like an excuse to me not to take a bath." He scooped a spoonful of beans in his mouth. "You know, them gals in Fort Worth ain't going to want to get near you if you smell like sweat and horses."

"Fort Worth?"

He nodded while gulping another spoonful. "Biggest town there is in Texas, next to San Antone. And it's full of women. Sometimes there're more of them than they is steers. Makes for an easy ride home." He winked at Les. "They make a fellow forget all the aches he's got. You know what I mean?" He threw more beans in his mouth, the sauce dribbling from his lips in his attempt to blow off the heat.

Les sat still, trying to decide if what he said was meant for a boy, or to tease the girl pretending to be one. She'd seen enough drovers cross the tracks in Abilene to Shenandoah's and other houses along the row to understand that men away from their homes paid women to act as their wives for the night, or so Miss Maggie told her. Les didn't

pay attention to his smile anymore, fearful it might lead
into a conversation she couldn't lie her way out of. Yet the
idea that Jody might know her secret forced her to dole out
her portion in a bowl and find a corner by the boulders.

Smith helped himself, and the two men commenced
their usual conversation of the night about people they had
met while driving cattle, mostly men of ill repute worse
than Les had ever heard of from Shenandoah. The sun set
and Les edged herself into a corner where the campfire
would illuminate least. Once the beans were gone, she took
the pot to rinse in the creek while listening to Jody's harmonica tunes. When she finished, he played the same one
that had made Smith stay so silent and still. As before,
when Jody completed the melody, Smith went to his horse
to start nighthawk duty. She wasn't sure that was the true
reason or just the excuse to leave.

Jody yawned long, which instantly made Les tired. As he
unfurled his bedroll, she did the same, and stretched hers as
far away from him she could out of fear he would spy on
her while asleep. The last thing she remembered when she
lay down was the black sky above with all those white dots.

The first push to the shoulder irritated her. The second
nearly threw her head into the boulder. She blinked her
eyes open quickly. Smith hovered above.

"It's your watch."

She nodded and threw off the blanket. Another long
yawn and a firm snap of her head to the side shook enough
sleep away to stand. The warm night had made her sweat in
the clothes. The edges of the soiled sheet strips dug into
her skin like a saw. The cool night air chilled her wet skin
and made her shiver.

Smith wasted no time in throwing his bedroll to the
ground and climbing inside. She put on the coat stored in
the mule packs and went to the paint. Oddly, she felt alone,
even though it wasn't the first time she'd been by herself. It
was her second nighthawk duty, and the first time both men
would sleep while she was out with the horses.

She steered the paint through the trees and found the remuda in the moonlight. As she'd been told, she circled the
perimeter to keep a count and to scare off any predators
that might have worked up the courage to take a chance.
Not that she would know what to do should something
charge out of the dark except turn the paint in the opposite
direction. As far as a count was concerned, the numbers
only served to dull her mind and weigh down her eyelids.

More than once she shook her head and opened her eyes
wide in attempt to rid herself of the drowsiness. However,
the paint's slow and rhythmic amble gently rocked her in
the saddle like a porch swing. The soothing sway teamed
with the darkness to numb her mind. The last bit of aware-
ness screamed at her to wake up, but it would take more
than a scolding from her conscience.

The glistening of moonlight off water caught her attention. The paint had come to the far side of the remuda and
further up the creek. Les tugged at the reins to halt her
horse. If she took a bath, maybe it would wash all the sleep
away. She faced to the camp, which she couldn't even see
through the dark. It might be the only chance to enjoy
scrubbing all the dirt from her joints. Although a risk, if
she hurried, no one would be the wiser. The longer she
thought about it, the more time she wasted.

She slid off the paint and crept to the bank. The moist
air was heavy and hard to breathe for someone with a chest
so tight. Yet she was determined, and soon she shed the
coat and had the chaps off, then the boots. Quickly she
threaded the buttons back through the eyelets, but before
she took the shirt from her shoulders, she peeked in the direction of the camp again. There was only the black of
night.

One arm at a time, she pulled out of the sleeves and the
shirt was off. The sheet bandage was tied tightly. She bent
an elbow behind and fumbled for the knot. Finally seizing
the lace ends between fingertips, she yanked the knot free.
The slack was like a gulp of air. She grabbed under the
edges of each side and further spread the back flaps. With

enough slack, she loosened the strips and unwound the bandage. The edges initially stuck as if glued to the skin. Gradually, she eased it off her torso. The night breeze soothed the sting of the blistered skin.

Les knelt by the bank and scooped water and patted her chafed underarms, beneath her breasts, and as far as she could reach behind, further enhancing the effect of the wind. She couldn't wait for the rest.

She slipped off the dungarees and socks. Like a child, she dipped her toe into the cold water and recoiled. Moonlight reflected her pale nude figure and frightened her worse at the notion of her nakedness. Cold or no, she slid into the water. The chill first seized her breath, but after settling her feet into the silt, she bobbed down to her neck and relished the relief. When she grew accustomed to the cold, it was then she realized she had no soap.

There would be no scrubbing. Nevertheless, just the freedom to move without the bondage of the sheet strips felt like heaven. She found a slight ledge near the bank on which to settle and rest her head against the dirt. With the light twinkling off the minute waves, she soaked as the current rushed over every inch of her bare skin.

# 10

NOTHING COULD BE better. Warm in her bed, she sank further beneath the blankets. The room had grown chilly through the night.

"Les."

Jody's call for her seemed peculiar. Why did he want her? And she didn't remember when he'd moved into the boardinghouse.

"Les!"

Her eyes shot open. The water lapped over her chest; her bare chest. Despite arms and legs with tingling numbness, she sank to neck level while trying to peek over the bank to spot Jody. With the forest of horse legs in the way she didn't see him, but from the sound of his voice she knew he wasn't far. The first reaction was to stay in the water. He'd never find her there. An instant later, she shook the idea from her mind. Her clothes were on the bank. The white cloth strips shined like a mirror in the morning light. If he saw them, there was no explaining how they came to be there.

Again, she peeked above the bank. Still, she didn't see him, so slowly she crept along the edge of the creek, her feet slipping in silt. With a deep breath, she gradually extended her arm toward the strips.

"Les!"

She lurched from the water and snatched the garment. The dawn breeze wrapped its frigid fingers around every inch of her skin. Like a crawfish, she recoiled back into the creek. With the white cloth beneath the surface, Les heard the clop of hooves approach. She knelt in the mud bed, chin-high in clear water. A peek down showed two bumps of white. Quickly, she stirred the mudbed, swirling a cloud of mire around her while tucking the cloth between her thighs so it couldn't drift.

Jody's smiling face emerged from over the edge of the bank. "Now you take a bath?"

"I thought it'd keep me awake." She looked to the rising sun. "I guess I was wrong."

"Yeah. You're right about that. Smith is madder than a wet hen over not having hot coffee." He dismounted and came to the bank extending his hand. "Come on out. We got plenty of ground to cover today."

Les didn't extend her arm. Instead, she cowered in the water knowing she had little excuse for not leaving.

Jody arched a brow. "Come on. Ain't like I ain't seen before what you got down there."

Whether it was true or not, she didn't move. "I ain't used to that. Not that. Not yet. You go on, and I'll be along."

He curled a corner of his mouth and gave a quick nod. "Still shy? All right, but don't take too long. Like I said, we got a heap of ground to cover." He mounted and turned his horse. The clop of hooves faded.

Les came near the bank, shivering only in part from the cold water. She wouldn't have long to think about which way to plan. With the sheet cloth wet, it wouldn't dry in time and she wouldn't be able to put it on herself. From now on, she would have to keep the coat buttoned and hat low over the brow. She eased her thighs and let the bonds of disguise drift away.

* * *

Rance splashed water over his face, then straightened, rubbing the refreshment over his freshly shaved cheeks. Ruth came to the creek bank. Rance turned to see her carrying a plate.

"I am obliged to your uncle for the loan of his razor."

"This is some of my aunt's cornbread. It's the last day it can be ate."

He accepted the plate with a tip of his hat. "I'm beholden to your kind aunt. What a sweet woman." He took a bite and swiped his sleeve across his lips. "Mighty tasty. You know, the truth be told, I didn't think we had time enough to eat. I just came here to wash the dust from my face."

Ruth knelt next to him. "Well, I think Uncle Thomas got us lost. He's up in the wagon right now staring at the map. He said according to it, this creek shouldn't be here."

Rance peeked at the stream. "Never known water to be in the wrong place."

Ruth laughed, her smooth cheeks receding into gentle folds to show an angelic smile. "He thinks we've come too far south. If this is the creek he thinks it is, it joins up with the Arkansas River."

The prospect of being no closer to the Kansas cow towns than when he'd started didn't appeal to Rance. However, he couldn't argue with fate's choice of company with which to wander. He reminded himself exactly who he was to them. "I wouldn't worry. The Lord has a way of making his point. If he had wanted you folks somewhere else, he would have put you there." He took another bite.

She inhaled a long breath and sighed it out. "He sure has made a point with us."

The comment had him stop chewing and swallow the mass whole. "What does that mean?"

She faced him without her usual spirit. "We're leaving home because we can't live there anymore. I wish it weren't true."

"Why?"

With her head slightly dipped, she took in another deep breath. "My pa was killed in the war. Yankees charging through Tennessee on their way to Chattanooga. My pa, he took up with the militia to stop them. I didn't know at the time. My ma had took sick and passed just before the war. My pa, he gave me to Uncle Thomas and Aunt Abby to see after me when he left, and they didn't tell me anything so as not make me fret. But I knew what was happening. I never let on to it. All the children at church were talking about how the Yankees were going to turn us into slaves like the black folk."

She paused only a moment before sucking in more air. Rance had heard many a sorrowful story about the war, but never allowed himself to take sides. War was fair only in that it didn't spare misery from either side. However, hers was the first such tale from such a young girl.

"Uncle Thomas and Aunt Abby's oldest son, Tom Jr., my cousin, he died too. Not in the same fight as my pa, but two weeks after. They didn't even know he left to fight. Tom Jr. told them he was against the war and was going west to New Mexico to start a new life. It was the only way they would let him leave in peace. Aunt Abby still believes he was coerced into joining. Tom Jr. was a friendly man, she said. He didn't have the hate in him that the others had." She paused to swab the single tear from her right eye. "That's why we left Tennessee. Just too many things to look at. Too many memories."

Rance's gut felt as if it had sunk to the dirt. Not knowing what words to say to change the girl's mood, he patted her shoulder. "I know this doesn't sound right at a time like this, but to me it makes sense that you're moving on. Sometimes the best thing to do is to cast all that behind you and seek more bountiful times. It's been my practice on a number of occasions." Astonished that his speech actually held a profound tone, he tried to leave the subject before he sullied it.

She smiled again, tucking her long strands behind her ear. "You have a way of saying the right thing with comforting words. It's a shame that your congregation cast you away. I don't think they appreciated what they had in you."

"Why, thank you, Miss Ruth." He looked into her eyes. In them he saw a young girl anxious to experience womanhood. Although it wouldn't take much effort to help her in that quest, he also saw that she was still a girl, and it would be a sin against his own nature to pick such a young bloom. "You shouldn't trouble what's inside that pretty little head of yours with my matters." He glanced at the creek, then back at her. There was something in her curious eyes that made him want to talk more than he should.

"I admit, my journey here hasn't all been filled with heavenly delight. Despite those hardships . . ." He paused, desperately in need of something noble to satisfy her worry without confessing. "I always maintained faith that wherever it is I end up, it will be preordained by the man above that I be there. No matter the means." He shrugged. "Call it luck. If there's such a thing." Again proud of his quick thinking, he filled his mouth with the last of the cornbread before any foolish words were to leave it.

Her eyes eased and her lips held contentment without smiling. "Sounds much like the 23rd Psalm."

He turned to her, his mouth full of cornbread, and nodded.

She put her hand on his arm. "Would you say it with me, Reverend? I know I would like to hear it. I think it would give us strength."

Rance's eyes widened. He pointed to his plump cheeks. The excuse didn't work. She was willing to wait. The handicap of the food-filled mouth might be his sole savior. He shrugged and gently took her hand in his, bowed his head, and closed his eyes. He mumbled random words as she recited the verse.

"The Lord is my shepherd; I shall not want. He maketh me to lie down in green pastures: he leadeth me beside the still waters. He restoreth my soul: he leadeth me in the paths of righteousness for his name's sake."

Although the words were familiar, Rance didn't know

the next one. He peeked to the side and saw Ruth with her head bowed and eyes closed. Surprised at the girl's memory for the psalm, he silenced his own mumbling to listen to her.

"Yea, though I walk through the valley of the shadow of death, I will fear no evil: for thou art with me: thy rod and thy staff comfort me."

As she continued, he opened both eyes, more amazed as she spoke each word with such faith and devotion. Bible preaching was never a priority during his young years. Yet he had enough manners to respect those who took the beliefs seriously.

"I will dwell in the house of the Lord forever." Ruth opened her eyes and turned to him. As she smiled, he couldn't keep from doing so also, nor did he desire to stop. He met Ruth's eyes and although he'd previously swore to restrain his attraction, he leaned closer with thoughts of stealing a kiss from the young beauty. He peered deep into those hazel eyes. His lips only an inch from her, he saw those eyes dart to the side. Her smile vanished. In an instant, he pulled back and followed her stare over his shoulder.

Four riders approached from the north. He could see the small dust clouds from the horses' trot, but they were too distant to recognize. Rance stood, but kept a watch on the strangers as they neared. "Well, now," he said, taking a glimpse at the wagon loaded with mother, father, and son. Another quick turn of the head spotted the white gelding with reins tethered to tree limbs. "Seems we have callers."

"Do you know who they are?" Ruth asked as she stood.

"I wasn't formerly introduced, but I have confidence I know what sort these men are and why they are here."

"And why is that?"

He faced her. Her innocence triggered his smile. "Like I said, you shouldn't burden yourself with my matters." He glanced at the approaching riders. "Those men are likely to tell you some awful untrue things about me. If you wish to help, what I need for you to do for me is tell your aunt and uncle to tell them fellows that you never seen nor heard of me." He went up the embankment toward the gelding.

"You want me to lie, Reverend?"

If he turned to face her again, his wits would be lost in her eyes. "Don't think of it as lying, Ruth. Think of it as a neighborly gesture."

"But why?" The sound of her voice hadn't faded. She was following him up the incline.

"As you know, the Lord works in strange ways." He patted the gelding's neck and took the risk of looking at her once more. "Believe me when I tell you, a young girl as yourself shouldn't know what strange ways he's led me through."

Ruth lurched at him and hugged his chest. "Take me with you, Reverend. I don't care where you are going."

In reflex, he put his hands on her shoulders to push, but his arms were paralyzed when his palms felt the soft flesh beneath her cotton dress. In an instance of consideration, her proposition opened his mouth, but seized his tongue. Rance stared in her eyes until she closed them and puckered her lips awaiting his kiss. About to accept her offer, he glanced at those four riders.

A gambler would take any such opportunity with great haste, but a man of the cloth had to be held to a higher standard. "What about your family?"

She opened her eyes and shook her head quickly. "I don't care. I'm only a burden to them. An extra mouth to feed. I want to go with you." She closed her eyes and prepared herself for his kiss.

There was only one thing to do. He pursed his lips and tenderly kissed her forehead. She opened her eyes in surprise. "Nothing would give me greater glee than to take the prettiest girl from Tennessee with me. But your time has not come for me or any man to take you away from your family." With gentle but firm pressure, he escaped her embrace. "Time is not a friend now. So all I can ask is for you to pass on to your aunt and uncle what I told you." He stared again into her eyes, only this time he was immune to their invitation. "Will you do that for me, Ruth?"

It took a moment, but she nodded her head, her cheeks sagging with disappointment. Rance took the reins from the limbs and mounted the gelding.

# 11

RANCE STEERED THE gelding through the trees and up a small hill. He yanked the reins and turned the horse to view the open plain below. While watching the four riders surround the wagon, he stifled his breath. Ruth stood next to the wagon where her aunt and uncle sat at the front. If she convinced her relatives to lie, all he needed to do was avoid the strangers' next chosen path. If she hadn't, he'd have to blaze one of his own for his life.

From afar the conversation seemed social. The men tipped their hats to the ladies and shook Fuller's hand. Although not a sure sign of success, it appeared a good start. In a short time, two of the strangers dismounted and walked to the back of the wagon. Rance couldn't recall any of his own items he might have left, and therefore finally let go of his long-held breath.

The two inspected the bed, then the underside, and last they completed the circle with the axles. Despite the peculiarity, there didn't seem any need to worry. He took confidence that Ruth had convinced Aunt Abby and Uncle Thomas not to mention his presence with them. He could turn his horse and hide further up the hill to wait for when the riders departed. Rance pulled the reins to the side,

forced the white gelding's head about, and readied his heel
to nudge the animal. He glanced over his shoulder. What
he saw had him hold the reins firm.

One of the strangers yanked Abigail from the seat to
tumble onto the ground. Ruth lunged to help her aunt, but
the stranger backhanded her. Thomas rose from the seat. A
whip lashed around his hips and wrapped him in its coil.
Rance looked to the third rider who threw it. A yank on the
whip pulled Thomas to the dirt.

Rance sat atop the gelding petrified. His usual reflex
upon sight of any trouble was to ride hard in the opposite
direction. His hand still squeezed the leather. He only had
the pepperbox in his coat, not a weapon to fire from any
distance. Yet with Ruth lying on the ground holding her
cheek, fire burned inside him. The third rider slipped from
his mount to subdue Thomas. As the two men struggled,
the fourth rider left his saddle with a roll of twine, no doubt
to bind hands and legs. Just as in a play of cards, he'd seen
the opponent's mistake and he'd have only seconds to take
advantage of it.

He kicked the gelding to run back through the maze of
trees. Once clear of them, he kicked the flanks harder to
have it charge straight at the attackers. The previous escape
from the train had taught him to wrap an arm around the
horse's neck while at full gait and without saddle. Not only
did it keep him atop the animal, it likely made for a harder
target.

He sank his right hand into the coat pocket and drew the
pistol. With a finger wrapped around the trigger, he attempted to steady it at the attackers. The bumpy view
through the white mane saw all concerned startled at his
approach, including the Fuller clan.

The two men securing Thomas with the twine now
stood and pointed. It would be a matter of seconds before
they fired at him. To beat them to the draw, he pulled the
trigger, doing his best to keep the barrel in their direction.
The shot rang out. The gelding veered right from the loud

pop so near its ear. Rance hung on with all the strength his left arm could muster. However, now facing the men broadside, he was an easier target. Again, he fired while the gelding continued its gallop.

Now the gelding reared from the shot and Rance dug his nails into its hide. With his view constantly blurred, he expected return fire any moment, so he aimed the pistol and fired once more. Just as the gelding set on all fours, he glimpsed a pillar of dust rising from the side of the wagon and heard a man's shout.

"The son of a bitch is shooting at the horses!"

Barely able to balance himself on the bucking gelding, he did see all four of the attackers scatter from the wagon. While three of them ran after their fleeing horses, the one who trailed knelt and aimed his pistol. Rance fumbled with trigger. The frustration forced him to kick the gelding. The horse reared again. A gunshot blasted out. With only a blurry image of the kneeling man, he pointed the pistol and squeezed the trigger. The slug kicked up more dirt in front of the shooter, who got up and scrambled after his friends.

Rance steadied the skittish horse enough to steer it toward the wagon, but it still wanted to run. As he passed, he yanked back on the reins, which only served to make it buck. Figuring he couldn't stop the horse, he yelled at the party while trying to hang on. "Get the mules running while they're after their horses." Still astride the kicking animal, he jerked the reins right and around the back of the wagon in a wide circle to the front. To keep the horse's spirit high for a long run, he eased the pressure, which stopped the bucking. When the animal strode past the front of the wagon, he yelled at Thomas.

"They'll come after me." He dropped the pistol in his pocket and quickly took off his hat for the ladies. "Much obliged for the hospitality. Good luck to you." He let the horse have rein and it bolted. His last glimpse was Ruth blowing a kiss his way.

\* \* \*

Les heard a rider approach from behind, and peeked over
her shoulder only enough to see Jody slow his mount. Still
sleepy and always tired, she was in no mood for more lectures on the importance of staying awake during
nighthawking. "What do you want?" she snapped.

"Well, I did come to be neighborly and offer you some
of my chaw," he answered, drawing the large cake of dried
tobacco from his pocket. "But seeing how you're acting
like you must have a burr in your butt, I believe I'll take
back the offer." His smile never completely disappeared.

"Ain't you afraid you'll be hollered at for riding off
from the herd?"

Jody shook his head, clenched his teeth on the chaw,
and tore away a sizable portion, which poked his cheek and
gave his voice a flappy tone. "Don't plan to be here long
enough to be hollered at."

Les pointed her eyes front. "I wish I could say the same.
I must admit some surprise Smith hasn't made it a point yet
this morning to come bawl me out for not having his breakfast ready." She peeked up at the clear sky. "Nearing midday, and I ain't even seen him, come to think of it."

"He ain't going to bawl you out."

"And just why would that be?"

Jody's voice took a stable tone. "'Cause I already took
it for you." Startled at the news, Les shot a look at him in
disbelief. He nodded. "Yeah, that's right, you're going to
owe me. I told him we made a deal, and I was to cook the
breakfast and plumb forgot."

"So he don't know about me in the river?"

He shook his head. "No, none of that."

Still in disbelief, she wondered the reason. "Why would
you do that?"

Jody dropped his jaw, but only to move the wad from
one cheek to another. "I figured you didn't have much further to go before he kicked you to the first town we came
by. If he was to do that, then I'd be stuck with all the cook-

ing and cleaning." He looked at her. "Couldn't have that. So I storied to him. He can't kick me out."

Unsure if the excuse was genuine, or if he had seen more of her in the river than she thought, Les kept her questions to herself. However, there was one answer she was anxious to learn. "So Smith, does he think better of me now?"

Jody huffed a laugh. "He thinks of you as a pox. Something to be survived." He leaned slightly to the right and spat a stream of brown spittle to the ground. "There are some things you do that puts him loco and I can see why."

"And what that be?"

"Like bringing green wood for the fire. Limbs and branches that have leaves on them ain't going to tinder no flame. It's the ones below without them leaves be dead dry enough inside to catch fire quick." He spat again.

Les considered the remark and once she tossed it in her mind, she didn't object to the criticism. After a moment, she was actually anxious to get to a camp to try out the new technique at building fires.

Three loud pops rippled through the air from the east. Jody reined in. "Pistol shots." He glanced at Les, then back in the direction of the shots. "Who could be out there shooting?" he said with a hint of reserve in his voice.

"Are you going to get Smith?"

He turned his scowl at her. "What? You don't think I can find it out for myself?" Before she had a chance to apologize or explain, he continued barking at her. "You just be careful in that saddle, little boy. I'll be the one finding out where them shots come from and by who without the help of that old man. Could be Indians or some other marauders after the horses. He'll just have us turn further west." Jody drew the pistol from his belt. "I have a notion to go and have a look for myself. And don't give no thought to joining me. You'll only slow me down. I'll be back before Smith knows I'm gone." He kicked his mount and headed to the east at a gallop.

Les watched him ride atop hill after rolling hill until she couldn't sight him anymore. She looked back over her shoulder and squinted into the sun. It didn't appear directly overhead, which was the usual signal to ready a camp for dinner. Again, she looked to where she'd last seen Jody. Perhaps she did have time to ride to atop a few hills of her own, if only to sight him again and be sure no harm had come his way. It wouldn't take her that long, and the remuda had to be at least a half mile behind.

As she gave it more thought, she nudged the paint and steered to the east, figuring if she had reason to stop, she wouldn't have traveled that far and would be able to return quickly. Even the mules didn't seem to object to straying from the course due south.

When she reached the first hill, only further hills were in view. Individual trees spotted the plain and small valleys. She didn't slow the paint, and the mare didn't stop on its own. The distance to the top of the next hill seemed to take a mite longer than the first. During the trip, the gentle sway in the saddle got her insides sloshing. Soon, once the idea of shedding her water came into her mind, the pressure to do so built faster than it took to fill a bucket under a pump. Just that idea was enough to give her pain and force her to make a decision.

Normally she had waited to do her business in the privacy she enjoyed more than a mile in front of the men. It must have been her late start of the morning, all the coffee she'd made a practice to drink, and this detour that had made her lose track of the day. A quick glimpse of the sun showed it near overhead. Les nodded at the notion it would be about that time.

With still some worry as to the whereabouts of Jody, she looked from atop the second hill and noticed a suitable spot. She nudged the paint down the slope toward a wide arroyo where a dry gully ran surrounded by a cluster of tall trees of various leaves. She halted the paint and mules under the canopy and dismounted.

The need hurried her into the shade. Quickly, she unthreaded the knots holding the chaps to her legs. Once done, she unbuckled the belt and pulled loose the buttons in the center. With her pants loose from her hips, she gave a last look for Jody, bent her knees, and commenced. Relieved from the duty of nature, she pulled the pants to her waist.

"What a delightful surprise."

The strange voice stopped her heart. She faced about in search of the source. From one tree trunk to next she darted her eyes, until from behind one stepped a man dressed in a black hat and coat.

# 12

"DON'T BE ALARMED, miss. I mean no harm."

The girl dressed as a cowpoke appeared undecided whether to run for the horse and mules or take the time to buckle her belt. In her panic and with eyes bulged from the sockets, she stammered in reflex while backing away, "Who—who are you?"

In need of an ally, the man realized the truth was a poor choice. Having enjoyed previous success with a new identity, it seemed wise to try the same play. "Reverend Josiah Hanks. I am a man of the cloth." The ruse showed little sign of soothing her fright. "I apologize for scaring you. It wasn't my intent. I just meant that it was a surprise to come across a fellow Christian in this wild country."

In a daze, she looked at her pants, then at him, her jaw dropping, then closing, her cheeks blushing red. Although he'd seen many a vain female, even he knew fate had put him in a position not many men with wives knew. He had some explaining to do.

"Forgive me for disturbing you. You must believe me it is not in my nature to pry on a lady during her private time." Her trembling hand wasn't a good signal. He needed to deflect blame. "It is only the Lord that put me here." The conversation with Ruth came into his head. "I wouldn't be here if he didn't want me here. It must be in his divine wisdom, a purpose known only to him." The notion seemed to calm her hand. The jaw slowly closed and her eyes returned to their normal size.

"What you doing out here?" Her voice was filled with jitters.

Again, divulging the truth seemed complicated and unwise. After having slapped the gelding's rump to mislead his pursuers, he was now afoot and destined to be discovered. This girl held the key to his continued escape. "My horse ran away some miles from here while I had to take care of nature's calling just as you. Now, I am at the mercy of a kind soul who could take me to the next town where I can purchase another horse and be on my way."

Even without her initial horror evident, she eyed him cautiously. In a rush, she scampered to her horse and leapt into the saddle like a cat. In a second she'd be gone.

"Please, miss, I beg of you to help me. I can pay you." He reached in his pocket and pulled out a wad of bills. The show of money kept her from galloping away. The few moments of her eyes darting from his to the money and back gave him the same confidence as at a card table. "You wouldn't abandon a man of the Lord, would you?"

"You don't look like no preacher."

He peeked at his clothes. "Actually, I was traveling to meet a new congregation and wanted to look my Sunday best." The girl didn't change her wary face. She peered about as if searching for someone, but when he did the same, he saw no other riders. "Someone else lost?"

She nodded. "A friend of mine." Her distracted expression changed instantly to a threatening stare. "He's a giant. And he's got a giant gun just as big as him that will blow a hole in a man a cabbage would slide clean through."

"Oh." Another quick scan still showed no one. "Well, perhaps I can help you look for him."

Her apprehension returned. "No. No. I wouldn't want the two of you to meet."

"And why is that?"

Her face turned sullen. She took a long gulp, then with enough courage built, she looked into his eyes. "He—he doesn't know—what you know."

Rance studied her face, then her heavy coat. "I see."

"You wouldn't have to tell him. You being a preacher and all. It wouldn't be a lie. There are secrets preachers have to keep, right?"

When playing a strong hand, it was always best to keep it for as long as possible to produce the greatest reward. "Of course, child. On my honor, I will hold it in confidence between only those parties."

She raised an eyebrow.

"That means, I won't tell another soul. It will remain a secret—if I can get you to help me."

For a few moments her reply seemed in doubt. Her eyes were careful to keep from his, giving the appearance that she was in the throes of indecision. Finally, she looked at him and nodded. "I guess we can ride double. Only, there ain't no towns near here that I know of. I can take you back to a camp I was to make about now. That fellow I was looking for and another are herding horses back to Texas. They might know of a town near here."

He smiled and walked toward her. "Bless you, child." He offered his hand. "I didn't get your name."

"I'm called Les."

When he saw a lone white horse peacefully grazing on the grass of an open expanse, Jody reined in from the gallop. Pistol still firm in hand, he slowly approached the bridled animal, which had no saddle. It was understandable why someone in a hurry might take a treasured if not expensive saddle, but this horse showed no evidence of being lame. The need for setting it to run free puzzled him. It didn't spook when his horse walked next to it. He twisted his neck in all directions for anyone close by that might be hurt or simply taking a nap. No one was to be seen. Curiosity got the best of him, so he tucked the pistol in his belt and dismounted.

When he reached for the reins, the horse didn't shy away. He patted its neck and ran his fingers along the girth. It was well cared for and didn't seem the type of mount used on a range. It appeared more of a riding horse, one used for pleasure. He lifted the tail. As suspected, it had been gelded.

"Hello." As soon as he called, he heard the click of gun metal.

"Don't move a muscle or I'll put a bullet in you."

The voice was low and gruff and came from behind.

"Get your hands high in the air. Any move for that pistol will be your last."

Not skilled in gunplay, Jody complied. Nervous, he found his throat choked with tobacco spittle, and spit out the wad to be heard clearly. "I ain't done nothing wrong. I came upon this horse by chance. Wasn't going to take it. I heard shots. Thought someone was in trouble."

"Where's the gambler?" said the voice, closer this time, and in an instant, a hand snatched the pistol from Jody's belt.

"Who?" Jody was grabbed by the shoulder and twisted about. Four men surrounded him, all with rifles aimed at his head.

"Don't play us for fools, son," said the one holding the pistol. He had a beard trimmed close to the cheek, wore a bowler with a taut fit just over the eyes, and a brown waistcoat. The others were dressed alike, but Jody didn't dare cast his eyes too far from the nearest muzzle. "Where's the man riding this horse?"

"I'm sorry. I really don't know what it is you think I should tell you. If you tell me what it is, then I'll tell you."

"He don't know nothing. Let's just shoot him and be back on the trail."

"Wait now," Jody stuttered. "No call for any of that. If you want my horse, take it. I ain't done nothing to hurt nobody."

"No, we're not going to kill you. Unless you don't tell us where the fellow went that was riding this horse."

With his heart pounding through his chest, and arms tingling from being raised so long, Jody inhaled deep to have enough breath to speak his mind. "Let me say this again. I heard shooting. So I rode fast to see if somebody was in trouble. There are still some wild tribes around these parts and I thought folks may need help. I didn't see nothing until I got here and seen this gelding. I figured it ain't no mount a buck would ride 'cause it's too clean and looks to have been eating oats real regular. Then you fellows came. Now, I'm here facing four gun barrels and my arms are about to fall limp."

The closest one nodded. "How is it that you were out here?"

Eager to answer any question that would lower the rifles from aim, he began with the truth. "I'm bringing a herd of horses. . . ." An instant later he reconsidered. Although these men dressed too well for horse thieves, the opportunity to steal fifty head of prime saddle ponies might be too tempting and bring trouble to Smith and Les. "Horses back to Texas. About twenty-five drovers are just over those hills. Likely they're wondering where I am. Might be riding in any minute with guns drawn and no mood to dicker after being slowed up from getting home."

"Is that a fact. We may just have to wait on these men. Maybe they've seen who we're looking for."

"Let's just shoot him and be done with it. We're wasting time. The trail is going to be lost."

"Nobody is shooting anybody," said the one with the neat beard. "I'm in charge, Swanson. Remember that. We're not murderers. It was bad enough what you started with that family. There was no reason to be rough. That's not the reputation we want burning like a fire in the minds of folks around here."

Jody appreciated the bearded one taking up for him. Maybe if he could strike up a conversation, he might make friends and be on his way. "Just who are you fellows?" The rifle muzzle was pushed closer to his nose.

"Not business of yours to know. We're on private business of Mr. Hiram Schaefer."

"Whoa there," said Jody, holding out an open palm. "Sorry. No offense meant. I just thought that if I was to know about who you were, I may be able to help."

"The way you can help," said young Swanson, "is for you to tell us where we can find the gambler that took advantage of Mr. Schaefer's wife."

"Close that mouth," ordered the one with the beard. "The next one that opens his mouth will get shot." He turned to face Jody. "Now, like I said—"

Blood spattered the beard. The one with the pistol fell like a rock. A bullet hole in the neck spewed blood a foot in the air just as the gunshot echoed about.

Jody cowered at the sight. His mind jumped from thinking one of the other three had fired to seeing all of them scatter for cover. With the horses scampering away, he crawled on the ground trying to retrieve his own pistol from the dead man's hand.

"Them damn drovers are shooting at us. He wasn't lying," yelled a voice.

At first confused by the panicked guess, Jody thought it could be Smith come to his relief. When a bullet popped dust too near his face, he thought again. Being in the open made him an easy target. Once he had the revolver, he ran at a crouch for the cover of a small tree. From the corner of his eye he saw another of the men running for the same tree, which was too small to hide two men. Jody saw the man's brow furrow, and in an instant the rifle was aiming directly at him. His instinct was to point the revolver and shoot first, but suddenly the weapon seemed too heavy to lift. He cringed, expecting a bullet to tear into his gut. A gunshot crackled.

The man stopped running and took a jolted step back. The front of his shirt turned red. After another wobbly step, he collapsed on the ground.

Jody never stopped running. He dove for the tree and scrambled to place his back firm against the trunk. Whoever was shooting was a crack shot. He didn't want to show any more of his body for someone to use as a target.

He peeked around the trunk. The only other one of the original four still in view was lying flat in the shade of another tree. It wasn't a hard shot to try. Jody himself had hit tin cans from longer distances, but trying to hit a man and take a life was a different matter. He'd heard stories from those who'd done just that, and thought the experience of battle had to be one of excitement. Now that he was in one, the only excitement was in his nerves shaking the revolver so bad he'd never be able to steady the aim.

For that matter, Jody didn't know for sure Smith was the one shooting. Trying to call for the old man might draw gunfire his way from either of the sides trading bullets. The best idea was to sit tight by the tree and wait for a chance to run to a horse.

The blasts of gunfire made him turn his head and wince. Two shots, then three, then one, then none. Seconds went by and no shots were fired. He craned his neck around the trunk. The one lying flat hadn't moved. A focused stare showed the rifle lying on the ground too, near a bloody hat.

Jody faced straight ahead. He cocked the hammer of the pistol and waited for the next sound. Moments went by like hours. Whoever it was that killed these fellows knew how to handle a gun. Jody tried to steady his breathing to slow his heart. If he was to survive, he'd have to rely on calm nerves to steady the barrel.

The snap of twigs yanked his attention to the left. A different voice came from the right.

"Drop that pistol, boy."

# 13

JODY RELEASED THE weapon and slowly turned his head to the right. Above him stood a man with more than a week's stubble splotched about his face. He wore a tattered cloth Panama hat and an old gray coat. Even though Jody's nerves twitched and he didn't think there was much reason for glee, this man smiled.

"Ain't you going to thank me?"

The question took Jody by surprise. "For what?"

"For saving you from being robbed. When we saw them pointing them rifles, we sized them as a bunch of carpetbaggers out to steal even more from another Southerner. And so, we ended their days of thieving."

Jody nodded as to the truth that the three bloody corpses sprawled on the grass wouldn't be thieving or breathing in this world again. One word puzzled him. "We?"

The man nodded and pointed the barrel of his rifle. "Me and him."

Jody peered over his left shoulder. A man in identical hat and coat, without the beard and only shorter in stature, approached while poking the barrel of his rifle between the ribs of the sharp-tongued Swanson.

"What'd you catch, Eli?" the taller one asked.

"Looks like I got me a yellow snake. Was hiding in the grass looking to take a shot at my back, brother." With a final firm shove, Swanson crashed to the ground. Upon turning faceup, he found a muzzle pointed at his jaw. "Weren't you, snake boy?"

"My name's James Swanson. If you're going to kill me, at least you should know who it was you murdered."

The shorter one glanced at the corpses. "Don't care to know their names. Don't know why I'd want yours." He pulled back the hammer of the rifle.

"Hold on there, Eli. Can't help but have some admiration for a man that shows some spine."

"You can save your admiration," Swanson said defiantly while propped on his elbows and observing his friends' bodies. "You two are a gang of cutthroats. I'll accept none from murderers who gun men down in ambush." Jody bit his tongue remembering only a few minutes before it was this kid that wanted to shoot him like a skunk with mange. However, he wasn't sure how these brothers would react to such remarks. He didn't want Swanson dead, even if it was a fair and even play.

Eli let show a wide smile minus three bottom teeth and two uppers, giving him the appearance of a beaver. "I take that as a compliment for my mark . . . markin . . . what did the sergeant call it, Levi?"

"Marksmanship. But I don't know if I can let you get all the credit. Some has to go to these Spencer rifles. Even if it is a Yankee arm."

"I was the one behind it lining up those shots, let's not forget."

"That you were. Just as I. Remember, I put a slug in this fellow's chest at more than a hundred yards."

Jody's gut became more queasy listening to the brothers brag like kids while holding deadly weapons and allowing the aim of both to wander in his direction. Swanson put it in words.

"Are you two finished? What is the purpose of your acts?"

The shorter Eli looked to his brother with a confused stare. It wasn't clear whether he hadn't an answer for the question or just didn't understand. An instant later, he relied on every man's reply when at a loss for words, and propped the muzzle against Swanson's forehead. "What about you, James Swanson? What about your acts? What was their purpose?"

With a glare first at Levi, then above at Eli, he lastly looked at Jody. "We saw this drover come after the gelding owned by Mrs. Hiram Schaefer and thought he might know where a gambler by the name of Cash might have gone."

"Hiram Schaefer?" Levi looked to Eli. "Brother, I've heard that name."

"Mr. Hiram Schaefer," Swanson said in a loud, precise, and rude tone. "The president of the Eastern Pacific Railroad, of which I am employed as were those men you murdered."

"I knew I heard that name," Levi said with a growing grin.

"What's he got to do with this?" asked Eli.

Swanson inhaled deeply. "Almost a week to the day, we've been chasing this gambler Cash ever since he was discovered by Mr. Schaefer himself in Mrs. Schaefer's private train car, after having forced himself upon the lady by threat of violence. The gambler nearly killed her bodyguard when thrown off the train. Then the gambler Cash escaped the train and stole Mrs. Schaefer's horse, a white gelding. Mr. Schaefer said he'd personally pay five thousand dollars to whoever brought back the gambler who defiled his wife."

The amount no doubt was the reason both brothers began chuckling. Eli prodded the gun muzzle firmer against Swanson's forehead. "That's a whole patch of money for a man who ain't even killed nobody or even stole nothing but a horse."

"He took the virtue of the wife of another man. That's reason enough."

Eli's chuckle slowed, but his grin remained. "What if

she liked it? Eh? Somehow this fellow knew which horse was hers?" The brothers laughed aloud.

"Mrs. Schaefer is a fine lady." Swanson made his voice loud and clear to be heard over the laughter. "True ladies don't enjoy the pleasures of the flesh. Everyone knows that."

"No. I guess you're right," Levi remarked. "Their delight is seeing to their husbands, or his money." He looked at his brother and winked. His face and mood changed when he peered down at Jody. "So, what is it you were doing out here? What's your name?"

Jody recalled his previous lie when faced with four riflemen. He still wasn't among friends. "My name is Jody Barnes. I'm part of a trail drive heading back to Texas with a herd of horses. There's twenty-five of us. I expect friends to come over that hill as mad as hornets they had to come look for me."

"Horses?" Levi looked to his brother, then at Jody. "How many horses?"

Jody blurted out the honest number. "Just over fifty."

Levi again looked to his brother. "Fifty?" He stared Jody in the eye. "You telling me it takes twenty-five drovers to wrangle just fifty horses? What do they do? Ride one apiece and lead the spare?"

The thought of wrinkling his nose when caught in the lie occurred to Jody, but instead he kept a straight face and thought of another. "All them fellows are anxious to get home. Only makes sense for them to pick up an extra wage doing it to bring their remuda home." Although it took more than a half minute, when the taller brother scratched his chin, Jody knew he'd come up with a good story.

"You better not be lying to me, boy."

"If you want, I'll take you to meet them myself."

"I wouldn't want to do that, brother," said Eli. "Texas cowboys ain't right in the head."

"Hush up," Levi ordered. He kept his stare at Jody. "Twenty-five, uh? All just wanting to go home? Well, so be it." The Spencer muzzle propped in front of his nose, Jody

kept his eyes on the man holding it and listened to every
word said. "Jody Barnes, you are going to fetch us fresh
horses and enough food to last us to Texas. Hear?"

"Texas?"

Levi nodded. "We're going to follow you to be sure you
don't breathe a word of us. If you do, I'll snatch you from
your sleep and gut you like a hog for Sunday supper." He
leaned closer. "Which offer would you rather take?"

With the weight of two guns trained at his front and
back, Jody gulped. "How do you expect me to get the
horses?"

"That," Levi began with the point of his finger, "I leave
to you. But see to it you will. Or face the wrath of two hungry men on tired horses. I'll give you until nightfall to
come up with them and the food." He raised the barrel as a
signal to rise.

On his feet, Jody brushed the dust from the seat of his
pants. Even though he was given the choice of leaving with
life and limbs intact, he didn't rejoice at the notion of riding away with his back to these two strangers. His eyes
darted to his Remington revolver tucked in the taller
brother's belt.

"If I go back without my pistol, I'll be asked questions."

"Tell them you lost it and it can't be found."

Jody found the reply easy to speak. It was the honest
truth that spilled naturally from his gut and out his throat.
"Mister, that gun cost me better than two months pay, and
it weren't new when I bought it. Now, I don't know about
you, but eighty-five dollars is a whole heap of money to
keep looking for. I show without it, I'll be asked where I
lost it and it will be thought queer of me to give it up so
easy. So if you want me to keep your whereabouts secret,
you'll have to give me the gun back."

Again, he took confidence he'd made his point from
Levi's chin scratch. The brothers glanced at each other as
if in a silent vote on the matter. Levi nodded and pulled the
Remington from his belt. Jody opened his right hand, anxious to receive the prized pistol, but Levi calmly kept it. In

a methodical routine, he opened the chamber and one by
one extracted all the cartridges. Once he raised the pistol
and angled it back to see through the empty cylinders, Levi
snapped the breech shut and handed the firearm butt-first to
Jody.

"Here you have it. Now put it in your belt. Remember,
we'll be watching as you ride from here. You draw it just to
rub your nose, much less seem to stuff more bullets in it,
and we'll kill you. Hear?"

Jody nodded. There was no sense protesting. He turned
to scan the prairie between the sparse trees for his horse.
As he searched, a familiar voice spoke up.

"What about me?"

All eyes went to Swanson still on the ground. Eli placed
his left hand under the barrel of his Spencer to fire a bullet
into the brain of the railroad gunny. Levi didn't object, but
Jody couldn't watch another man's blood splattered before
him. Swanson closed his eyes.

"Wait."

Now all eyes turned to him. Jody cleared his throat for
time to come up with another excuse. "No telling how
many riders are out there. They're probably chasing down
the shots you've already spent. Another will just bring
them closer."

Levi slowly cracked a grin and nodded. "You might be
right. But why wouldn't you want that? It would favor you
if they come."

The question made sense. All Jody could come up with
was the same reason that had stopped them from shooting
Swanson. "There's been enough shooting. I wouldn't want
any of them to get shot on my account."

"Hell, brother," Eli said in frustration. "Let's shoot them
both and be done with it." Jody looked at the smaller
brother in silent anger. It was the second time in less than
an hour that his life was considered a puny bother.

"No. I think what he said makes sense." Levi stared at
Jody. "You go and find these friends of yours, if they exist.
If you draw them to us, we'll kill Swanson here, then high-

tail it faster than you can count to ten. But it will have been you that killed him just like you pulled the trigger yourself. Hear?" He waved his hand. "Now, go on. Be about your way to them."

"Without my horse?"

Levi frowned. "I can't cure all your problems. Some you're going to have to fend to yourself."

"What about your friends?" Eli asked. "You can take one in their string."

"No." Jody shook his head. "That will be as queer as not having my gun." By the disappointment etched in their faces, Jody felt like a schoolboy talking to elders. The more thought he gave it, the odder it seemed that these bandits weren't the hard cases they'd first appeared to be.

"I ain't giving you mine," Eli said.

"That would do me no good neither." Jody looked about, but the hills with trees didn't reveal any horses. "I'm going to have to find it." After few moments of silence, Levi waved his hand again without a word. Slowly, Jody turned his back to the pair. Once a few cautious steps away, he made his way up the incline, sensitive to every sound from behind. At the top of the first hill, he saw his horse. He exhaled in relief at the welcome sight, but the relief was gone in a flash with Levi's shout to turn around. The horse was too far away. If he ran, they'd have little trouble riding him down. Without a better option, Jody gradually faced about.

"You say you're from Texas?"

Confused as to the reason for the question, Jody shouted back, "Yes."

The brothers looked at each other, then at Jody. "You know of a fellow name of Marcus Broussard?"

More confused than ever, Jody wasn't sure which answer they preferred. The truth was the only one he knew. "No. Never heard of him."

It only took a moment for them again to glance at each other. Then an instant later, Levi waved his hand for the last time.

# 14

"DO YOU THINK we ought to turn back and find out who's doing that shooting?" Les asked over her shoulder.

"Not unless you have an arsenal of guns of your own."

The preacher's answer didn't calm her fears about Jody. "What about my friend? He could be shot, or hurt bad and needing help. My help. Our help."

"I understand, miss."

"Don't call me that," she snapped from fear this man would reveal her secret to Smith or Jody.

"I beg your pardon. Les. But the fact of the matter is that I am only one man. And, well, you are pretending to be one. Whoever is shooting back there likely is a better shot than both of us. Especially since we don't have much to shoot back with. I think it wise if we found some of your friends and have them ride in the direction of those gunshots."

Although his idea made better sense than hers, it didn't keep her stomach from churning. The more she tried to steer her mind away, the more she found herself back where she started. "Are those the same men that was after you?" There wasn't an immediate answer. With him perched on the cantle and snug against her back, there wasn't room for her to turn her shoulders. Besides the trouble it made for having conversation, she didn't get to read his face. Although when she first laid eyes on him she didn't have time to stare, she did get a good look at his sharp chin and smooth skin. His hat hid most of his hair. What she did see was black and combed neatly behind his ears, unlike most men, who didn't have their hair regularly barbered. She waited for what she thought ample time for a reply. "Well? Are they or are they not?"

"Most likely there's a fair chance of that."

"How come? What did you do?"

Another longer-than-normal pause ensued. It was the kind of pause she often needed to think of what to say. It occurred to her then she might have uncovered a secret about this man. However, she didn't have the courage to ask a grown man if he was lying. "Is it because you don't know?"

"Oh, I know. They were bandits. After the money I keep to do the Lord's work."

If he was lying, she admired his calm voice while doing so. "From what you showed me, it looked like a heap of work was going to get done."

"I was hoping to go west and find a cow town and settle there. Part of that money would be to build a new place where the people could do, uh, do, uh—"

"You mean a house for the Lord's work?"

"Exactly, Les. Hey, does this horse go any faster?"

"She is going as fast as she can with two people. She ain't used to the weight." Les wanted to keep to the point. "So, you wanting to build a house where people can go and give their money and feel better in their lives doing it?"

Unlike her previous questions, this one was answered quickly and with some cheer. "Les, I think you hit that nail square on the head."

From the top of a hill, she saw the remuda herded in a circle and the skinny spiral of smoke. "Hang on tight," she said as she kicked the paint and set the animal running at a gallop. Still not used to riding at such a gait, she found it doubly difficult to manage the mules' reins and her balance with his arms wrapped around her belly. Down the slopes and up the inclines they both bounced in the saddle until they came to flatter ground. In little time they rode straight at the smoke. The fast ride brought fresh wind inside her lungs, but it quickly sailed out of her and into the breeze at the sight of Smith with his hands on his hips. She reined in, stopping the paint just feet from him.

Smith put his right hand on the butt of his holstered pistol.

"Wait, friend," the preacher said sliding off the saddle. "I don't mean any harm. I wish to thank you."

Smith raised an eyebrow. "Thank me?"

"Of course." He pointed at her. "For allowing the young mi—Les here—to ride to my rescue and save me from certain harm by bandits."

"Bandits?" Smith turned his head up at Les. Her stomach churned worse. "Where's Jody?"

"I don't know. I was looking for him when I came across this preacher here. He thought it was best if we came back here and got you. We heard shooting."

"Shooting?"

Les nodded. "That's right. Jody and me, we heard shooting. Jody rode after it and told me to stay behind. But when I couldn't see him no more, I rode down a bit to see if I could catch sight of him again. When I didn't"—she paused, reminded of exactly how she'd met the preacher—"I did—"

"He found me," said the preacher. "I was on foot and was fearing those men might come after me. But Les was first to come to my aid."

Smith kept darting his eyes to the man in black, then to Les, as if confused they might be the same person, or unsure who to believe. "You're a preacher?"

"Yes, sir." He stepped forward and offered a handshake. "Reverend Josiah Hanks is the name."

Smith didn't take his hand off the butt of his pistol. It

was more than a minute before Preacher Hanks withdrew
the offer. Smith peered at Les. "Get down off that horse."

Without pause, she slid from the saddle. When he arched
his thumb for her to walk a distance behind him, she knew
the old wrangler meant to scold her worse than Miss Maggie
had ever done. Yet she marched with Smith close on her heels
as far as she thought necessary so the preacher couldn't hear.

"Now, tell me what's this about?"

Standing stiff, she noticed his tone wasn't the one she'd
expected. "Like I said, Jody and me were riding. When we
heard the shooting, he rode off. That's when I found Reverend Hanks. He said they were after him, and would pay
me to take him to the next town. I don't know no towns, but
I thought you might so I brung him back. While we were
headed this way, there was more shooting."

Les looked into Smith's red leathery face. Any second
she expected him to let loose with a windful of barking for
leaving the herd. Instead, his brow eased. He appeared to
take in what she said.

"This man you brought is no preacher," he whispered. "I
guess I can't fault a kid for not seeing it and believing
everything you're told. But when you get as old as me, you
can spot someone claiming to be something they're not
from a mile away. You know what I mean?"

Les wasn't sure if he was talking about her, so she nodded to keep him talking. "Yes, sir."

"Now you might need to stay with the herd by yourself
while I go look for Jody."

"What about him?" she said, pointing at Hanks.

"I'll handle him. You just stay at my back. Did you see
if he had a gun?"

"No." She shook her head. "He said he didn't have one
or he'd go and shoot back at who was shooting."

Smith nodded. "Good enough." He faced about and
marched back in front of the preacher. With his hand back
on the butt of his pistol, he lined his shoulders at the man in
black. "All right. So what's the truth?"

Hanks's mouth fell slightly open. "I don't understand."

"You ain't a preacher any more than I am Sam Houston. Now, state your business why you're out here and why you made this boy bring you here."

Smith's question scared Les. She looked into Hanks's eyes trying to tell him without words that she hadn't brought this tirade on him. If he thought she did, he surely would tell Smith the truth about her.

Hanks's eyes wandered. A grin soon grew from his open mouth. "I didn't get your name."

"I answer to Smith. Now, what is your business?"

Hanks gave Les one last glance and let out a long-held breath. "Mr. Smith, you are a shrewd judge of men." His eyes darted to the pistol. "That appears to be a fine weapon you have there. Looks like a cap-and-ball load?"

Smith drew the gun and pointed it at Hanks. "Walker Colt forty-four. You're going to get a show on how fine it fires if you don't tell what I asked you."

"There's no need for that," Hanks replied with an open palm. "The truth is, I have some acquaintances that I just as soon not get reacquainted with, if you know what I mean." He paused for a reply. It took a few moments before Smith did.

"Go on."

Hanks took in another longer breath, glancing at Les before he spoke. "My trade makes me an unpopular person with those I deal with, Mr. Smith. You see, I am an investor in odds. I'm rather good at it, and when I take the reward that is due me, I often encounter those that aren't as agreeable as to the outcome."

"Mister, whatever your name is, I have to get these horses to Texas in less than two weeks and I haven't got time to bandy words. You either talk straight, or I'm going to take it you're a man wanted by whoever it is shooting at you and shoot you myself and take what reward they're offering."

"I'm a sportsman," Hanks blurted.

"You a gambler? A cardplayer?"

"Cards, dice, faro, horse races. I make wagers on most things people hold opinions on."

"So, the ones after you, they folks you cheated?"

"No," Hanks said looking over his shoulder. "If I had to guess, those men after me are working for someone who doesn't like me very much."

"Who might that be?"

"Railroad man name of Schaefer."

Smith let out a breath in a huff. "You got the railroad after you?" He shook his head in disgust. "You need to take that kind of trouble away from here." Smith waved his gun as a motion to move.

"I'd like to do just that. But, you see, I don't have a horse."

"Well, then you better start walking."

Hanks chuckled, until he noticed Smith didn't. "I wouldn't get very far. At least not far enough away to lead them away from you. It be a shame if they came across you and this herd. You know railroad agents. Not much better than the outlaws they claim to hunt down." Hanks's eyes drifted to the herd. "I'd be glad to buy one of these fine animals from you. Maybe a saddle as well?"

Smith took only a moment to look in the same direction, then shook his head. "Not mine to sell."

Hanks pulled the wad of paper money from his coat pocket. "Sure about that? I can make you a handsome offer."

"I gave you my answer. There are fifty saddle ponies expected back on the Cooper ranch. It ain't up to me to sell them for profit." Smith waved the gun again.

"An honest man. I admire that." Hanks thumbed four bills from the wad and held them between his fingers like bait. "I'll tell you what I propose, Mr. Smith. Since you can't sell me one of the horses, how 'bout I rent one from you. Say, to the nearest town where I can purchase one of my very own. I think one hundred dollars is a fair price under the circumstances."

Smith's shoulders sagged just a bit. The aim of the pistol dipped slightly off its target. The two men stood directly in front of each other without making a sound for nearly a minute. Then Hanks waved his fingers. The paper flapped like a flag during a parade.

"Mr. Smith? What do you say?"

The old wrangler put the pistol back in the holster and snatched the bills out of Hanks's fingers. After eyeing each bill, he folded the four and stuffed them in his vest pocket. "Only to the nearest town."

"Deal," said Hanks. "So, which one should I get?"

"The first one you can catch."

Hanks appeared surprised by Smith's remark. "You mean, I have to catch my own?"

Smith nodded. "Don't recall agreeing to wrangle one for you. Oh, I don't own no spare saddle neither."

Les bit her lip to keep from laughing. She wanted to see the same show she'd put on back in Abilene. When Hanks looked to her, she shrugged. When his frown tickled her ribs, she bent and faced away so as not to laugh aloud. She caught her breath, straightened, and saw Jody.

He rode his horse at a casual lope from almost the same direction as she and Hanks had. It was then Smith saw the horse approach and tipped his hat back. Hanks turned around. Jody pulled up on his horse and slid off the saddle before his mount came to a stop. Without anything said, he walked directly for the fire and took a coffee tin. Les wasn't sure what was on his mind, but she noticed the smile he always wore wasn't there.

# 15

THE DROVER WITH the blue shirt knelt by the fire. Rance peeked at Smith and Les. Their expressions showed that their friend's behavior was unusual.

Smith walked toward the fire. "Where you been, Jody?"

Jody rose and shrugged while slurping the coffee. He swallowed the hot liquid and let out a pained huff. "Went out looking for who was firing a gun. Thought somebody might be in trouble. Didn't find none, though."

Smith shook his head. "Don't know why you want to find trouble if ain't already yours."

"I thought if it was going to be mine, I'd better find it before it finds me." Jody eyed Rance while taking another slurp. "Who are you?"

Before Rance could step forward and offer a hand, Smith made the gruff introductions. "His name's Hanks. He says he was chased by bandits." Smith peered over his shoulder at Rance. "Maybe with good cause. I'm letting him ride a horse from the remuda until the next town."

"Next town?" Jody asked in surprise. "Don't he know where it is we're at?"

The answer to the question seemed written on both of

their faces. It didn't appear promising. "I'm afraid I'm at a loss," said Rance. "Is another town very far from here?"

Smith hung his head for a moment, then lifted it and inhaled deeply through his nose. "We're coming into what's known as Indian Territory. Ain't many white folk live in these parts and those that do, well, most of them that do so are avoiding the law, for good reason. Now, we come through here twice a year without any trouble. As long as we don't cause a ruckus, the locals here don't harm us none." He turned to face Rance. "That means you ain't to practice any of your trade with any of them we might come on. Understood?"

"Understood." Rance felt the older man's stare down through his boots. "So, am I to understand that there are no towns near here?"

"Not for two hundred miles or more."

Smith snapped his head at Jody. The action was meant to silence the young cowboy, and it did the trick. Rance peeked at Les. Her eyes were wide, giving the impression she was unaware of the distance as well. Smith looked back at Rance. "Grab yourself some coffee and a roll. We're moving on." He walked to his horse.

When Smith mounted and rode away, the three remaining stood for a moment as if they were left in a void. Uncomfortable with that feeling, Rance relied on instinct. He approached Jody with an open hand. "I am Josiah Hanks."

"Jody Barnes." Both men shook hands, but Jody cast a wary eye at Rance, then at Les. "You an undertaker?"

Rance peeked at his own clothes figuring they'd sparked the question. He didn't know how to explain without more questions asked. "No. I'm not."

"How is it you came along?"

"Well, as your boss said—"

"He ain't my boss." Jody's tone was defiant.

"I apologize. As Mr. Smith said, I was making my escape from bandits after me. Your friend and mine, Les, came to my rescue and brought me here."

Jody again gave Les a long look. "I thought I told you to stay put."

"I did." Les darted her eyes between both men. "For a long while. But when I heard more shooting, I got scared something happened to you. I only followed a little. Mr. Hanks here—" She eyed Rance and paused. "Well, he surprised me while I was resting in the shade. I couldn't just leave him there."

Jody resumed his wary stare at Rance. "Hanks? That's your name?"

Rance wondered why he'd asked. "Of course."

Jody poured the coffee from the tin to the dirt. "Where you from?"

"New Orleans. But I haven't been there for some time." With accusing eyes still focused at him, Rance thought more explanation was needed. "You might be wondering why I'm here." Jody nodded. "Well, I wanted to see more of this great country of ours. To experience the West and see the wonders others described to me." The bright speech wasn't received as hoped.

Jody gave Rance a last glare, then looked at Les. "You heard Smith. We're moving out." He went to his horse and soon was riding out to the herd.

Rance watched Jody leave, then turned to Les. "Nice friends you have."

She shrugged as she kicked dirt on the small fire. "I never said they were neighborly. I didn't think Smith would let you ride along."

"So speaks the power of financial incentive." When she looked puzzled, he knew it wouldn't do any good to explain. "Never mind." He looked out to the horses.

"I guess I need to thank you," said Les.

He looked at her. The glimmer of a genuine smile crept across her lips. "Why is that?"

"For not telling Smith."

He nodded his head. "I made a promise. Friends keep their promises." He held out his hand to her. "We're friends, right?"

It took a moment before she accepted his hand. "You promised me money if I brought you here."

Rance nodded and pulled the wad from his pocket. When he thumbed a single bill out for her, he pulled it back. "I'll double it, if you help me snatch a horse."

Once again Jody rode flank, the horses to his right, but he couldn't help glancing to his left. He settled his breath after eyeing Smith, sure the old wrangler would spot something wrong in his own manner. While spying Smith across the remuda, he considered how to comply with the bandit pair's demands. Saddle ponies weren't something to be hidden under a shirt, and Smith always took count, making it a matter of pride to bring back the full herd.

It was also his habit to only buy enough supplies from town to town so as not to be dragged down by the unneeded weight. Surely there wasn't enough that some wouldn't be missed.

More than once Jody decided to fess up to Smith, and every time he changed his mind. Part of his worry was the warning not to talk. If Smith showed he knew, those bandits might shoot him. The same for the kid Les. The guilt should something happen would be too much to bare. The other part was shame. He'd been made to look like a child. It wasn't an easy thing to admit to another man.

While Jody continued to scan, he caught sight of the distant stranger Smith had let tag along. That fellow appeared the very one the railroad agents were looking for, but since they were dead except for Swanson, it wasn't a matter needing to be settled. However, the man in the dandy duds didn't seem the type to be trusted.

The more Jody thought about what to do next, the more he was convinced there was nothing he could do at the time.

Once more Rance found himself astride a horse without a saddle. With a light grip of the mane, he evaluated what five dollars had bought him. With the help of Les, he'd caught a red dun gelding after nearly twenty minutes of the both of them tossing ropes from the saddle of the paint.

Ambling along behind the group, he steered away from the dust kicked up from the herd. The clear sky made for little wonder why the grass stood yellow and dry. The more he thought of the lack of rain, the hotter he became in his black coat. He sniffed the crevices between the coat and shirt. More than one bath would be needed to rid himself of the sweaty stench.

In an attempt to keep his mind off his misery, he weighed the options. By joining this group he was slowly moving south toward Texas. Never had he heard a nice word said about the state. Besides it being a land of tumbleweeds, all he knew was it was packed full of cows and cowboys with no money. It only made sense that they drove their cattle to the Kansas railroads for the reward of raising beef. It was the lure of Kansas that had set him on this journey.

He peeked over his shoulder. Although he figured it was more than two hundred miles, it would still be worth the effort to get there. An instant later, he realized just what effort it would take. He was on a borrowed horse. To turn back to the north would only put those two cowboys on his trail. Since he was riding without a saddle, fortune would have to smile brightly for him not to fall off the mount, much less evade their pursuit.

If he was to get to Kansas, it would have to come from a better plan. For the present, he'd have to follow this outfit further away from his desired goal. While he pondered, the reason he joined the group came to mind. The railroad agents who had pushed him this far south couldn't be far away. Should he be on his own, he would be easy prey to chase down. It was a poor gamble. His luck wasn't that good.

As the day passed into night, the horses were herded along a small creek. While Smith and Jody circled the animals near the water, Rance rode to the small campfire, where Les knelt next to the tripod. A kettle hung from the

metal rods. The smell of beans grew stronger the closer
Rance came to the fire. Despite holding no affection for
beans, just the aroma of food cooking made his mouth
water.

"At last," he said, sliding off the horse. "Something to
eat."

"You need to tie your horse," said Les. She rose from
the fire and tossed him a six-foot length of hemp twine.
"You don't want to go hunting your horse in the middle of
the night."

"Good idea," he answered, a bit surprised at the girl's
advice. Rance took the twine and tried to loop it around the
dun's neck. It reared its head. Rance again attempted to secure the rope, but the animal kept stepping away while nibbling grass.

"Here," she said, rising from her knees and walking to
him to take the rope from his hand. "You got to be gentle."
Carefully, she patted the horse's flank and eased the loop
around the neck. She cinched a quick knot with slack
while the animal grazed. With the other end, she went to a
low tree branch and tied it. Les rubbed the dun's belly once
more, and returned to the fire to stir the beans. Rance admired her skill while shaking his head at his own novice
ignorance.

"You must know what you're doing." He took off his hat
and sat on the dirt next to the fire.

Les shrugged. "Ain't much. If you watch, you learn a lot
of things." She continued to stir, keeping her eyes on the
kettle.

The odd silence made Rance uncomfortable. "So, how
long have you been with these two?"

"Almost two weeks."

Her quick answer didn't satisfy his curiosity. "Why are
you with them? And why don't they know, as you put it,
what I know?"

She twirled the ladle, all the while staring at the pot. "I
want to go to Texas. If they knew I was a girl, I don't think
they would take me."

"You want to go to Texas? Why? You have family there?" Again, her answer didn't come as rapidly as desired. He was unsure whether Les had more secrets or the subject was difficult to discuss.

"I ain't never been there." She lifted her eyes to him. "I ain't never been nowhere."

The answer brought a single chuckle from Rance. "You must be from somewhere."

"Abilene, Kansas."

"Kansas?" His curiosity was piqued. "Why would you leave there?"

"Why would I stay?" She took a bowl and poured a full ladle into it.

"What I know of Kansas, it must be full of money what with all the business these cowboys bring. And the trains bringing in new wealth, it seems to me the best place to be."

She ladled another bowl and gave it to him. "Then why ain't you there?"

He was caught in his own web. "Well, you should know why. I was ambushed and without a horse. Otherwise, I would be making tracks to be there."

Les shoved beans into her mouth. Since it seemed it would take at least a minute for her to answer, Rance shoveled a spoonful into his. The old beans tasted like warmed dirt.

"I don't know what you heard," she said, scooping more beans onto her spoon. "But the Abilene I know ain't like that. At least it ain't like that for long. People come off the trains, and some stay at Miss Maggie's boardinghouse. That's where I'm from. But most of the time there ain't much of nothing there. Now, on the other side of the train tracks, a lot goes on, but Miss Maggie, she didn't like me over there." She paused and a sheepish grin cracked her face. "But I do have some friends I made there."

A grin grew across Rance's face. "Would that be an area most of the men in town go to?" Her reply wasn't instant, but she nodded within a reasonable time. "I think I understand," he said. "So, you were born and raised in Abilene, Kansas."

She shook her head. "I wasn't born there."

"Then how did you end up there?" The inquiry, although meant in a polite way, brought a somber reaction. Les filled her mouth with beans to escape doing so with words. Rance ate as well. The second bite was worse than before, only now with the thick sauce, it was more like mud caking the roof of his mouth.

"Miss Maggie, she's the one that raised me in Abilene, she would always say that it wasn't nice to ask questions about people." He was sorry for asking, not wanting to pry into the girl's past. It really wasn't a matter he cared to know. She dragged her spoon through the beans like a plow. "I'm from back East. I was sent West by the sisters."

The news surprised him, but it explained why the girl was here by a campfire in the midst of wilderness, and perhaps why she was dressed as a man, but it still wasn't plain why she wanted to go Texas. He was intrigued by the possibilities, and another question came to mind, but then he heard the splash of a horse trampling through the creek. The younger drover dismounted and walked to the fire.

# 16

JODY WALKED BETWEEN Les and Hanks the gambler. It was the first she'd seen him since the midday coffee. She hadn't seen his smile since morning. He picked up a bowl and hurriedly ladled it full of beans. While he did, he eyed the gambler with the curl of his brow.

"You got the horses bedded down?" she asked.

Jody looked to Les. "Smith is with them. I came in to get something to eat quick, then I'm going back out to spell him."

"Seems it would be easier if the two of you came in together." The gambler's comment didn't change Jody's face.

"There's a whole lot of money on the hoof out there, mister," Jody said as he dug out another ladleful and slung it in the bowl. "Anything could spook them off. Snakes, coyotes, even seen a possum make them scamper. I guess it all looks easy for a fellow like you, dressed in your dandy duds." The sharp tone of the remark made Les's stomach stir her beans. "Where is it a fellow gets those?"

Hanks cocked his head. "In some of the finer haberdasheries in St. Louis."

"That where you been?"

"I've been there and some other places." Hanks propped

his spoon in front of his open mouth as if he was going to take another bite, but stopped, looked at it, and put it back in the bowl.

"You get to them places by train?"

Hanks glanced at Les, then pushed back his hat. He put his hand to his chin while giving Jody's question thought. The fire's glow against the orange sky lit up his blue eyes. She couldn't help staring at them, but his voice broke her trance.

"I get to most places by train. Or riverboat." The gambler put his right hand in his coat pocket as if he was reaching for something, but he didn't take it out. "I'm curious, Mr. Barnes. Why would you want to know?"

Jody shook his head. "No reason. Just curious myself." Jody hooked the ladle to the spit and slid his spoon into the pile. "I figured a fellow like yourself ain't much for horses."

"Is it that plain?" Hanks said while grinning at Les. Before she could answer, Jody did.

"Yeah. You ain't much for riding. Them clothes, don't see them out here. Normally men wearing them are in the saloons at the railheads. Cardplayers wear those clothes. That what you are? A cardplayer?" Jody stuffed the spoon in his mouth, but he didn't take his eyes off Hanks. Les's stomach rumbled worse.

Hanks paused before he answered. "As a matter of fact, I have played a game or two. Why? You want to play a hand? I have a deck right here in my pocket." Hanks pulled out the box of cards.

"No," Jody answered, swallowing and shaking his head with a hint of a smile curling each corner of his lips. It disappeared in an instant. "Your kind already has all the money in Abilene. I just don't understand what a cardplayer would be doing stumbling along a cattle trail."

Again, Hanks glanced at Les. She darted her eyes at the both of them. There was a purpose to what Jody was asking. By the look in Hanks's eye, he wanted her to tell him why. She did her best to cock her head to the side for

Hanks to see, and Jody not, and indicated that she didn't know the reason. He put the deck back in his pocket.

"As I was telling Les," Hanks began, then placed his bowl on the ground with his left hand. "I was trying to get to just such a place as Abilene. Sounds like a town where I could do some business with men that are in your line."

Jody shrugged, all the while shoveling beans in his mouth. With his tongue busy, Les spent the time to finish her bowl. Hanks left his on the ground. Still not quite sure what all the questions were about, she didn't mind that it kept Hanks from asking any more about her. She never liked talking about herself.

Jody dropped the spoon in the bowl, then the bowl to the ground. He swiped his sleeve across his chin. "Well, I got to get to Smith. You have a nice night, Mr. Hanks." He looked to Les. "I'm coming to get you in three hours. Better stay awake at your turn this time. Get your sleep in camp." His tone wasn't the friendly tone she'd known at the start of the day. Without more said, he strode past them both and into the darkness.

"Why do you suppose he was asking all those questions?" Hanks asked, removing his empty hand from his pocket.

"I can't tell you," she muttered. She turned to look at Hanks and thought aloud. "It ain't like Jody. Of the time I've known him, he's been almost like a brother, watching out for me. I thought he'd kind of took a liking to me."

"As a boy?"

Her first reaction was to assume Jody only knew her as a boy, but once she let the idea simmer, her gut churned gas up her throat to erupt from her mouth like a dog's growl.

"My." Hanks leaned away from her. "That sounded like it hurt." He looked at the bowl on the ground, then back at her. "If you're going to cut wind, please point away from my direction."

"Ain't something to laugh at. I think I may be sick." She held her aching abdomen.

"Little wonder if all you've been eating is this excuse

for food. I recommend a little meat in your diet. Maybe an apple or two. It helps the digestion."

She was in no mood for lectures. "I think I'll lie down. Jody was right. I'm going to need my sleep." She unfurled her bedroll along where the fire would provide warmth. At home, whenever she was ailing, she always felt better the next morning when she slept downstairs near the heat of the stove. As she lay down, she fixed her eyes on the stars. Miss Maggie sometimes would say the future was written in how they were strung along the night sky. She wished she could read what it was they had in store for her. "Good night, Mr. Hanks."

"Good night, Les. All I ask is I hope you don't snore."

Sunshine brought Rance out of a restless slumber. He rolled onto his back, wiped the dew from his face and lips, and yawned in the day. Smoke pierced his nostrils. He craned his neck over his chest to see Les kicking dirt to snuff the flames. "What are you doing?"

"Leaving," she answered. "It's been morning for five hours. It's time to get the day started."

Rance peeked at the sun creeping over the horizon. "Five hours? It's just now light." The protest didn't sway her from putting out the fire. Then he focused, and saw the cooking irons poking from the bundles on the pack mules. "What happened to breakfast?"

"Done had it," Les answered with her back to him while tying the final knots to secure the packs. "Smith said we should make the river today, and he wants to get there while the sun is high overhead so as not have it in the eyes of the horses when they cross."

Rance sat up, still pinching the sleep from his eyes. "Why didn't you wake me?"

She faced about. "I tried." She walked to the paint and jumped to put her foot in the stirrup, then settled in the saddle. "You were snoring so loud I couldn't get much sleep. But *you* sure did." She took the mules' reins from around the horn and turned the paint mare for the prairie grass. "Better get to your horse. The herd left near an hour ago."

Rance watched as she rode off. The sudden shroud of solitude wrapped over him with the morning breeze. There was no time to dawdle. He stood, brushed the dust from his black pants, and went to the dun. He untied the hemp knot from the tree branch. With no time to struggle getting the slack knot from around its neck, he thought to use the rope as means of a bridle to stay atop. In an instant he hopped across the dun's back and steered it after Les and the mules.

Hunger pangs twisted his belly as the morning wore on. Since he'd missed breakfast, the thought of the midday meal pushed him to come alongside her. "How long do you think before we eat?"

"Not for a good stretch." She squinted into the sun. "I'd say more than an hour." He watched her stare at the sun. A round blur stained his eye. He blinked to clear it. Once the stain faded, he focused on the tall figure of Smith riding toward them.

"There's a spot to cross about a quarter mile upstream," he said, his voice booming louder as he approached. He turned his horse in circles, never coming to a stop. "It will take us some time to get them bunched so we don't leave any strays. You two go first and get as far ahead as you can. When you get maybe a mile, start setting up camp."

Les nodded, and Smith turned his horse back toward the rising dust. She looked at Rance. "I guess that's your answer."

"At least now I know." He followed as she steered the paint and tugged the mules to the west. "Did Jody say why he was asking those questions last night?"

She shrugged. "He didn't say nothing. He just woke me up as usual. Seemed kind of tired."

"That normal?"

Another shrug. "I know I was. Every day gets longer than the one before it." Her slumped shoulders showed the proof of that statement.

More questions of the girl didn't promise any better answers. Rance let the dun's pace sag behind her lead as he
pondered just how safe he was traveling with this pair of
cowboys and Les. If he believed what she said about the
change in Jody's manner, it may have been due to some influence by others. Or if the young drover was suspicious of
men in finer clothes, he might hold a grudge against all
gamblers for his losses at the games of chance. Without
more information, Rance was left to guessing as to the actual reason. The uncertainty had him peek over his shoulder at the two wranglers chasing the herd into a tight pack.

Water lapping against rocks turned his attention forward. Les had stopped the paint at the shore of a river.
Rance took another quick peek behind to see the herd
forming. From the force of Smith's words, he expected
him and Les to be across far enough ahead to have a meal
ready by the time the remuda crossed. Minor guilt formed
in his gut for slowing her with questions. He kicked the
dun to come alongside her.

"You better hurry," he said. "They are almost here."

She faced him with her mouth slightly open and her
eyes in a dazed stare. "I never done this," she said with a
quivering voice.

Recognizing the fright etched in her cheeks, he reached
for the mules' reins. "Here, give them to me." Once he
gripped them, he first nudged the dun to enter the water.
When it hesitated, he kicked its flanks. The stubborn mules
pulled his balance backward while the dun bolted forward.

His hand clutched the hemp twine. Water drops sprinkled his face as he lay near prone on the horse's back. Before he could right himself, the chill of the river wrapped
around his legs, filling his boots. In seconds the crashing
tide was at his waist. The cold gripped his chest, squeezing
his ribs and lungs.

"Hang on tight," Les yelled from somewhere near. He
couldn't see her.

The dun struggled against the current. It rolled its shoulders, further throwing him side to side. The mules didn't

follow as fast as the dun nor as straight. Their reins pulled
his right arm around over his head, dragging him shoulder-
first to the left. The heavy animals were swept further
downstream. If he released the reins, all the food for the
group would be lost. Rance clenched his right fist to keep
the leather secure. The dun veered to the right. His boots
weighed like lead anchors. He couldn't stay on the dun.

Without a splash he sank into the green-tinged waves.
Water ran over his nose and mouth. Both arms were outstretched. In his left hand he held the hemp twine attached
to the dun, in his right, the mules' reins. While all three
beasts instinctively thrashed against the raging current,
Rance sensed the icy tug of death pull him deeper. His wet
clothes kept dragging him down, the saturated fabric keeping his arms from pulling, his legs from kicking, and his
chest from expanding. A choice had to be made, his life or
the food.

He released the reins. The jolt of the dun swimming tore
the hemp twine from his left hand. The horse's legs
churned the water. The void of their wake sucked him further down. He flailed in the water. His fingers clawed for
any progress up.

The pressure against his ribs pushed the air from his
lungs. He watched the bubbles reach the surface. Although
the cold seized his arms and the relentless current pushed
him further away from the scrambling animals, the need to
survive surged through his body. One last kick and throw
of his arms to the side sent him up.

He broke the surface. Instantly, he inhaled life. Water
lapped in his face and over his head. His heavy legs
couldn't kick any harder and his shoulders were bound by
the wet coat. He couldn't tread fast enough to keep above
the waves for air.

About to submerge again and likely for the final time,
he heard the piercing whir of a rope. In an instant he felt
the tight cinch of a lariat surround his arm and neck. The
jolt of the rope choked his throat. Reflex had him grab the
rope and pull for slack in order to breathe.

He didn't mind the overwhelming tow. It kept his head above the water and although water crashed against his face, slowly he felt the sun on his neck, then chest, waist, and finally legs while sliding through the mud of the river-bank. His vision still blurred by the water droplets, he swiped his face clean to see Smith astride his horse above.

"You all right?"

With water still in his throat, Rance could only nod. He coughed out what was left of the river from his lungs and squinted up at the old wrangler. "I'm beholden to you."

"What the hell were you doing out there?"

"I was trying to cross the river," Rance huffed out.

"I told you and that fool boy the crossing was a quarter mile up the river. Hell, you still had half the ways to go to get there. The water ain't two feet deep at that spot."

The realization he'd risked his life in vain had him col-lapse to the mud. While still introducing his lungs to fresh air, he watched as Jody led both mules onto the bank. Not too far away, the dun grazed on the green growth near the shore. Les kicked her paint mare to take its final stride out of the water. Rance couldn't decide to scream in anger at her or laugh at his own foolishness.

"Looks like we may have trouble."

Jody's warning brought Rance to sit up. Again, he squinted into the bright sunshine. The clop of horses ap-proaching made him stand. Three riders came over a small hill. Rance reached in his pocket. The pepperbox was still there, but the river surely had ruined the loads. As he watched them come near, he saw all three were dressed in coats and trousers and wore hats with wide brims. None of them appeared familiar.

"Do you know who they are?" he asked Smith.

"Yeah," he answered with a sure tone. "I was expecting them."

"So? Who are they?"

The reply was short and held a hint of concern. "Indians."

# 17

RANCE PEERED FROM side to side looking for any other strangers to arrive. None were in view. The middle of the three riders was an older man of slight frame. His two friends were dressed in similar coats and trousers, but distinctive long braids drooped under their hats. All three reined in their mounts just feet away.

"Good afternoon," the older Indian said in a polite voice. "I am Robert Whitedeer, member and counsel to the tribal chiefs of the Cherokee Nation, which owns this land." Rance was impressed at the correct English diction. All he had ever heard of about Indians was their savagery.

"I know who you are," Smith replied in less polite fashion. "And I know why you're here. Been expecting you at some time during this trip."

Whitedeer nodded. "To pass through this land the tribal council requires two saddle ponies as tribute."

"Two?" Jody's alarm brought Smith's scowl upon him.

"I thought it was one," said Smith, turning his attention back to the older Cherokee. "Two horses is a high price."

"You know the council guarantees your passage throughout the nation. For that it takes the Cherokee marshals to ride great distances. They need fresh horses at the outposts."

The numbness in Rance's toes gave way to a biting pain. He sat and pulled off each boot to pour out the water. Smith dismounted.

"Well, I guess I got no say in the matter." He motioned with his hand. "Don't guess you're going to want me to pick them out for you." With that, all three Cherokees nudged their horses forward into the river and toward the remuda still on the opposite side. Smith began looping his rope in tight coils when Jody slid off his mount and Les steered her mare close enough to hear.

"You going to let them have two?" asked Jody.

"I don't like it neither, but I ain't got much choice. Mr. Pearl told me to expect it. When the drive came north through here, they took ten beeves. If you don't give them what they want, then they'll take them in the middle of the night, so this way at least we can get some sleep. The law and the Army says it's Indian land, so they won't help none. Just the cost of doing business was Pearl's words. Told me they may have wanted five, so we got three more to return than first thought."

Jody shook his head. "Just seems like they're stealing."

"Ain't no matter." Smith took his rope and tied it to his saddle. "It ain't like those are ours."

The three Cherokees drove their two choices back across the river. As they passed, Whitedeer pulled his horse near Smith's. "I will tell the council that you have paid for safe passage through Cherokee land. Tell Frank Pearl he is welcome to bring his cattle through our property next spring."

Smith nodded, and Whitedeer turned his horse to join his friends.

"All right," Smith huffed. "Come on, Jody. Let's get the rest across before they scatter." He stepped into the stirrup and pulled himself into the saddle. He looked at Les. "You have caused us to be at least an hour behind schedule.

Make some tracks." Yanking the reins, he steered his horse about and he and Jody entered the river.

With both men gone, Rance looked at Les. "The next time you need help crossing a river," he said, prepared to finish by telling her he should be one state away, but his tongue was seized by her solemn face. After a moment's recollection, he realized that he'd put himself in the predicament of charging into a river atop a horse with no saddle. "Ah, forget it." Drops pelted the dirt beneath him turning the ground to mud where he stood. "You go ahead without me." He pulled the socks from his feet and wrung enough water on the first fold to fill a small pail. "I'm going to take the time needed to get dry." He looked at her. "You're welcome to stay while I remove my pants, but since you have a meal to cook, I suggest you heed Mr. Smith's command."

"That's good with me," she answered. "Ain't like I never seen a man with his pants down before. Seen one, seen them all."

Surprised by her wit, he stopped unbuttoning his shirt and watched her lead the mules south. However, his amusement quickly turned to worry when he pulled off the soaked coat. It was heavy enough on its own dripping wet, and he feared the cargo inside the lining was somehow damaged. He glanced up as Smith and Jody drove the remuda further to the west, no doubt to the crossing Smith had first recommended. It might take them more than thirty minutes to get to this side. Although tempted, if he tore the lining to inspect the money, he wouldn't have the time nor the secrecy to repair it. His inspection would have to wait for more suitable surroundings.

Jody slopped beans into the bowl and topped it with a biscuit. Despite the slivers of bacon in the pot, the taste wasn't much improved. The evening's supper wasn't the worst thing troubling his mind.

It had been nearly two days since he'd encountered the

two bandits. Each time he glanced into the darkness, he readied himself for their arrival. He almost wished they'd come and get their vengeance so he could be done with the affair.

Since the afternoon and the encounter with the Cherokees, an idea had plagued his mind. With the Indians only claiming two horses rather than the expected five, three were left to dicker with, and it wouldn't cause a concern once the remuda returned to the Cooper ranch. If he brought two ponies to those men, perhaps they'd leave him and his conscience alone.

He swiped the bread into the sauce to soften it, and his nerves. As with most nights, the day's toil had left every mouth speechless. That was fine by him. Normally, it was his nature to bring conversation to the fire, but during the last two nights words hadn't come easy to him.

Les huddled in a corner as was his habit. The gambler reclined against a log with eyes closed. Jody wasn't sure, but it only made sense that this was the man the first group of men hunted. Whether the gambler was guilty wasn't a matter for Jody to ponder. His only care was to rid himself of his own guilty silence. He put down the bowl of beans. The food did little to settle his qualms.

Resolved to go through with his plans, he first needed to see if the opportunity allowed for it. He stood and went to the string. He felt both Les and the gambler watching his back. Once he pulled the knotted reins free and mounted, he steered his horse into the night. Beyond the fire's glow, the light of the full moon illuminated the field where the remuda had settled.

He slowed his mount and circled the herd so as not to spook them. Halfway around, he recognized Smith in the saddle, positioned far enough away to see the entire herd like a shepherd with sheep.

"What are you doing out here so early?" asked Smith.

"I couldn't sleep. I knew I had to be out here in little more than an hour's time. So, I thought to give the time to you."

The orange luminance from Smith's pipe showed his face for only an instant. Smoke gently billowed into the breeze. "You feeling poorly?"

Jody took a moment to think of a suitable answer. "I can't tell for sure. Maybe the boy ain't cooking the beans long enough. Or maybe I've ate all of them my body can stand. Anyway, I thought the night air might help. Wasn't doing me any good sitting next to that pot."

Smith chuckled. "I know what you mean. Try eating them for ten years straight. After a while, you don't remember what real food tastes like." He inhaled deeply and let it all out at once. "Well, if you're offering, I'm accepting." He turned his mount in direction of the camp. "I can't say I mind the extra sleep. Don't get enough of it at my age. Try to keep them quiet. I saw a fire of a camp through those trees less than a mile on the other side of a creek. Be careful. You don't know who that might be."

The news tightened Jody's chest. "Did you see how many they was?"

"No. I didn't want to get that close. And you don't neither. Just keep the herd on this side of that thicket. This ground is higher than theirs. You can't be seen through the trees. I already looked myself." Jody watched Smith ride until his figure faded into the surrounding grass. He tried to take a deep breath but couldn't.

He peered into the eastern darkness. Convinced the campfire must belong to the two bandits, he wanted to get his part over with as quick as possible. He took both lariats and widened the loop. He nudged his mount to walk among the herd with confidence the horses wouldn't startle with his approach as long as he was slow and deliberate. There wasn't enough light to judge which two were best, so he used his calm voice to ease each loop around the first pair standing on the outer edge of the herd. He led both away at a slow walk. Each step brought him a mite more comfort that by morning he'd be done with this affair.

Once past the first trees, he steered left and right as needed to brush against as few as possible. The further he went, the thicker the brush became. When a limb swatted his face, he realized he couldn't ride through the thicket. He slid off the saddle and led all three horses by foot.

The flicker of a fire caught his eye. Although it was distant, it was clear to see it was a campfire on a lower plane. He took a moment to consider what next to do when the sound of water running through a stream had him tie the reins and rope and survey his next path. He crouched so as not to misstep on the sloping ground, and came within view of a small ravine where the creek ran. While he thought about how to traverse the incline, the sound of a voice humming crept into his ear.

The closer to the edge he came, the clearer he heard the humming. Thorny limbs blocked his path. Carefully, he pushed them aside one by one with the heel of his hand. The new growth was limber and he was cautious not to force them to snap.

Jody snaked through the branches. He knelt on one knee on the high embankment overlooking the creek. The water glistened with moonlight. He saw a young woman alone in the stream wearing only white underclothes. She wasn't aware of his presence. A small thought in the back of his mind told him to leave, but not a muscle complied.

She stood just a few feet from the shore. The waves cascaded around and through her thighs. Her hair was loose and reached the center of her back. The humming stopped. She dipped her hand into the water. He knew it was cold, and she showed it with the shiver in her shoulders. Twisting about in each direction, she appeared to look for anyone who'd be watching. Afraid he was close enough for her to hear a whisper, he hushed his breath.

With both hands, she took the bottom of her camisole top and pulled it up and over her head. His heart pounded. The gray light gleamed off her round and firm female contours. She faced to the side. Her front in silhouette, she cupped water in her palms and splashed her chest, arms, and shoulders. As she rubbed the cold water about, Jody's nerves made his own gut and ribs quiver.

She stepped to face straight away from him. Quickly and delicately, she edged the pantaloon bottoms from her hips, stripping them from one leg at a time, then tossing them to the shore, and finally kneeling beneath the surface. As he watched her undress, he gauged the woman to be in her twentieth year by the reflection of her skin in the light. All the women's backsides he'd ever seen were of those working the bawdy houses. Their old sagging folds didn't compare with this one's form.

He wiped the sweat from his brow. The crazy notion of actually trying to introduce himself to such a beauty left his mind as soon as it entered. Her screams would be heard for miles and wake every man with a shotgun. Yet he wanted to meet her. He wondered where it was she was traveling and needed to know her name.

A horse's neigh shattered the silence. Jody froze every joint still. The woman sunk to the shoulders, her head bobbing and twisting in every direction. His stomach ached as if punched, apologizing in his mind for the intrusion. Her fright had to be ten times as great and he was embarrassed for her.

Her bath ended with the interruption. She rose from the stream and retrieved the white undergarments from the shore. She stepped into the pantaloons and slipped the camisole over her top all faster than he could admire. Into the shadows she scurried up the small incline and through the high grass on the far side. Only flashes of her presence were left to him, until long enough had passed by he was sure he would see no more.

Jody inhaled deeply for the first time in nearly ten minutes. The night air had a greater kick than any whiskey shot. However, he didn't regret the lack of breathing for the chance to view a little bit of heaven. Still in a crouch, he stepped back through the thorny brush, remaining careful not to snap any branches. It wouldn't do for her to hear one break and know she was watched. She was a lady, and thinking himself a gentleman, he owed that to her.

# 18

LES MADE IT a point to be out early ahead of the herd. For some reason her body was full of spirit. Perhaps it was due to the bacon she'd sliced into the beans for breakfast as Hanks had suggested, or maybe it was the five hours of sound sleep. She wasn't sure which. There was another pleasant surprise that greeted her this morning, the return of Jody's bright smile. Just as uncertain to that cause as she was to the crisp air on the bright cloudless day, she didn't trouble her mind as to why and just enjoyed the result.

Behind, the remuda moved at a slower pace a half mile away. She took advantage of the distance to search for a spot to start a fire for dinner. She found one along a line of trees that would make for pleasant shade during the meal. When she got off the paint, she removed the cooking irons from the packs and found the rocks needed to surround the prospective flame. Needing kindling and tinder, she searched and found limbs and branches already scattered beneath the trees. A welcome sound pushed her further under the canopy. A small brook threaded around the large trunks. She couldn't believe her luck. Now, she wouldn't strike camp with less than full canteens.

When Smith and Jody arrived in camp, she had the beans at a bubble. Each of them wasted little time in grabbing a dish and serving themselves. The good weather and tall grass kept the herd calm, grazing, and easily in view.

She couldn't keep from admiring Jody's sheepish grin. As he swirled the beans inside his mouth, he spoke using only his lips while his jaw kept chewing. "You ain't going to believe what I saw last night."

Smith didn't raise his eyes from his bowl. Les took the bait. "What is that?"

"A beautiful woman."

Suddenly, Les didn't know if she wanted to hear more, but it wouldn't seem normal for a boy of her age not to. Jody didn't need further encouragement to tell all.

"And she was naked as the day she was born."

Les's gut stopped her chest from taking in air. Smith stopped his spoon and faced Jody with an inquiring arch to his brow.

"Ain't lying. There she was taking a bath in that creek you told me of. And she weren't no old woman." His pause only allowed him to enjoy each word. "She was big where it's best to be and skinny where need be. And she looked to be just a year under me." While still grinning from ear to ear, he managed to slip his spoon between his teeth.

Smith returned his attention to the bowl.

Jody's grin faded. "It's the truth. The God's honest."

"Where'd she come from?"

Les felt better with Smith's question. She'd like nothing more than to think it wasn't true.

"From a camp on the other side of that creek. She scampered back to it when my horse neighed. I was just getting up the gumption to walk down to there to get her name."

Smith swallowed, then glanced at Les and winked. "Why didn't you?"

Jody seemed ready to answer. However, he held his mouth open, gasping the air as if the words he wanted to say were stuck in his throat. He aimed his face back at his bowl of beans. "I was afraid she'd be scared and run off screaming. It being night and all. What else would you think a woman would do by herself?" He quickly shoved his spoon in his mouth, as if he felt that if he couldn't speak, he wouldn't have to answer any more questions.

"If it was me," Smith said, doling out another ladle into his bowl, "and I saw a pretty woman without her clothes, I'd've found me a way to get down to the water and get her name. Might even help her with her dressing." Smith gulped some beans. Jody rolled his eyes at the brash brag. Les felt a grin crease her face. "But," Smith continued, "seeing it was you there, then I think you did right. Yes, sir, if that female got one look at you she'd run screaming into the next county."

Smith's guffaw caused Les to laugh also. Jody didn't appear amused at the remark until only a few seconds had passed. Then the approach of a rider wiped the smile from Jody's face. "Don't say nothing."

Hanks came to the camp appearing like he hadn't slept a wink. Although it was mid-morning and they'd covered a good six miles, the gambler wiped the wrinkles of slumber from his black-stubbled face. He stopped the red dun just short of the camp. His unbuttoned shirt showed his hair-matted chest, while his coat was folded in front of him across the dun's back. "It isn't polite to leave a man to sleep alone in the wilderness."

Les stoked the fire, eyeing the faces of Jody and Smith. When she'd left well ahead of the herd, she'd thought it fell to them to wake their guest.

"You slept more than all of us stacked together. Didn't think it our duty to start your day," Jody said with a hard-tack roll stuck in his cheek.

"Did you get lonely?" Smith asked. The innocence of his question forced a laugh from Jody that spread to Les.

"Very funny," Hanks said sliding off the dun. "I don't suppose we had an agreement."

"The deal was for the use of the horse until the next town. Not to act as no nanny." Smith's gruff tone seemed to settle the matter.

Hanks slipped the coat sleeves on his arms and took a
tin to fill with coffee. Pops and cracks could be heard while
he stretched his jaw and craned his neck. As he twirled his
head about, he stopped it when facing the tree limbs above.

"Do you smell that?" he asked as he flared his nostrils.

Les sniffed the air and watched Smith and Jody cease
their gulping and do the same. Again, Les snorted. Only a
hint of a scent of something cooking crept up her nose. She
peeked at the pot. The smell wasn't from the beans.

Smith was first to angle his head around until he stood
and faced about to the southeast. He drew in deeply
through his nose and exhaled out his mouth. He looked at
Jody and Hanks. "Somebody is boiling mash."

"I thought I recognized that odor," Hanks said with
pride.

Jody stood and copied Smith's stance and action. "I
don't know what that is." Les was glad he'd admitted the
same ignorance.

"Hooch," said Smith, again facing the southeast, until
he returned his attention briefly to them. "Moonshine."

Les looked to Jody, then to Hanks. Both men shared the
same wry smile. She wasn't sure exactly what was the
source of their delight.

"Why would they be out here?" she asked.

Smith glanced at Jody while answering the question.
"Because there ain't no law out here. No real law. Them Indians don't matter. They probably take it as 'tribute' to the
tribe."

"Why does that matter?"

"Ain't legal to still your own whiskey. Not and pay no tax
with it." Smith sat down and poured more coffee in the tin.

Jody remained standing, twisting his head back and
forth to the southeast and to Smith. "You don't want to
know where it's coming from?"

Smith gave him a quick glance, then turned his eyes to
the fire. "Nope. I don't. I'd think they don't want no visitors. None they didn't invite personal."

"That would be my bet as well," Hanks said.

"How do you know?" Jody asked, facing Hanks. "They may want to sell some. Hell, they can't be making it all for themselves."

"They're outlaws most likely. They still it here, then take it into Texas or Arkansas to sell to sutlers and such to pass it on to white folk who don't know the difference."

The silence that settled between the men didn't last long. Jody poured what coffee was in his cup to the dirt and started toward the string. "I'm going to have a look."

"No, you ain't." Smith's rebuke only stopped Jody for a moment.

"Yes, I am. You ain't my boss or my keeper, Smith."

The two cowboys stared at each other for a long moment. The only sounds came from doves cooing. Smith's jaw clenched as a sign he wasn't used to defiance of an order, not from a kid half his age. Jody stood firm, his eyes glaring at the older man. Hanks reclined on the ground with a sly grin enjoying the show. Les huddled her shoulders. The sight of the two men she was dependent on to get her to Texas arguing with the snarls of mean dogs made her queasy.

Finally, Smith nodded, then stood. "All right." He looked at Les, then at Hanks. "We'll all go." He turned his eyes back to Jody. "There's no sense having to look for your carcass after you're shot. Might as well see it when it happened." He started walking to the southeast closely followed by Jody. Even Hanks rose off the ground and swiped the dust from the seat of his pants. Les got up to join the group, but was torn about what to do with the camp.

"Should I put out the fire?"

Smith shook his head while keeping his eyes on where he was walking. He only spoke over his shoulder. "No. We ain't staying long. Just enough to see who it is to satisfy Jody." His tone held a hint of disgust. Les ran to catch them, skipping over the small brush growing under the trees.

Jody pulled the pistol from his belt and gave a puzzled

face to Smith, whose gun stayed in the holster. "Better have it ready."

Smith then gave Jody a confused twist of his brow. "Why? You expecting somebody you know?"

"You're the one said they was outlaws. I just thought it best to be ready to shoot back."

"I don't expect to get that close." Smith followed the run of the brook, bending under the wider branches and sliding past the longer ones. Les stayed at the rear where she felt most safe. If there were outlaws in these woods, she wanted to be first to leave.

As they went further into the thick foliage, Smith's pace slowed to a creep. With every third step, he angled his nose up like a hound. Jody and Hanks mocked each move of the old wrangler. When the leader stopped, they all stopped just like a train. Sunlight that sprinkled through the leaves above appeared as patches against their clothes, becoming smaller with each yard or so they went. The density of the thorny brush hid Smith's tall shape when he changed direction. The air was heavy without the breeze to move it. It was as if the woods were in a big pot and the sun cooked them like a fire. Les could taste the white bark of the cottonwoods. Sweat streamed down her nose at a rate that made her think her hat was full of it.

She knelt under a large limb and came in line with the other three. As she rose, she heard a long hollow click.

"Nobody move or I'll scatter all of you to the next county."

Les didn't move a muscle, but closed her eyes. It was more than a single second before she couldn't leave them closed anymore. Through her squinted eyelids, she saw Hanks two feet ahead. In front of him stood Jody, his blue shirt lighter than the darkness behind. She couldn't see Smith, but the voice wasn't his. She lowered her eyes to the dirt. If she didn't look, maybe nobody would be scattered.

"I've heard that before," Hanks said in a kindly fashion. Les cringed even more. The gambler's charming tactic had

worked on her, but if she'd had a gun aimed at him when
they first met, she couldn't swear she'd resist pulling the
trigger. Yet he was a gambler.

"Thomas Fuller, is that you?"

Les opened her mouth, ready to take in a deep breath to
run if needed. A reply was long in coming.

"Parson?"

"Why, yes, it is," Hanks replied. "What a divine event to
find friends here deep in the woods of wilderness."

Usually sickened by false charm, Les finally inhaled as
she took stock of Hanks's confident tone.

"Who is it you got with you?"

"I'd like to introduce some new friends of mine. However, I am wondering if I might do this under more pleasant surroundings. Could we be allowed to leave these
stifling conditions for where you are?"

Again, the reply was not immediate. "Come out of there.
But only one at a time until I can get a good look at all of you.
Remember, it only takes one barrel to tear apart three men."

Adhering to the order, Les stayed in step behind Hanks.
She carefully pushed the thorns away from her path, catching the ones that swung back at her from the gambler's
clumsy lead.

Fresh air was the first sign that she was nearing a clearing. As the branches thinned, the splash of the breeze
against her face was as cool as any water. She wiped the
sweat from her eyes and focused on a short-statured man
with a bushy mustache holding a shotgun. Les took a place
in line with Jody, Hanks, and Smith.

"Reverend Hanks," came as a squeal from a feminine
voice. To the right, a girl not many years older than Les ran
with open arms toward the gambler. In a brown dress with
white spots, she jumped into his arms and planted a kiss on
his lips.

# 19

"RUTH! GET OFF him."

"But Uncle," said the long-haired girl while keeping her eyes staring into Hanks's. "I never got a chance to thank him proper for saving our lives."

The surprise of the announcement turned Les, Jody, and even Smith with furrowed brows to the gambler.

"It ain't proper for a young girl to be hanging all over a grown man who's half dressed. Even if he is a preacher."

When the girl released her arms from around Hanks's neck, Jody opened his mouth. Les thought he would set the man with the shotgun straight to the truth about Hanks, but the gambler was quick to button his shirt and even quicker with his tongue.

"No thanks needed. Although I couldn't imagine a better reward. I was just doing what I was called to do by the man above." As Ruth stepped back, Hanks pointed at the shotgun still steadied at the four. "There's also no need to fear, Thomas. These men mean you or family no harm."

"Just who the heck are they?"

Hanks turned his finger to Smith and pointed. "This man's name is Smith. This young man is Jody Barnes, and this 'boy' is called Les. I was able to join them when I left your company in such haste."

The shotgun didn't waiver. "What are they doing out here?"

"We ain't no law, if that's what you're asking," Smith said. "We're part of a cattle drive went to Abilene. We're bringing back a remuda to Texas. We found the"—he hesitated—"reverend in the woods some miles back. I told him we'd take him to the next town." He pointed at a metal can as big as a keg with a cone-shaped lid, all of it sitting on an iron stand above a small flame. From the can, a coiled tube spiraled down to a wooden bucket. "The smell of the mash brought us here."

Hanks nodded. "There you have it. Now, you can put down the gun before something happens I know you wouldn't intend."

Slowly, Fuller lowered the weapon. "Ordinarily, I'd say you folks are a little too nosy for your own good. But seeing you're with the parson, I guess I'll have to trust you."

Les exhaled in relief.

Another woman and small boy walked from the cover of the trees at the far side of the clearing. "This is my wife Abigail and my son Horton." With Hanks's lead, all the men removed their hats. Les took a moment before realizing she needed to comply with the respectful gesture. The woman nodded in recognition.

"Good afternoon, gentlemen. I'm so pleased to see you safe again, Reverend Hanks."

"And I you, Mrs. Fuller." The gambler's sweet tone hung in the air while the woman turned her eyes to Les.

"What a handsome young man."

Les was hit in the head by the compliment. "What?"

"That young fellow's name is Les, Mother," said Fuller.

The woman giggled. "And shy too." She looked at her son. "Horton, maybe Les will tell you about being a cowboy."

Horton didn't show the same enthusiasm for the idea as Hanks. "I'd think that would be a fine idea," said Hanks. "Don't you, Les?"

Unable to say what truly was on her mind, Les shrugged and forced a polite smile. "I don't know what I'd have to say. This is my first time."

"Modesty is a fine quality," Mrs. Fuller said with some pride. "Les, ain't you uncomfortable with your coat buttoned to the top like that?"

Suddenly, all eyes looked her way. She didn't know what would make sense to say, so she relied on the excuse of being a kid. "No, ma'am. I'm cold-natured."

"Heavens to Betsy," Mrs. Fuller chortled. "I don't want to share a bed with you when it's really cold." While others joined her in laughter, Hanks cast an eye at Les.

"No risk in that happening, Mrs. Fuller." His statement hung in the air for a moment while all but Les wondered what was meant. Hanks was quick to change the subject. "Is that your wonderful cooking I smell on the fire?"

"Why, yes, it is, Reverend. Thomas got me two big rabbits to stew. There's more than enough. Won't you and your friends join us for supper?"

"We don't have—" Smith started, but Hanks again was quicker to speak.

"Of course we would love to accept your invitation. I know these fellows have suffered enough with nothing but beans and hardtack. I can heartily recommend your cooking as some of the best I have ever tasted."

Mrs. Fuller flapped her hand at Hanks. "Reverend, you are too kind."

"Not at all, Mrs. Fuller. Not at all." He looked at Smith, who appeared as if his breath had been stolen. It was the first time Les could remember the old wrangler not getting his way twice in the same day.

When dusk settled over the prairie, Les steered her mare to the string near the opening in the woods. She had taken the first turn mainly to avoid having to spend time with Horton, and now followed the smell of a woman's cooking through the branches.

Once she entered the clearing, the fire had taken over as

the sole source of light for the camp. Smith sat on a log that he'd no doubt pulled to that spot. Hanks sat to the right with Ruth close to his arm. Jody sat to the left, his eyes firmly planted on Ruth, but she didn't seem to notice his attention. The Fullers with their son sat opposite their guests. Abigail rose upon sight of Les.

"There looks like a boy with a mess of hunger stirring. Can I get you a plate of stew? Do you like dumplings, Les? I've been holding some back for you."

"Yes, ma'am. All that would be much appreciated." She took a place next to Jody. Everyone appeared to have already enjoyed their meal. Smith pulled his pipe from his vest and took the tobacco pouch from his pants pocket.

Thomas Fuller lowered his brow at Hanks. "Parson, looks like you have need of my razor again."

Hanks rubbed both stubbled cheeks with his right palm.

Fuller then smiled and lifted a jug from the ground and yanked out the cork. "This is the batch I was telling you about. Been sitting in the fruit cellar back home for over six months. Should be just about right." He passed the jug to Smith. "I'll let you do the honors." At first, Smith didn't appear willing to accept the privilege, but holding the jug for more than a minute tempted him more than he could resist.

Smith hooked his finger through the handle hole at the top and propped the jug on the side of his right elbow. Slowly he angled it up until his lips kissed the opening. For two gulps he held the jug in place, then put it to the ground. "That tasted ripe." Fuller grinned at the compliment.

"I'll have a taste." Jody hooked a finger into the jug and took a swig of his own. He held it in place for three gulps, rapidly slinging the jug off his shoulder. He squinted hard, gritting his teeth like he was in awful agony. He exhaled in a gush to the guffaws of Fuller and Smith.

"First taste of backwoods mash?" Fuller asked as Jody continued to wheeze air. He nodded, then offered the jug to Les. "Go ahead, young man," Fuller said with pride. "It'll put hair on your chest."

Unsure how to refuse, Les sat still. Mrs. Fuller arrived

with a plate of stew, three dumplings, and a soft bread biscuit. Les accepted the plate as a rescue from the pain the men encountered sipping the jug. She enjoyed the aroma. "Much obliged, Mrs. Fuller." She sunk her spoon into the gravy, dumplings, and meat. The taste instantly took her mind back to Miss Maggie's boardinghouse, and for the first time she wished she was back in her own comfortable bed, eating dinner promptly at six o'clock. More fireside chatter interrupted her remembrance, bringing her to the present. Jody still sat next to her. She edged her elbow against his arm. "It's your turn," she said. "Ain't you going to go?"

"In a minute. I'll know when it's time to go," he answered with a sharp tone. He didn't waste a second in putting his eyes back on Ruth. It was hard not to notice the girl's eyes sparkle with the flicker of the flame. Jody obviously did.

Les felt her stomach sag. She ate more of the meal, and although the taste was as good as she'd known at home, it didn't displace the empty feeling in the pit of her stomach. She chided herself for thinking something she'd no right to assume. Yet the more she looked at Jody looking at Ruth, who looked at Hanks, Les couldn't help running through her mind that she should have met him when she wore a dress. How would he have looked at her then. The other half of her mind argued that it wouldn't have mattered.

While dressed as a boy, she was thought of as a kid by Jody, and he wouldn't think her any older as a girl. Ruth, although not more than two or three years older, didn't act any more mature. While Les cut into a dumpling, she angled a view at Ruth's protruding top. Recollection of the men's reaction to the women at Shenandoah's reminded her of the appeal of the buxom gals. Les stabbed the dumpling with her fork and bit into it.

Hanks picked up the jug and took his swigs. After a long gulp, he sucked in wind and blew it out. "Some of the best I've had in some while. I didn't know you had such a talent. Your blend must be known throughout Tennessee, Mr. Fuller."

"I didn't know a man of the church as yourself would take to sipping whiskey with such an open mind."

Hanks grinned, hesitating before he spoke. "I have imbibed some of the finer libations on occasions. Of course in limited quantities." He darted his eyes around the camp, no doubt to see who believed his excuse for drinking liquor.

"Truth be known," Fuller said with a hint of shyness, "I don't make it to sell. I just keep enough for my own use." He paused. "My son and I used to sip some from the porch."

The gambler's grin faded quickly. The mention of the dead son took the smile from Ruth's face as well. "I again mourn your loss," Hanks said. He looked to Ruth. "All of your losses."

"What happened?" asked Jody, appearing eager to learn as much as he could about anything to do with Ruth. Smith once more showed his scowl to the young cowboy.

"My son was killed in the war, as was my brother, Ruth's father," said Fuller.

Jody's head shrunk beneath the bend of his shoulders. "Sorry," he said while looking at Ruth. She replied only with a smile lasting just a single instant.

Fuller's voice broke the silence. "I guess it can be talked about now, with the war being over four years." He looked at his wife. She wiped away a tear with her apron. "Tom Jr. snuck from home and joined up with the First Tennessee Regiment. I guess due to all the rabble-rousing about Southerners' duties to their states. My brother was an ardent defender of states' rights, and he signed up to fight as soon as news got out about the South firing on Fort Sumter. So we figured Tom Jr. went off to fight with his uncle. It wasn't long before we heard the news of the battles in the East and the First Tennessee joined with General Lee's army." He hung his head.

Les felt as uneasy hearing the story as she sensed Mr. Fuller was telling it. A quick glance around the camp showed the giddy faces present only a minute before were gone. Ruth wiped a tear from her cheek. Hanks drew a handkerchief from his pocket and gave it to her. Jody watched her accept it and shook his head.

Fuller continued. "The last letter we got from him said he was marching north. It said not to worry about him, that he'd be home by the fall to harvest the corn." He inhaled sharply. "It wasn't until the fall that we learned he was killed in Maryland near a town called Sharpsburg."

Silence stole over the camp. Smith struck a match and lit his pipe. The smoke puffed out in large clouds as he sucked in the flame.

"He sounds like he was a brave young man," Hanks said. "I can admire his sacrifice for what he believed. I've heard many a story from the soldiers of the South. All of them tell of the heroes they fought with that gave their lives in the glory of battle."

"Glory?" Smith said in a loud voice. "Hell, you don't know what you're talking about when you say glory." He nodded toward the Fullers. "I'm sorry about your son. I saw many of them myself." He faced Hanks. "And as far as glory, there weren't none. Not with men screaming from their wounds."

Mrs. Fuller rose. "Horton, Ruth, it's time we tended to the plates." Horton's pleading face gained no favor with his mother. She pinched his shoulder to make him stand. She offered her hand to Ruth. The girl gave Hanks a longing stare, then went with her aunt. Mrs. Fuller looked at Les. "Would you like another dumpling?"

"No, ma'am." Les handed her the plate. "That was a mighty fine dinner, Mrs. Fuller." The older woman nodded in thanks and left the surroundings of the fire.

"My apology if I upset your wife," said Smith.

Fuller shook his head. "I take no offense. She just can't stand to hear what really happened on those fields. But I guess you do, Mr. Smith. If you don't mind me asking, what part of the war were you in?"

# 20

SMITH TOOK SOME time to answer. "I was in the Second Dragoons of the Fourth Texas Brigade."

A surprised Jody turned to him. "You were?"

Smith nodded and drew on the pipe. He took it in hand and pointed at Hanks. "You talked about the glory. There were some in Texas that said the same thing. So I joined up to serve my state, although many others including Sam Houston thought it a poor reason to fight. But I knew many a man that signed up and I felt it was my part to join them. We went east and served under Colonel John Bell Hood."

"I've heard of him. One of the South's great commanders."

"He was a damn fool," Smith said, chiding Hanks. "He was another one seeking glory. Oh, he was bold, give him that, riding ahead of us, calling on us to fight. We went to battle many times when we weren't ready." He nodded his head and looked at the dirt. Only moments later, he stuck the pipe between his teeth and peered up at Thomas Fuller.

"I was at Sharpsburg. The Federals called it Antietam Creek. We licked them that day, but it cost a bunch of our boys." He took in a long pained breath. "And I was with the Fourth when we hooked up with General Lee too. Killed a mess of Yankee boys at Fredericksburg, and later at Chancellorsville. It filled us with fire. Convinced us and the generals we couldn't be whipped." Smith drew on the pipe, as if he had something to say but didn't know the right words.

"Marching up north, we got into Billy Blue's backyard. Came to the town called Gettysburg." Murmurs like moans came from Fuller and Hanks as Smith took another breath. "The first day was nothing but a scramble of lines looking to outflank the other. The second day was our best chance. We joined Alabama Regulars to charge up a hill next to what's known as Roundtop. Charge after charge we went up that hill. But the Yankees kept firing and pushed us back. Before we could make one final charge to break their line and take the hill, a Northern officer charged down the hill. Surprised us like a bolt of lightning. I retreated before I was taken prisoner. But that just saved me for the third day."

"The charge of General Pickett?" Fuller asked.

Smith puffed out smoke, waiting before nodding. His voice was low and in a monotone, speaking in sharp-cut sentences. "Orders came down General Lee had ordered an advance against a fortified line of Federal rifles. There was a heap of brash talk about how we would take them down that day. When we marched, it felt like there was more soldiers in that field than wheat stalks. Then the Yankee guns opened up volley after volley on us. Like a scythe being swung, Southern soldiers fell to the dirt. Cannon on Roundtop Hill fired grapeshot." Smith's voice quivered. "Men cut in half. Bellies split open, bowels spilling out. Heads and arms lopped off by the dozen like they were cleaved by a butcher. But we were ordered to keep marching. A slug nicked the side of my head and my legs buckled. The blood blinded my eyes, but I heard the whir of bullets just over the stalks. It sounded like bees buzzing. It didn't stop for an hour."

When Smith tapped out his pipe, Les took a breath for the first time since he began. She needed the fresh air to keep from throwing up the dumplings she'd just enjoyed.

Jody too appeared ill, while Fuller and Hanks sat with somber faces.

"I was taken to a wagon where my wound was dressed. General Lee retreated back south. When I healed, I rejoined the brigade. And I fought, even though we fell back further south. Chattanooga, Chickamauga, and the Wilderness where Lee himself commanded us. And Petersburg, which is where I took my last days sitting in a trench, picking vermin out of my rations while waiting to die. I'd had my fill of fighting and seeing men shot to pieces. Becoming food for varmints to gnaw on and rot into the soil."

Smith stared into the fire. "No, sir. No more. I went home. I'd done my duty. I'd given them my years. Desertion ain't something I took pride in, and some of the folks I knew didn't want to know me no more. But it weren't a fight we were going to win. I missed my wife." His chin trembled just a bit as he paused. "But before I got there, I found my Deborah buried in a church grave. They told me she came north to join me, sick with worry about me. She was sicker than she thought 'cause she didn't make it two hundred miles. God took her there, so the folks she traveled with didn't think it right to move her. They placed her in that churchyard." With eyes still on the fire, he nodded his head once. "When my days are done, that's where I'll be. I seen to it."

He looked at Jody. "Next fellow tells you about the glory of war, fighting and killing other men, you keep in mind, when you draw aim on a man, you're about to end his life. Make his wife a widow, his kids orphans. And he'll be shooting back, planning to do the same to you. It's a bloody and miserable business. And the ones you love will die in the same numbers next to those you're fighting." He ended his story with a loud exhausted huff. "And now they recite poetry about it."

A calm settled on the camp. All those around the fire darted eyes at each other, not comfortable with breaking the silence by intruding with conversation. More than a few minutes passed before Jody drew his harmonica. He

licked his lips and put the reed organ against them, ran the
scale of notes from low to high, before beginning one of
the tunes he'd played on the trail.

The start of the lonely melody seemed to accompany
the fire's dance in the air, bringing a soothing warmth to
chase the chills from the skin. Les took a deep breath, ex-
hausting the nervous shakes that had built inside with
Smith's story. The old wrangler's face dipped toward the
ground, as if he was listening to a lullaby. Thomas Fuller's
voice sung words in a soft hum to the notes.

> *"A hundred months have passed by, Lorena,*
> *Since last I held that hand in mine.*
> *And felt that pulse beat fast, Lorena,*
> *Though mine beat faster far than thine."*

Smith peered up with just his eyes, a grin slowly creasing
his lips. When he nodded, so did Fuller, as if they both
shared the same memories of the war.

"You were at Chattanooga?" asked Fuller.

"Yup."

"My son, Thomas Fuller Jr., was lost in that fight. I was
told he was brave until the very end."

Smith shook his head. "I can't admit to knowing him.
There was a lot of units from many states at that one and
what seemed every fight we were in."

"We met up with two fellows yesterday," Fuller said. A
pause succeeded the casual mention. "They spoke of the
war. They said they too were at Chattanooga. And Petersburg. I don't know if I remember their names. They were
traveling to Texas."

Jody stopped playing the tune.

"I overheard them talking about a man." Fuller
scratched his head. "Marcus some such. Marcus Broussard, that was it."

Les looked at Hanks, who looked at Smith, who looked
at all those in the camp and shrugged. "You heard that
name?"

The gambler was first to shake his head. Les followed. It wasn't a name she'd run across. Jody took a moment before mumbling, "No. I don't know anyone by that name."

"They appeared to be what I would call on the shady side. Most of the questions we asked them, they didn't speak about and only asked us more questions. It was like they were hiding something."

"When was the last you saw them?" asked Jody.

"We shared dinner with them yesterday. They were appreciative Southern men. Then they left."

"Did you see which way they headed?"

"Can't tell you. By the time we were packed back up from dinner, they both had left. I'd have to believe they went on their way to Texas."

"I wouldn't pay them much mind," Smith said. "The war has scattered a mess of folks to the wind wanting something better in front of them than that they left behind."

"Yes, sir," Fuller agreed. His wife and Ruth emerged from behind him. "Back home there are more carpetbaggers now than there are folks who grew up there. The missus and me, we thought the better place for us was west. Heard from a cousin of mine said New Mexico is territory needing more white people to settle it." He looked upon his family's women fondly. "We were following the Santa Fe Trail, but somehow or another strayed too far to the south."

Ruth resumed her seat next to Hanks, who didn't appear to want to notice. However, Jody did. Les nudged her elbow against his. He scowled at her interruption. When she arched her thumb to signal it was his turn at nighthawk, he shook his head angrily, then instantly changed his attitude and interest back to a kind manner directed at the host. "Y'all ought to come to Texas." he suggested.

"Why is that?" Mrs. Fuller asked.

Jody gulped. "Well, there's plenty of land there for one reason." He paused as his head turned from the Fullers to Ruth, whose attention was fixed on Hanks in a dreamy-eyed fashion. "Plenty of opportunity for those that live there. It would make a fine home for anyone looking to make a fresh start of their lives." Again, he stopped. Ruth's eye remained on the gambler.

Hanks didn't return her affection. He appeared purposely distracted by the fire, until Jody said, "And there's plenty of money there too."

"Money?" Hanks asked. "How so?" The gambler's question brought all eyes Jody's way, including Ruth's.

"Well, like I said, there's plenty of land. And a mountain's worth of cattle growing like the grass. Just waiting for someone to round them up and form a herd."

"But someone owns this cattle," Hanks said.

Jody had to admit the fact with a nod. "Whoever's land they're on. But some stray off that land. It's who brands them first gets to claim them."

Hanks shook his head. "Still, the fact remains, they don't turn into money until they reach Kansas cattle towns. That's the way I understand it. I'm looking to go to one of these cow towns. It's there the money is minted rather than straying wildly with horns." Hanks and Fuller chuckled at the comment.

Jody frowned at their scoffing. "Ain't no bigger single cow town on the prairie than that of Fort Worth."

The chuckles stopped.

With all attention firmly on him, Jody continued. "Most of the cattle drives headed north go by way of the Chisholm Trail, which passes right through Fort Worth. You never seen so much cattle in one place at one time."

"And who frequents the local establishments?" asked Hanks with renewed interest.

"Just about every cowhand in Texas." Jody looked at Smith, who nodded the truth of the statement.

Hanks pointed his chin in the air, then pointed at Jody. "So, you're saying there is one cow town in Texas where every cowboy driving cattle with a dollar in his pocket ends up?"

Jody nodded. "Both coming and going. It's the God's

truth. That's where we're going. I still have saved up just for the pretty . . ." He paused with his mouth open. "Pretty—paintings there is to see on the walls of—churches."

A smirk grew on Hanks's face. "If ever I recognize true intent, that must be it." He leaned back and slapped his knee. "Well, it seems fortune does find a way. I was to ask the folks if I would be allowed to follow their trail. But it appears I was heading in the right direction all along. When do we get to this Fort Worth?"

"It's at least a week away," Smith said in a dry tone.

Jody's voice was still full of spirit. "But it's an easy trail. The further we go south, the greener the grass will be compared to here. And we'll be crossing rivers so there's plenty of water. You should follow us."

Despite the encouragement, Fuller shook his head with a smile in place. "No, thanks, young fellow. I've heard of some of things you're talking about in Texas. But my cousin has already staked a claim in New Mexico for us. He put down cash money in our name. I couldn't go back on a promise. Not on family." Fuller looked at Hanks. "Parson, I'm surprised at your interest in money. Most of your kind that I've known are more interested spreading the Gospel. New Mexico may be a place for you to find new souls to save."

The gambler's mouth fell open. Les had to bite her tongue to keep from giggling. "You are a keen judge of men, Mr. Fuller," he said. "I just know that wherever there is monetary splendor, there will be a higher number to the congregation. Of course, as you so aptly stated, my only purpose for asking is to reach as many followers as possible at one time."

"Reach into their pockets," muttered Smith. Neither Hanks nor Fuller heard the remark as evidenced by their congenial smiles.

"Come on, Ruth," said Mrs. Fuller. "It's getting late and time for us to get to bed." She held out her hand for the young girl to follow. Reluctantly, Ruth stood. Hanks, Smith, and Jody rose in gentlemanly style. Les felt a swat

to her shoulder from Jody, and she joined the group in the
show of respect.

After a long last glance at Hanks, Ruth finally left his
side and went with her aunt. "Good night, everyone," said
Mrs. Fuller. When the women departed the fire's glow for
the darkness, Les swatted Jody back and again arched her
thumb.

"I know," he said with disgust. He leaned closer to her
ear. "That was the girl I was telling you about. The one
bathing in the creek."

Les's eyes widened. "The one you saw naked?"

He covered her mouth. "Hush." He then nodded. "I'm
going to try to talk to her." He tapped Les on the shoulder
and left the camp with a sly smile.

# 21

JODY THREADED HIS way through the thorny brush. For him to get to Ruth, he figured he would need to ride at least a half mile behind the woods and across the stream to approach their wagon. He found his horse in the moonlight and mounted. With spirited purpose, he kicked the flanks and steered north.

With only mild attention given to watching the remuda, he convinced himself the late-night meeting wouldn't take him long enough to be missed. He followed the same path as the group had traveled that day, and recognized landmarks to guide him.

The breeze whistling through the leaves signaled the spot he knew to cross. The horse leapt the small width of the stream, and he ambled around the thicket searching for the path back toward the camp. Clouds drifting through the night sky obscured the moonlight. The dimness shrouded the surroundings in shadows. He leaned forward in the saddle to focus while the horse ambled forward. A limb scraped his head.

Cursing under his breath, he dismounted and led the horse into the bushes and trees. He was still a considerable distance from the camp, and his mind wandered with thoughts of again catching sight of Ruth in her loose underclothes. The thatch of limbs and branches blocked his path. Rather than retrace his path, he tied the reins to a limb and went further into the thicket on his knees.

The smell of the night's supper was still in the air. He followed that and the limited view to the front. He pushed a limb from his face, bobbing his head between branches for a less obstructed path. With the appearance of a small patch of brushless grass ahead, he slipped between branches and stepped into the clearing. A rustle of limbs came from the right. A voice came from the left.

"Don't make a sound or you're dead."

Jody froze. The accent was one he'd heard before. "Who is that?"

"Why, hello, Jody Barnes," said the voice as it came closer. A hand patted his ribs and belly until it found and took the revolver in his belt. "We thought you forgot about us."

"No." Jody drew a shivered breath. "Been thinking about you two longer than I wanted."

"How come you ain't been out to see us?" asked the other.

Unable to see either one, Jody stared straight ahead. "I tried last night. I thought you were camped by a creek. I brought the horses. I couldn't bring food. Don't have none to spare without it being missed. But it weren't you two."

"You were out watching that girl taking her clothes off."

Jody felt insulted, even if it were the truth. "I didn't go to see that. She was taking them off when I got there."

"Yeah." The voice chuckled. "And you didn't complain none. Don't blame you. I saw her pretty little daisy. I wouldn't mind a turn or two at that." More chuckling.

"You hush up about her. She ain't no dance-hall gal. She comes from a respectable family and she shouldn't be talked about that way."

"What's she to you? You sweet on her? Are you out here to bring her flowers?"

"That's enough," came from the left. "Now, you remember that boy Swanson, don't you? We let him go on your word that you'd come through with your part. Now, we come to get what we want."

"You did? You really let him go with no harm done?" Jody's question hung in the night air before it was answered.

"Sure we did. Just like we promised. Now, it's your turn."

"All right," Jody said with some relief, anxious to rid himself of these two. He took some confidence he could explain to Smith about the missing horses. "Follow me back to the herd and I'll cut out a couple for you."

"We already got the horses."

The answer seized Jody's chest. What else did they want? "I told you, I can't get you no food. All we got is beans."

"Forget the beans. We want our cut into that fancy dude you all are carting around."

"That gambler?"

"Now you're talking," came from the right.

"He ain't with us. He's just getting to the next town." The shove of a barrel pressed into his ribs.

The one on the left spoke. "Well, he ain't going to make it. You're going to see to it. He's the one those railroad men were wanting. The one with the big reward pinned to his ears. We aim to claim it." The barrel edged up to Jody's throat. "Tomorrow you're going to parade him out in the open. Make sure he ain't carrying no gun."

"How am I going to do that?"

"You just find a way. When you bring him out, we'll do the rest from there. And then, Jody Barnes, you won't have to see us no more."

The offer to rid himself of these bandits was inviting, but the cost was a man's life. "You're going to kill him?"

"Ain't your concern. He ain't nothing to you, you said. What does it matter?"

"You're asking me to help you kill someone."

The barrel poked the back of his head. "Ain't asking.

I'm telling. You do this, Jody Barnes, or I'll be looking for you and him. Better to save yourself."

A weight slammed onto his boot. The rustle of branches came from the right and left. Soon, the sound faded, but he waited until he was sure he stood alone. With his breath slowly returning, he took it in deep. Gradually, he knelt and touched the dirt to steady his balance. The revolver dimly shined in the moonlight. Like in a daze, his head wobbled to the side and his gut churned. The order to provide the bandits what they wanted now felt like a noose around his neck.

With the herd clearly in sight less than a quarter mile ahead, Rance thought about his future during the cool dry morning. The time alone allowed recollection of his parting from Ruth.

Although he was experienced with leaving women, most of those occasions were with mutually agreed haste, normally to avoid bodily harm to one or both of the pair. In some cases, it was the fairer gender wanting to take a piece out of him. Yet slow, peaceful farewells were not something easily accomplished. For the second time he'd had to disappoint the young girl with her dreams of a new life on her own.

Upon remembering the sight of her teary eyes, his heart ached just a bit, but the decision couldn't be regretted. Despite her eagerness, he resisted the temptation to steal the young beauty from her family and rob her of the happiness destined to her as a wife and mother. His destiny was not one to share. He grinned slightly upon realizing that truth. There he was in the middle of the wilderness on a rented horse with no saddle.

He rubbed the grit from his eyes and once his view was cleared, he saw Jody riding toward him. Delight filled him for an instant as he anticipated the plans for the midday meal. However, a second thought reminded him they'd only been on the trail for less than two hours.

The young cowboy reined in his horse without his usual smile. "Smith said he wanted you to ride to the east and scout for water."

The request seemed odd. "He wants *me* to scout for water? The only place I know to look is in a canteen." The attempt to amuse didn't show on Jody's face.

"Just do it. It time you earned some of your keep." The tone was brash and curt, not one he expected from the younger cowboy. He rationalized that he was the only one without a true function and could ride and report what he found. "So be it," he relented. "How far do I have to go?"

"At least two or three miles. If there's not any, then come back and we'll know we have to look further south." With that, Jody rode at a gallop back to the remuda.

Rance did as he was asked and steered the dun to the east. As he lost sight of the herd of horses, the day became hotter. He removed the coat to allow the breeze to cool his chest and arms. He reached a hill only to find more yellowing grass blowing in the wind like waves in a river. Small trees dotted the grass every ten feet or so. It was the first time he took notice of the fact that this wasn't Missouri, Tennessee, or Louisiana. The dry dirt underneath the dun's hooves showed that water didn't visit the region on a frequent basis. At least, not at the end of August.

Unsure of the distance covered, he gauged he'd traveled nearly an hour and might have ridden the first mile requested. From atop hill after hill, there was only grass to see. He continued onto the top of another hill. Once there, thirst pushed him to the next one. He wasn't just looking for the glint of a running stream for the benefit of the group now.

A large plateau jutted out from the prairie on the left maybe a half mile away. He licked his lips in hopes it might hide some small pond or creek on the far side. He led the dun in that direction while rethinking his encounter with Jody.

Although it wasn't beyond the realm of possibility that Smith had told Jody to relay the message, Rance couldn't remember witnessing the older man ever giving an order such as that. He tried to rid his mind of the insignificant fact, but couldn't. All his life, he had paid attention to just those types of signs, and been rewarded for it with bills and coins. This was no gambling parlor and he had no cards in front of him, just the approaching plateau. Nevertheless, no matter the game, there were always nuances that figured heavily in every outcome.

Slowly he rounded the plateau, and the initial view was the same image he'd seen for nearly two hours. The large rocky rise might have served as a fork in a giant river centuries before, but it only served now as the shepherd of these plains of swaying grass and brush. A peek at the sun showed it overhead. Morning had passed into afternoon, and he let out a long breath as a signal of his frustration and increasing thirst.

Pain stung the back of his neck. The crackle of a shot echoed in the air. His eyes stayed fixed on the dun's mane, unable to move another muscle. The pain subsided into cool refreshment, like water dripped down his nape. Unable to stabilize his balance, he listed to the right and collapsed into the high grass.

His hat was crumpled under his head, allowing the sun to beat on his left cheek. The dun remained in its place, satisfied to take the break from the weight on its back by nibbling the grass. Rance took his first breath. More than thirty seconds had passed when he realized he'd been shot. But he could still breathe, and feel the sun's heat. If this was death while still experiencing heated discomfort, all the warnings of damnation to the infernal region must have come true.

The more he heard the horse snort, the wind whistle through the weeds, and his own breathing, the less he was convinced he was dead, but he could be dying. He tried to move his arms, but neither of them complied. Stranded on the grass, he decided to close his eyes and rest in hopes that in a few minutes the condition would pass. The more he let his mind wander, the more he thought all of this might be due to his great thirst.

While he was pondering the possibility, an unfamiliar noise grew in the distance. He kept his eyes closed, trying to rely on his ears to tell him what was approaching. As he centered on the rhythmic pattern, he recognized footsteps striding through the grass. The stems rippled off the pantslegs. As they neared, the dun's low grunt convinced him someone was coming toward him. Hooves cracking the brittle stems meant it too was moving, likely from the appearance of strangers.

The heat from his left cheek vanished. He sensed shade, but he couldn't hear the dun snort, so the emergence of the source wasn't from the horse. A peek through the eyelids showed a blurred silhouette of a man in a coat and hat. The object in his hand extended too far to be focused on. Odds were great it was a rifle. Rance did his best to relax and hold his chest firm. The best strategy was to play the part of a dead man until he knew who was standing over him.

# 22

"DO YOU THINK he's dead?"

Rance listened for a reply as his fingertips tingled. The sensation gave him thoughts of reaching for the pepperbox pistol, but his coat had stayed on the dun. The poke of a muzzle against his ribs didn't bring him out of the pretense, but the click of a hammer made his heart race.

"There's only one way to make sure of it."

"Wait," pleaded Rance, holding up an open palm. For the first time he saw two men both dressed in coats and wide-brimmed hats. The rifle's muzzle pointed at his head. "I believe I can offer you a better solution."

The bold proposition brought a chuckle to both men. "And what is that?" said the one with the rifle.

Rance needed time to think. Just as in a poker game, the best way to distract opponents was with a smile. "It appears you gents are after a better future at my expense. Am I right?"

"Yeah," the shooter said with a nod. "That's just what we are thinking of doing." He raised the rifle to the shoulder.

"Killing me will only cost you money." Rance stared at the barrel, his eyes cowering from anticipation of a bullet between the eyes. After more than a second passed, he focused more clearly on the confused shooter.

"What are you saying?" the man asked.

At last, the conversation was turning his way. "I have no money," he said, gulping the large lie down his throat. "But I can work for you fellows to get all you'll need for the rest of your life." Both men laughed. Rance too joined them, although he wasn't sure what he said that was so amusing.

"Mister, you're already worth all the money we need. Hear?"

Now, Rance lay confused on the ground. "Wait. Why do you say that?"

The shooter lowered the rifle. "Because a railroad man name of Schaefer is going to pay us five thousand dollars to bring you back dead."

Rance shook his head. "Hiram Schaefer? Do you know him?"

The shooter shook his head. "No. I don't have to know him. All I need to know is he's willing to hand over a pile of cash for you."

"I don't understand. Why would he do that?"

"Because he caught you coupling with his wife," said the other in frustration. "Come on, Levi. Let's shoot him and get the reward." The one with the rifle again poised the rifle at Rance.

"That's not true," Rance said with a cocky chuckle. "That's just a lie." He looked up at the shooter, who'd closed one eye in careful aim. With a sense for the curiosity of human nature, Rance continued slightly shaking his head while maintaining his smile. In a few moments, his confidence wore on the two men's nerves.

Levi dropped the rifle to the side. "What do you mean it's a lie? I don't think railroad agents chase a man over a hundred miles due to a lie." Once more he pointed the rifle, but Rance didn't lose his confidence.

"Were there four of these agents?"

The rifle wandered from any careful aim. Both men looked at each other and nodded at Rance. "So?"

Rance inhaled deeply. "I was in a poker game with those fellows. I was holding a pair of deuces and the best hand against me was a queen jack straight. During the play, I engaged the boys in a little talk." Levi had a grimace building on his lips. He put his other hand on the gun appearing ready to resume its deadly aim. A diversion was needed. "So one of them started bragging on how he had seen Hiram Schaefer's wife without any clothes on."

Both ambushers stood with jaws ajar. A lesson learned while growing up on the banks of the Mississippi was when a baited hook is thrown in the water, more fish are caught when it's allowed to hang in place.

"So what'd you say?"

Rance shrugged. "Naturally, I was intrigued by such a claim. I asked him to prove it."

The other man looked skeptical. "How would he do that?"

Rance used his best honest tone. "I told him if it was true, then he should be able to describe what she looked like."

"Well? Did he?" The question was asked with eagerness.

"Oh," Rance began, "yes, he did. The story went that he hid in her private car, and Mrs. Schaefer, thinking she was alone, didn't bother with standing behind her partition. First, she put one leg on a chair, to delicately remove the garter from her right leg. Then she did the same to take the other off her left leg. Next, she slowly took down her stockings, but not too quickly."

"'Cause she'd put a hole in them and they'd ruin, right?"

Rance nodded at the attentive remark. "Precisely. You obviously have been in the company of finer women."

Despite his partner's modest smirk, Levi growled. "He don't nothing about fine women. A fine woman to him is a whore with a day-old bath."

"Ain't so."

"Is too, Eli. Remember the fat German woman? The one with more hair on her body than you? She stank worse than a pen of hogs."

While the two quibbled, Rance sensed the chance to get off the ground. Slowly, he went to one knee, then stood.

Eli shook his head. "Ah, nah. You're wrong. She was a Swede woman."

"Hey, where you think you're going?"

Rance looked at Levi. "I was just getting stiff laying down." Pain throbbed from the back of his neck, but he feared rubbing the wound would remind the two attackers of their business. "So anyway."

"That's enough talk, mister," Levi said, aiming the rifle from his hip.

Rance opened his palms to them. "You don't want to hear when Mrs. Schaefer slid the dress off her shoulders?" The suggestion faded their mean resolve. "How she wiggled it down to her thighs? What her milk-white flesh looked like when she delicately peeled her shimmy from off her top?"

Despite Levi's head shake, Eli licked his lips. "Was it really milky white?"

"Every inch," Rance said to keep these pigeons enamored as he edged toward the dun and the coat. "Well, of course, for that one spot."

Eli hooted in giddy laughter. Levi appeared irritated at the partner's lack of attention. "Would you stop? It ain't like the woman is standing in front of you."

"Yeah, but just the thought of that little gal in the naked milky-white flesh. I can taste the cream," Eli said, staring at the sky. While both were distracted, Rance casually lifted his coat from the back of the horse.

Levi slapped Eli. "Get her out of your head." He looked to Rance, the barrel of the rifle still aimed straight. "Getting comfortable?"

Rance nodded. "Just felt a bit of chill." He slipped on the coat over his arms.

Both of them looked to the sun on the clear hot day. Levi put the rifle to his shoulder. "I'm going to shoot you dead."

"I told you, it wasn't true. Those fellows only told you

that because they had a grudge against me for taking their money in the poker game."

"Hold on," Eli said, holding out a single open palm. "I thought you said you only held a pair of deuces while the other fellow had a straight."

"That's right," said Rance, sinking his right hand into his coat pocket. He took a firm grip of the pepperbox. "That is what I said." He took a step closer to Eli.

"So, how is it you won the game?"

Rance drew the pepperbox and jabbed the barrel against Eli's forehead. "I bluffed them." He faced Levi and ordered in a stern tone. "Put down your rifle or your friend here will have a bowl where his brain once was."

Levi darted his head from Eli's wide eyes to Rance's determined scowl. "You damn fool. I told you to get that gal out of your head. Look what you done."

"Kill him, brother. He ain't got the guts to pull a trigger."

The dare forced Rance to straighten and set his feet in a stance ready to fire. He'd not yet shot a man, but like all things, he knew there had to be a first time. He prepared for that, but put his bet that one brother wouldn't gamble with the life of the other. "It's not likely that I'll miss," Rance said, peeking at Levi while trying to keep the six-barreled pistol pressed against flesh.

"No," said Levi, squinting an eye down the line of the barrel. "Neither will I."

Another peek at the muzzle targeted at his own head meant a raise in stakes was in order. "You know the chances of this gun not going off should you shoot me are very slim. If I were you, I'd reconsider."

"Mister, if you're meaning to pull that trigger, I suggest you do so, 'cause either way I plan on pulling this one. Hear?"

Rance took a deep breath. Normally when his play was called, he had calmly showed his winning hand, sometimes with the help of a hidden card slipped in the deck. Now, he had to use what he held. If he fired quick, he might be able to get another shot off at Levi. As he prepared to shoot,

Smith's lament of the consequences of taking a life swirled in his mind. Yet when faced against a better hand, all he could do was let the cards decide.

Levi's finger edged closer to the rifle trigger.

Rance closed his eyes and squeezed the trigger to the pepperbox. He heard the hammer rise and fall. The sole noise was a harmless click. There was no explosion. No recoil. No burning stench of gunsmoke. He squinted one eye open.

Eli appeared as surprised as Rance. They both looked at Levi, who after being surprised by the dud load, cracked a smile. Again out of options, Rance closed the eye accepting the fate of a bullet.

A loud crackle broke the air.

Rance flinched. There wasn't an immediate pain, much like the wound to the neck. Instantly, he figured the shot had killed him and no pain should follow. Another shot echoed. If he were dead, how could he hear two shots? He opened both eyes. The brothers crouched in a cowering stance while looking up at the plateau.

"Who the hell is that?" Levi screamed. Dust popped a foot in the air, quickly followed by the crackle of another gunshot.

Never so happy to be in the midst of battle, Rance ran for the dun and jumped across its back. When he swung about, he was noticed by Levi, who once more aimed the rifle. A different shot rang out, attracting all eyes to the base of the plateau.

Jody came at a gallop toward them. Pistol in hand, the young cowboy fired, smoke puffing from the muzzle to hang in place as he rode past. The attack sent the brothers into bewildered frenzy, their heads twisting about in all directions. More bullets pelted the ground.

Rance kicked the dun to escape out of range. The brothers sprinted in panic to the pair of horses calmly grazing on grass. Rance gripped the dun's mane to stay aboard. At first he gazed at the welcome sight of a friend charging his way, then glanced over his shoulder and saw his two ambushers mount up.

Jody reined in as he approached. "You shot?"

Rance shook his head, and both of them looked toward the fleeing brothers already at a gallop. He looked at his young friend. "Never thought I'd say this to a man, but you've never looked prettier."

A grin cracked Jody's face, but only for an instant. "I should have been here long before now."

Unsure of the reason, Rance nodded in acceptance of the apology. He looked at the plateau. "Is that Smith up there?"

"Yeah. He was firing to keep them pinned down while I flushed them out."

Rance swung his horse toward the rocky rise. "Well, then, I have another person to thank." He nudged the dun and Jody followed. Once Rance reached the base, Smith stood atop two bottom boulders. The smile on his face was unexpected and pleasing to see.

"Just that scratch on your neck?"

Rance peeked at the small trail of blood on his coat and shirt. "Seems my luck is holding out. Especially with the help of two friends like you."

Smith held up his rifle with a single hand. "That fact and this yellow boy will send most scampering." He pointed. "Did you use that pepperbox?"

Rance dipped his eyes at the pistol he still clutched without realizing. "I tried. But the damn thing didn't fire. Must not have cleaned it well enough when it was wet."

"You let me know when you plan next on firing it. You'll be lucky if all six barrels don't go off at the same time." As Jody arrived, Smith looked in the direction of the distant riders. "Do you know them fellows?"

"No," Rance replied. "Never seen them. They bushwhacked me while I was riding—" He paused to look at Jody. "While I was looking for water."

"Water?" Smith said with surprise. "What the hell for? There's no water out here."

"That was my doing," Jody confessed, darting his eyes to Rance. "And I feel plumb awful about it. They ambushed me too. About three days ago. At first, they told me they wanted horses, then last night they found me again and told me they wanted you. They said if I didn't send you out to them, they'd kill me and the Fuller family." He offered his hand. "I come to my senses after I told you to look for water and told Smith you were out here. That's when we came riding hard to find you and saw they had you at gunpoint."

Initially, Rance felt betrayed that his life had been sacrificed so easily. However, a moment's thought made him realize that if faced with the same deal, his solution might have been the same. He accepted Jody's hand.

"Can't blame a man for choosing himself first. Only natural. No offense taken. Just glad you changed your mind when you did."

A small grin creased Jody's face once more. Rance imagined the relief to the young cowhand must have rivaled the same he felt on seeing his rescue.

"I heard them call each other by name. Levi and Eli. One referred to the other as brother," Rance said, facing Smith, who seemed interested at the names, but his attention quickly turned to the western sky.

"We better get back fast."

"Oh, damn," Jody said with concern. "Les is alone with the herd. They'll start stampeding at the first strike."

Confused as to what worried them, Rance decided to show his ignorance. "You two mind telling me what is so bad?"

Smith pointed. "You see them clouds? Especially that big one looks like an anvil?"

Rance sighted the cloud. Just as described, its orange base had a form much like the plateau. The color turned gradually to a brilliant white at the flat top. "What's that mean?"

"A storm is brewing. The winds are blowing the tops of

them clouds and are fixing to whip up something awful down here. Rain, hail, lightning, all spilling out of the same pot. We've got to get back fast. With lightning flying, there won't be a remuda to bring back."

# 23

THE DEEP BLUE sky was shrinking. Les sat astride the paint mare mesmerized by the massive tide of clouds rapidly consuming the sunlight. The once-muggy air was swept away within a blink of an eye by a cold gale, chilling her skin worse than any winter morning.

The herd scurried to the far side of the clearing. Alone, she held the reins firm, unsure which way to go, how to turn them back, or whether to seek shelter herself. This wasn't her first blue norther, but this storm was the biggest, and the first one headed directly for her while on horseback in an open field.

Lightning streaked overhead. Branches from the initial bolt grew in a single second to resemble a ten-year-old tree. This time thunder rolled immediately like the crack of that old tree being split apart. The final boom shook every blade of grass.

Instead of circling, the horses fled to the south like a flock of birds, each of them running wild with the same speed used to escape a lariat. Les, the wind whipping against her cheek, was even more petrified by the sight of the stampeding remuda. They'd been left as her responsibility. She'd lost them.

When she finally decided she'd rather be lost chasing them, a shout came from the east. There was Jody, his hat's brim bent up from the force of his horse's gallop, riding down the far slope. She didn't understand any words, but his action fueled her courage to release the mules' reins and kick the paint's flanks.

While matching the mare's stride, she saw Smith riding further ahead of Jody at an angle toward the front of the herd. She faced straight. A cluster of trees to the southwest barred the herd like a fence and kept them running to the southeast. They appeared like leaves being scattered by the fierce wind.

Black sky lit up bright with the flashes. Clouds like puffed cauliflower emerged as white mountains and were gone within an instant. The storm shoved her forward against the saddle horn. She grabbed the mane to keep her balance. The hat's floppy brim curled over her right eye, so she cocked her head left to see.

Drops streaked just ahead of her. Hundreds appeared thrown from a giant arm, each leaving a visible trail in the air. As they fell, the numbers increased until the clearing filled with rain. Her coat became soaked in a breath's time. Water pelted her face. The felt hat drooped, blocking her view. Although she was not in a tub, her saturated pants, coat, shirt, and hair rivaled any thorough bath.

She peeled the brim up, and had to hold it in place to see. A wall of falling water obscured all but the paint's neck. The only sign she was riding was from the hooves' splash hitting her boots.

More loud calls came from the left, but she couldn't see who was yelling nor make out what she was being told. Just as with the brief shower weeks before, she relied on the mare's instinct to follow the herd. All she concentrated on was not falling off the saddle.

From under the edge of the brim, she saw Jody cut in front of her and into the herd. At most, only three horses could be seen. Not wanting to be left behind, she yanked the reins right to follow him. The change of direction put her face in line with the rain. The drops stung her cheeks and eyes.

Despite squinting, she recognized the tail of Jody's horse. He hollered and whistled in an attempt to drive the horses in a circle, but he was no match for the fury of the storm. The three joined four more, all of them running west and away from the herd.

A lightning bolt stabbed the cluster of trees. All in front of her turned brilliant. Sparks shot into the air. Her wet hair tingled.

The explosion forced the horses to veer back to the left and return southward. Jody followed them and she followed him. Again, with her back to the wind, something hard struck her ribs. The pain made her wince, but it was more an irritation and not severe, until the next one slammed against her shoulder.

Like white stones, hail pounded the ground all around her, bouncing up several inches. Just as the rain had streaked in front of her, the rocks of ice filled her view, pelting her back and neck. The paint neighed and bucked. Les grabbed the mane and the horn, thrown forward and back in the saddle. Her heart raced in fear of falling under the hooves and being trampled.

"Head for the trees!"

Jody's voice was loud and clearly understood. At once, the paint resumed its stride, as if it understood. In a sprint, the mare followed the rest of the horses under the canopy of limbs and leaves. Jody spanked their rumps to force them between the trunks and brush. Just when he was under the cover, he swung his leg over the saddle to dismount. It was a long moment before Les joined him.

She enjoyed the relief from nature's assault, deeply inhaling the frosty air. The hail careened off the wood above to spill through the branches. Jody quickly ran through the trees with coiled rope in hand. Even though some of the horses ambled about, none seemed willing to abandon the safety of the trees. Once he shepherded a few from the other edge of the cluster, he walked back to her. The wet shirt clung to his muscular chest.

"You hurt?"

It was a few moments before she could answer. Despite her sore back, she nodded. "I think so." When she lifted her right leg over the saddle to slide down, the pain she hadn't discovered before rippled through her nerves. With another deep breath, the pain subsided and she faced Jody. "Where's Smith?"

He shook his head. "I don't know. I lost sight of him when it started pouring." He quickly scanned to the left and right. "I only count twelve. I hope he's got the others somewhere." They both paused as they caught their breath. She followed his gaze out onto the open prairie. Like after a night's snowfall, the entire field reflected solid white in the dim light.

"How long do you think we can stay here?" she asked.

"As long as it keeps hailing down. Until then I ain't going nowhere."

"What about Hanks? Do you think he's with Smith?"

"Don't know that either and don't care. I saved his skin once for this day. He'll have to fend for himself for the rest of it."

The comment confused her. "What you mean saved him?"

He first looked at her, then darted his eyes away. "He strayed his way into some robbers. Me and Smith found him and chased them off."

The explanation surprised her. When Smith had left her to watch the herd, he'd said they had lost sight of the gambler and were going to find him. "Robbers? Was there shooting?"

He nodded. "Some of that."

Curiosity gave her an excuse to further gaze at his body. His arms bulged the sleeves. The ripples of his upper chest still showed through the shirt. The chaps, although wet, still hid the shape of his legs. Satisfied she couldn't see any blood, she then shifted her focus to herself. The soaked coat hung like an iron weight from her shoulders, but it didn't reveal any of her shape. When he noticed her careful interest, she was reminded that she was a boy. "Everyone look as good as you do?" she asked, then shook her head. "I mean, anyone hurt?"

"Well no one got shot, if that's what you're asking."

His perturbed tone sent her mind into a scramble. She needed to divert attention elsewhere. "Did you know who the robbers were?" Her question did the trick. His eyes shied away once more.

"I don't want to talk about that."

She remembered the first time he'd ridden off after hearing shots. "Were they the bandits that Hanks talked of?"

"I told you, I don't want to talk about that," he said with a scowl. "Don't you listen?"

His anger scared her. "Sorry." The quick apology seemed to settle the matter, and even his temper.

The dull knocks from above quickly faded. Jody looked up. "Sounds like it's passed us. We're going to find Smith and hope he has the rest of the horses." Jody went to his saddle and unfurled his bedroll. When he drew the canvas slicker, Les thought the idea sound and did the same. They both mounted and threaded through the trees, repeating their steps as needed to account for the dozen ponies.

Again in open prairie, Les saw the dark cloud continuing ahead and stretched in a line beyond the western horizon. The ice began dissolving. Rain still fell, but at a gentler rate. The sky above was blanketed by thinner gray clouds, but bright enough to see a mile of grass in front of them. Jody rode on the far left of the small herd. She rode on the outer flank, yelling as loud as she thought needed to chase the strays nearer the rest of the group.

When she again made sure of the count, pointing at each horse, it occurred to her the other hand only held the paint's reins. Where were the mules?

Instantly she pulled back on the reins and sat in the saddle motionless. The impact of the realization struck her worse than any lightning bolt. Slowly, she peered behind. No animal lingered near the trees. Her gut rumbled once more.

She faced straight ahead and tried to breathe, but she couldn't get much air into her tight chest. She had lost all the food and the spare water. She had doomed all of them to starve.

Thinking she could do nothing to find them on her own, and that Abilene was more than three weeks away for her to hide back in her bedroom, she nudged the paint to follow the rest of the horses. She prayed Jody wouldn't notice the missing mules. It was a foolish prayer. As soon as he got hungry, he would notice she had no cooking irons or food to cook. She kept as far away from him as possible.

They continued over the marshy ground at the same slow pace. After some hours, the dark cloud edged further southeast, revealing hills and some escarpments of considerable height. She tried to let her mind be distracted by their beauty. There were no hills this size in Kansas. At least, none she'd ever seen. That notion made her realize just how much she had seen for the first time and how much she had learned during this trip.

Never had she ridden a horse this far. Never had she spent so many nights sleeping on the ground in her clothes. She'd also survived longer than first thought by others, and even by herself. Despite her accomplishments of starting campfires, cooking, and even eating beans for nearly a month, the sense of pride left her mind as soon as she missed the stubborn tug of the mules behind.

As the problem nagged at her, she noticed Jody rein in his horse and scan about. He appeared lost, which didn't settle her stomach. Any moment she expected him to call to her about the mules. She didn't have an answer other than the truth.

Jody pulled the pistol from his belt and pointed it to the sky. The shot echoed against the surrounding hills. Les turned in all directions. She didn't see any danger approaching, and was confused about what the warning shot was meant to frighten.

While she sat in the saddle looking for an answer, a distant shot rang out. Jody hooted and turned to her. "Over that rise," he shouted while waving his arm. Les nudged the paint, steering it to round the edge of the dozen horses so as not to lose any more animals.

The closer they got to the rise, the faster Jody's pace became. All the horses followed his lead, as if they sensed what he'd found. The notion finally slammed into Les's head.

When Jody reached the top of the rise, he let out another hoot. Though he stopped his mount at the top, the rest of the horses disappeared down the far slope. Les arrived last, reining in the paint's stride. When she got to the top, her lungs filled with the fresh moist air, she exhaled in relief upon seeing the rest of the remuda huddled in a circle. They calmly stood on a swale surrounded by a horseshoe cut out in a rocky cliff.

Smith stood with rifle in hand. "What took you so long?"

"We held up in some trees with the hail. Came out looking for you when it passed."

Smith nodded, then signaled to a large boulder. Hanks emerged from behind it. Les was glad to see the gambler was safe, but even gladder a second later when Hanks paraded out both mules. "These belong to you?" Smith yelled.

She couldn't keep from chuckling. "Yeah, I appreciate you holding them for me."

A pause came over all them, perhaps for each to give silent thanks for the safe deliverance after the storm.

"So, get down here and cook us some supper. We're not ten miles from the Red River. Tomorrow we'll be in Texas."

# 24

THE ORANGE-SOIL BANKS of the Red River were a welcome sight. Les had had her fill of three weeks of sweaty clothes, swatting mosquitoes crawling on her skin, and eating dust. The beans' only difference was they were warmer and wetter, but they were no more delicious.

As before, Smith told her where to cross, except now he made a point to show her the exact spot. Unlike the previous crossings, there didn't appear much water in this river. She led the mules down to the shore and onto the sandy riverbed. What flow there was didn't reach much above the paint's fetlocks.

When she reached the far bank, she kicked the paint and tugged the mules up a steep embankment. Once on level ground, she paused a moment, closed her eyes, and breathed deep.

At last, she was in Texas. She faced forward, then turned around. The scrubby brush, yellowing grass, and cracked ground were the same on both sides of the river. The air was no fresher, the sun no brighter. She was almost convinced she'd made a mistake, but decided that this was just the first few feet of the state. More wonders surely lay ahead in the next few miles.

Midday dinner passed and the group drove further south. By nightfall, Les slumped in a sleepy stupor. After serving beans and rinsing the bowls, she curled up into her bedroll. She didn't remember seeing any stars until Jody woke her to start breakfast.

By afternoon, the hills that surrounded the Red River crossing had given way to flatter ground. Mesquite and cottonwood trees dotted the grass prairie. Low creek levels made for a longer time to retrieve water, but there was plenty of deadwood for campfires.

One day's routine melted into the next. The cloudless blue sky allowed the sun full aim. Sweat poured down Les's face. She'd grown used to the odor from her own skin, no longer ashamed how badly she reeked. Everyone smelled the same.

Another supper, breakfast, and dinner passed. Les wiped the sleep and sweat from her eyes. Like a mirage, the glistening of water caught her eye. She faced about. The remuda was nearly a mile behind, barely cresting the horizon. She sat confused, unsure whether the drovers were aware of what appeared a fair-sized creek. As she pondered, the mules made up her mind for her. Their strong march toward the water couldn't be stopped. They jerked against the reins, snapping their heads to the side. She didn't have the spirit or the strength to hold them back. The paint was more compliant, but since the two ornery mules were loose, Les saw no reason to keep from joining behind.

The small flow didn't fill the bed, but the ripples over the rocks were a welcome sound. She slid off the paint as it drank. With the water soaking her knees, she took off her hat and stuck her head as far under the surface as she could.

As soothing as any bath, she enjoyed the chill against her forehead. With her nose pointed down toward her chest, her stench was stronger than during the whole trip. She didn't mind. The comfort of the water ebbing against her cheeks was too good to leave.

Despite the gurgle in her ear, she heard laughter. Immediately feeling a fool, she raised her head. Smith and Jody sat mounted on the embankment. "Don't let us stop you." Jody chuckled. "Go ahead and strip off your duds."

She didn't laugh much at the suggestion. "Where is this?"

"Trinity River," Smith answered. "Fort Worth is on the other side of the hill."

Les looked in the direction he motioned. Relief at the thought of a real meal and a night in a soft bed brought her to her feet in an instant. She retrieved the reins to the paint and mules, jumped into the saddle, and followed the men's lead. They drove the herd along the banks of the river, allowing the animals a fresh drink. Hanks remained behind to splash his face. No one was waiting for him.

Tree leaves were greener and more numerous as they approached the hill. Her heart pumped a little faster, tingling her fingertips and toes. The remuda continued along the banks, but Les went to the crest of the hill to get the first look at the town she'd heard so much about.

Once there, she gazed down upon Fort Worth. The wooden buildings didn't stand as tall as those she knew in Abilene, but she attributed the difference to the distant view. However, as she neared the town, the buildings didn't grow in size.

The one-story shacks appeared hurriedly nailed together, leaving gaps between the sun-beaten boards. Smith had steered the horses to the pens at the north end of town. With suspicious stares from the few men walking about in the street, Les reversed the mare and joined them.

When she got to the pens, Smith and Jody had finished herding the horses inside the wooden rails. The animals quickly gathered upon the three hay bales like starved dogs. Hanks slowly arrived and slid off the dun. Les stopped at the edge of the gate.

"Strip them mules of the bundles and get them inside," ordered Jody. He swatted his hat against his dusty sleeves, sending a brown cloud adrift in the slight breeze. Les dismounted and knelt under the paint to unstrap the cinch.

"Better leave that on, boy."

She looked at him confused.

"It's better than a mile to the Acre."

"Acre of what?"

"Let me guess," said Hanks. "Whiskey, women, and whimsy?"

Jody shook his head. "I don't know about the last one." He paused to smile. "But usually there's plenty of the first two."

"And with those three Ws, I would expect some 'wagering.'"

Jody nodded. "Some of that too."

Smith joined the group, leading his horse. "It cost twenty-five dollars a day to keep these horses corralled for the night. I'd say we make the best of it." He looked to Hanks. "Well, Reverend. Here's your town. I'll let you keep use of the dun until the morning."

"I appreciate the latitude. Where might a man get a bath, shave, and a haircut?"

"Follow me," Jody said with his smile. "The prettiest gals go to the ones that look the cleanest." He nudged Les in the elbow. "Come on, little boy. I'll spring for a bath for you too."

The offer scared her, but she forced a smile to hide the fear. "Maybe after you. I want to have a look about the town first. And I still need to get the bundles off the mules."

"Don't take too long or all the women will be spoken for." He mounted his horse. Hanks and Smith did likewise.

"I'll be along directly," said Les. "I also want to give the mare a share of that hay."

"Sounds like you're more concerned with them critters. Suit yourself." The three men nudged their horses and rode down the dusty street. Fearful of what would be expected of a young boy in a strange cow town, she found her imagination stirred by curiosity while the paint drank at the trough. She stood paralyzed as whether to follow her friends or linger behind to insure the safety of the horses. Smith had said they were staying the night, and a few moments' thought was given to throwing the bedroll out inside the small barn.

However, she hadn't come to Texas to sleep in a barn. Swiping beads of sweat from her brow reminded her that the horses might object to sharing a room with her stinking so bad. The least she owed herself was a decent meal cooked by someone who knew how. A dollar wouldn't buy much, but all she wanted was a plate of fine food. She made up her mind. She would find a place for a meal. And maybe a bath.

She stripped the mules of the bundles, then carried those camp provisions into the barn. When she was done, she mounted the paint and steered it into town. Not more than a few minutes had passed since the three men left. Yet she couldn't spot them among the cowboys already walking the street. Some sat idly on the individual boardwalks and watched her ride by them.

Most of the structures showed gray aged wood. Some appeared to have been painted by the same hurried hands that built them. The further south she rode, the closer the buildings stood to each other.

A sign for a mercantile hanging from a protruded beam swung in the mild breeze. While she was noticing it, the smell of bacon cooking wafted into her nose. Although she'd known that scent for nearly a month, just the idea she wasn't the one cooking it made it all the sweeter.

She followed the drift of smoke to a stack poking from the roof of a small shack. With a firm tug she slowed the paint, but didn't come to a complete stop. The unfriendly faces on both sides of the front door didn't welcome strangers to enter. Her stomach would have to wait.

Further down the street, a white painted shack with a single window without a front door sat to the right. Again, she steered toward the smell of food. Two long tables sat outside. Les studied the place as carefully as she knew how. A woman appeared inside with her hair in a bun. She stuck her head out of the window and returned Les's peculiar stare.

"What's the matter with you, young man?"

Les shook her head. "Ain't nothing wrong. Just wondering what this place is."

"It's a cookhouse! What, did you just come off the Chisholm Trail?"

Les nodded. "Yes, ma'am."

The woman quickly smiled. "How about a plate a beans with some cornbread?"

The mention of the food she'd eaten for three weeks straight soured her appetite. The offer was meant with good spirit, and Les felt guilty for refusing. "No, thank you, ma'am."

"Oh, but these are chilied beans. You know, like chili con carne."

Unsure of the difference, Les raised an eyebrow.

"Have some. It's only twenty-five cents. And if you don't think it's best, I'll give you the next plate for half price."

At first the proposal seemed sound. As Les dismounted and tethered the reins to a table leg, it occurred to her that maybe she didn't quite understand the deal. However, the price was smaller than the dollar she held.

The woman propped the plate out of the window and stuck a fork into the steaming pile of beans. They didn't appear any different than what Les ate every night, but she handed the coin to the woman.

"I'll give you the change when you bring back the plate."

Believing the condition a fair one, Les settled on the bench seat of the table. As she observed the beans and sauce more closely, she noticed bits of meat along with red and yellow slivers. Hunger put the wooden spoon in her hand, and eager to have a taste for something new, she sunk it into the pile and scooped it into her mouth. The instant impression of the beans-and-meat mix was how tasty it was compared to what she'd been eating. So much so, she shoved in another mouthful. About to scoop the spoon once more, she sensed the sides of her tongue singe. Like a fire, the heat went up in her nose like a flume. She sucked air, but that didn't keep her eyes from tearing. Again, she inhaled and got no relief.

Through the blur, she looked to the canteen slung around the saddle horn. Les scrambled to her feet and ran to the horse. She pulled out the cork and guzzled two gulps. The fire spread to her palate. Reflex forced her to dab her tongue to rub the irritation. Now the tip was infected with the burn. Again, she gulped water, then huffed heavy breaths. A tingle replaced the burn.

Once her breathing was steady, she peered again at the bowl of fire. Although she was still very hungry and it had tasted good, she feared another bite would bring flames from her ears. She picked up the bowl and went to the window.

"Excuse me, ma'am."

The woman emerged from the dark and came to the window. Her smile when she sold the plate was still in place. "What's the matter, hon?"

"I can't eat no more of this." Les put the plate on the sill.

The smile vanished. "We don't give refunds."

Les swallowed. A mild sting ran down her throat. "I wasn't looking for no money back. Just the change on account I brung the plate back."

The woman raised a suspicious brow. "You a cowboy? Ain't had no complaints from no real cowboys."

Les averted her eyes from the window. "I'm awful sorry. It was mighty tasty. But I can't eat food that hurts that bad."

The woman paused, then snatched the plate from the sill. It took several seconds before the change was slapped in its place. Les swiped the coins off the sill and went to the mare. She led the horse only to the next building. It was like a small house with a porch, two windows, and a door in the middle. She peered at the sign on the roof. BARBER.

Recollection of Abilene told her this was the place most trail hands bathed. She sniffed herself again. It was time, but the notion of taking off her clothes in front of anyone, much less strange men, was frightening. However, it might not hurt to look. Maybe Jody was inside with his clothes off.

She tethered the mare to the pillar and, one cautious step at a time, opened the door. A bell chimed, bringing a barber with a thick mustache to glare at her. "Be with you when I'm done here." Les looked at the single chair. Although a white cloth covered the patron's chest and a towel covered his face, she recognized the boots.

# 25

"HANKS? THAT YOU?"

"Who did you expect?" was murmured under the towel.

Les looked around the small room. The aproned barber slid a straight razor back and forth against a leather strap. "Where's Jody?"

Without looking at her, the barber pointed to a red drape at the back of the room. Slowly, she went to it, hesitated, then pulled the edge just far enough to peek. Jody sat bare-chested in an iron tub centered in a tiny room. She averted her eyes, but not fast enough not to be noticed.

"That you, Les? Come on in. I'm about done."

Although attracted to the bath, she wasn't ready to accept that offer. "No. I can wait."

She heard the slosh of water. "Come in here. I need to tell you something."

Her chest tightened. "Can't you tell me out here?" She glanced at the barber, who cast a suspicious eye at her just as the woman with the bun.

"I don't need all to hear," he said in a lower tone. If she didn't go in, her identity as a boy might be questioned further. Out of explanations, she pushed the drape aside just enough to sneak inside. Jody scrubbed his feet with a brush. "I want to tell you what to do while you're in this town."

She made a point to casually look at the boarded wall. "Oh? What is that?"

"First, you need to shed them clothes and take a bath."

Instant panic shivered her spine, until she realized it wasn't an invitation to join him. "Was planning on it."

"Good. 'Cause you stink worse than me. You need to wash the dirt and sniff all the places you know smell. When you're done, rinse them clothes out next and sniff them places too."

Les nodded, her eyes rolling to the roof. "Will do."

"When you don't stink no more, you ought to come to the south of town." He paused. "Maybe find yourself a young gal as young as yourself. Likely a few in this town. Ever bedded a gal before?"

She inhaled to stretch her chest. "No," she said, sensing her voice quiver.

"Don't take shame in that. Got to be a first time. Let me tell you what a gal likes best."

She cocked her head to the side, intrigued to learn his answer. "What might that be?"

"Tell her how pretty she is, even if she ain't. They all like to hear that. Whores most of all. But don't say you love them or they'll bend your ear about marrying and want you to take them with you."

A grin creased her face. "All right."

"The next thing is buy her a drink and yourself one too. It will help when you get her alone. Even whores don't like stripping off clothes. You get a drink or two of whiskey in her, and she'll strip them off faster than if they were afire." He chuckled. "Most will even drop your drawers for you."

Les held back a chuckle of her own.

"I know, even at your age, it gets stiff. When you're alone with that little gal, she'll want to be on her back, and then you'll see her little pocket for your pecker. Then let nature take over." He hooted. "Ain't nothing feels smoother in the world. Like warm churned butter. Don't worry none when she starts moaning. They ain't hurt. Every woman does. All of them do as soon when I start. Must be due to them liking it so much."

Les's eyes widened. She knew the tingle herself, but she couldn't imagine acting as he described.

"You'll be done before you know it. When you catch your breath, it's time to go. She won't want you to leave, asking to have another turn. Whores like it. But you'll find no matter how much you try, you ain't got it in you for another hour. So, pay her for the time, a dollar is plenty. And get yourself another drink."

She shook her head. "Ain't got that dollar," she lied, holding Hanks's ten in her pocket. She hoped the excuse would give her reason to avoid further conversation.

"I'll stake you." The water sloshed again. It splashed against the rim of the tub. Surprised, she glanced his way. Jody stood naked in the tub reaching over the side to grab his pants. Curiosity pulled her eyes down to his man spot. For the very first time, she witnessed a man in bare flesh. One second passed, but she couldn't keep from looking. She'd heard it described by Shenandoah's girls, but his wasn't as they said. Yet her tingle returned and bubbled through her blood.

He drew coins from the pocket and held them out for her. She met his eyes so to keep from looking down. She took the coins and nodded, gulping air to speak. "Thanks."

"I'll want it back whenever you make some money." He stepped out of the tub. Les again stared at the wall. In short time, she heard the jangle of his belt buckle. Gradually, she edged her head around to see him with his dungarees around his waist. He lifted his shirt and boots from the floor. "I'll leave it to you." He grinned as he left. "Remember what I told you."

Firmly securing both edges of the drape to stretch the entire width of the opening, she let out a breath. She couldn't decide whether to risk being seen. To help the choice, she looked at the dingy water in the tub. A bucket sat next to it with clear water in it. At first confused, she understood when she saw the sign above the drape.

FIRST WATER 15 CENTS. USED 5 CENTS.

"Meet you at the White Elephant, Hanks."

Chimes rang. Rance pulled the warm towel off his face. "Did he say White Elephant?"

"Ah-huh," the barber confirmed, then swirled a brush in a mug. "It's the biggest saloon in Hell's Half Acre."

"What a delightful-sounding place."

The barber swabbed soapy lather on Rance's cheeks. "There's a lot of delight going on there. Until all the drovers pass out drunk. Then they sober up and leave town in the morning, and it all starts over when a new cattle drive comes through." Finished lathering, he began shaving off the week's worth of whiskers.

While the edge scraped against his throat, Rance carefully lipped out another question. "Any games of chance played there?"

"It's all the place is good for, besides all the liquor being drank. Most all the high-stakes games in town are played there." The barber drew the blade up the cheeks.

"How would a man find this establishment?"

"Just follow Main Street," the barber said as he shaved the other cheek. He wiped the remaining lather with a towel. "Right across the street where they're hammering together that new dance-hall theater."

Rance sat up in the chair, took the hand mirror, and viewed his image. Sure both sides were free of any stubble, he stood, pulled the wallet from his coat, and paid for the service. With hat in hand, he turned for the door, but stopped. He faced about. The barber appeared busy wiping off the chair, so Rance went to the red drape. Carefully, he pulled the drape to the side.

Les reclined in the tub, her coat stretching over each side as a sort of canopy with only her head poked out above. Upon seeing Rance, she shivered in an instant as if awakening from a nightmare. "What are you doing in here?"

Rance put a finger over his lips, then spoke in a muffled tone. "I just came in to be sure you're all right. You got enough money to pay for this?"

Les nodded, darting her eyes to the drape. "Just 'cause you seen me—you know, once—don't mean you can come barge in here."

"I was only thinking of your welfare, Miss Les."

"Don't call me that. Just get out."

Rance held up his palms in surrender to the command. "I'm leaving. You need to watch yourself in this town."

"Jody has already told me what to do."

"Well, in spite of his best intentions, this isn't the type of town to wander very far from where there's plenty of folks. Men of despicable reputations frequent these towns. And it is in your best interest to stay as far away from them as possible. Understood?"

She curled her nose. "I ain't some little girl that needs her hand held. I'm from Abilene, Kansas. There's plenty of ugly men there and I watched them walk down the streets. I know what not to do."

Rance pursed his lips and nodded. "All right then. I'll leave you to your bath, *sir*." He grinned, then slipped to the other side of the drape. He walked to the front door, handing the barber a dollar. "See my friend isn't disturbed." The barber nodded. Rance waved and left through the front door.

With a clean body and face, Rance soaked in the fresh air, put on his hat, and sought the dirtiest part of town. A quick glance to the left and right showed more traffic to the south. He strolled from one raised boardwalk to another, noticing the fresh lumber being carted by wagon. It appeared the town was in the process of expanding.

The louder the voices, the nearer he felt to his goal. Around a wooden ring, men of different backgrounds and classes shouted and cheered. Rance angled his shoulder forward through the crowd to get a better view. In the ring two roosters flailed wings, beaks, and legs at one another.

No stranger to cockfights, he'd never seen the attraction

to the sport. It was a gruesome contest for the entertainment of the easily satisfied. While he watched one bird dominate the other, he observed the money eagerly exchanged with boasts of how much longer the loser would live. The flurry of feathers in the air made it hard to discern which of the similar-colored chickens belonged to whom. In short order, the victor stood atop his fallen competitor, its bloody beak pecking the victim as some sort of primal warning not to tread in his domain.

Cheers erupted from those obviously backing the winner. He gave mild thought to attempting to capture some of those winnings, but he was no expert in the sport. There was no edge to gauge. He was a better judge of how well men competed. He left the side of the ring as two more combatants were prepared to battle to the death.

On his way south, he wasn't sure he was on the proper route. He inquired directions to Main Street from those less than sober souls that sat or lay on the boardwalks. Most were only able to point just a few feet ahead from where they were.

A pounding echo distracted his attention. When he recalled the barber's directions, he followed the constant bang. He turned the corner of a tannery and saw carpenters hammering nails into beams of a framed two-story structure. He looked across the street and saw numerous men standing on a boardwalk beneath a shady awning.

He straightened his hat and proceeded on his way. Upon approaching the swinging doors, he noticed the painted sign propped on the roof. WHITE ELEPHANT SALOON. He took a breath of elation at finding the establishment, and politely doffed his hat to those loitering around the doors and entered.

A polished oak bar lined the wall to the right where a number of cowboys stood with one boot resting on a brass rail bolted a half foot above the wooden floor. No less than six tables filled the room, all surrounded by players adorned in the garb of cowhands. He moved further into the room, sensing eyes cast his way. With a confident flair, he watched his back through the image of a broad mirror behind the bar, went to the bar, and leaned his elbow against it. As he waited for service, he noticed a faro table on a raised platform across the room. Four drovers anxiously risked their money on the next card drawn in fool hopes of bucking the tiger.

Faro was a brace game in which the odds of winning were greater than being hit by lightning on a sunny day. The only side to play for was the house. Since he'd just arrived, there wasn't much chance of being offered such employment.

The bartender came his way. "A sample of your finest whiskey," said Rance. A bottle was drawn from under the bar and a shot glass was filled level to the brim.

"Four bits."

Rance deliberately took the wad of cash from his coat pocket so as to arouse attention. He handed the bartender a ten-dollar greenback. "I'll keep the bottle." The barkeep agreed with a nod.

He took the shot glass and sipped while watching the play at each table. None of the players appeared a gold mine in chaps. By the cards visible on the table, monte seemed the game of choice. The strategy of the game normally meant low stakes, not worth the hours needed for a worthy take.

He took his bottle in hand and threaded his way through the tables. A year's worth of wages needed to be present in order to make the game attractive enough to try one's luck. As he reached the end of the bar, he saw a small alcove to the right where three men of cleaner appearance sat without their hats. Sensing an opportunity, he slowly approached. Two chairs were unoccupied. "Gents, may I sit in on a hand?"

The three looked at one another without an objection. A silent motion indicated an invitation into the game. He sat with his back to the room full of cowboys. There would be time to change seats once he eliminated one of the contestants. A nervous silence reigned over the table as one player constantly shuffled the cards. Rance realized one chair was still empty.

"You gentleman waiting on someone?" No one replied. Uneasy, he thought conversation the best way to ease his way into their confidence. "Allow me to introduce myself."

"Rance Cash," said the slick-haired man entering the alcove.

# 26

LES TOOK ONE last breath. The water soothed her scorched skin so well, she had to muster the will to leave it. However, a half hour or more had gone by, and she didn't want to press her luck. Sooner or later, someone was going to barge in.

She lifted the coat as she stood, using it to shield her body. A moment's thought was given to washing the clothes too. She shook the idea from her mind, thinking if she did, she'd have to parade outside to hang them on a line without any to wear while they dried. They'd just have to carry the same smell.

Quickly, she stepped into the pantaloons, which were now flattened to the shape of her legs. Next, she had the pants on, and shirt, which remained the only cover for her chest. The door chime rang out.

The hollow pounding of boot heels approaching made her put the coat in her hand and turn her back. The drape was swiped to the side. Over her shoulder she saw a big burly man with a thick curly beard, checkered shirt, and suspended dungarees fill the threshold. "You done?" he bellowed.

With one arm in a sleeve, she slung the other through

and fastened two buttons, keeping her now-clean face angled to the floor. "Just leaving." She picked up her boots
and hat and headed for the doorway.

"Damn. It must be the hottest day of the summer. And
you're wearing a coat? What's wrong with you, boy?" He
arched an eyebrow.

She bent under his outstretched arm. "Just feeling a little feverish." Before more questions were asked, she went
into the front room, then stopped to dig into her pocket.
The barber shook his head and held out a palm. Blood
rushed to her head. What now?

"Been paid for by your friend."

Realizing he meant Hanks, she realized that suddenly
she needed a friend. "Do you know where he went?"

"White Elephant Saloon."

"Where's that?"

"About a half mile, next street over. Main Street.
Biggest place in town. Can't miss it."

She nodded and left the shop with a polite smile. When
the door closed behind her, the blistering heat of August
blew in her face. She looked to the west to see the sun still
had an hour to shine. The need to hide still existed. She
stepped into the big boots, put on the hat, and cinched the
chin cord.

Rance watched Colton Schuyler sit in the last open chair.
His heart pounded at the sight of a man he didn't care to
see again. Still with neatly slicked-back hair and a waxed
mustache, the gambler gunman aimed his steely stare right
at Rance.

"Mr. Schuyler, what a pleasure to see you again."

Schuyler grew a smug smirk from the right corner of his
mouth. Without words, he nodded to the one shuffling the
cards, who quickly dealt out hands facedown to the left. No
one picked up their cards. After two went to each player,
five more were snapped out in the center of the table facedown. This didn't look familiar.

"What's the game?" asked Rance with an eager tone.

The dealer glared at him. "Hold-'Em. You make your hand with the two you got and the five pooled on the table. First, you see three, then the last two."

Unsure, Rance nodded with a gleeful smile. Once the other players picked up their cards, he checked his. Five of diamonds, eight of hearts. While he was still trying to grasp the strategy, Schuyler took neatly folded greenback bills from his inner coat pocket.

"I'll open at one hundred."

The sign was clear. Just as on the *Robert E. Lee,* this wasn't to be a long contest over a few hundred dollars. The reaction of the players confirmed his suspicion. They all appeared spooked by the stakes. The two to the right immediately folded. Rance grinned. With only a few smaller bills still left in the wad, he removed his wallet and withdrew five more.

"I'll call," he said, placing one bill into the pot.

Les wandered between the buildings, fearful to enter any of those she passed. Loud voices erupted in cheers further to the south. When she followed them, she saw men crowded around a circle. Without much choice where to go, she slowly walked to the crowd. A gap between two men wearing chaps encouraged her to take a peek. Between the two cowboys, she saw a foot-high wooden-fenced circle. The squawking of chickens forced her further forward. She poked her head through the mass of shoulders and ribs to see two roosters fighting.

Back in Abilene, she'd seen roosters fight over the hens in the coop, but Les didn't see any hens, and these roosters didn't show the tall red comb of the ones she'd known. Normally, one would give ground to the other and the fracas was over. With these two fenced in, it appeared neither had a choice to run.

They flapped their wings and jumped at each other, pecking and kicking. One would be up, the other down, and in an instant, they traded places. The men, some white cowhands, some brown-skinned Mexicans in sombreros, others in Sunday-dressed best, shouted encouragement as if the birds understood what was yelled.

When she didn't see Hanks, she turned away, only to turn back on hearing loud cheering celebration. She poked her head through the crowd again. One rooster was pecking its motionless opponent, until a Mexican man took it away cradling it like a baby. A young Mexican boy no more than twelve went to the other bird, which appeared dead. He knelt for a moment, balling a fist to wipe his eye. Les's heart sank. A coin came flipping out of the crowd, hitting the parched dirt next to the bird.

A voice boomed. "Here you are, boy. Fry him up for supper for me." Loud giddy laughter followed the remark. The Mexican boy slowly picked up the bird, paused only a second, then picked up the coin. Les felt her gut boil up into her mouth. She couldn't watch anymore.

Running from the sight, she held her mouth to keep from gagging. Inhaling long and quick, she steadied her stomach. The cackle of other roosters chased her away from the crowd. She ran around the corner of another tall structure of hammered lumber. She stopped, wheezing while bending and grabbing her knees.

Peering up, she saw the swinging doors of the biggest building seen so far. A sign on the roof showed this was the place where Hanks had gone. She'd never been in a saloon due to threat of a switching by Miss Maggie. She'd always wondered what went on inside. She caught her breath and cautiously approached the men standing around the door. As she hesitated entering, a small wooden placard nailed to the wall caught her notice.

NO WOMEN ALLOWED.

At first, she wanted to turn around, but another breath later she stood steady. She'd traveled more than three hundred miles as a boy. That success gave her the right to walk just three more feet. She let out a breath and went through the doors.

Like a barn, the room was dimmer than the evening sunlight. Kerosene lamps hung from the wooden ceiling, but did little to penetrate the smoke-filled interior. She stepped in among the loud laughter and cries of success and failure. The view of many tables all squeezed full of men pushed her toward the wall. A long dark wooden counter caught her eye to the right, and she went to it as a place to stand and observe the room. When she leaned against the counter, more than one eye was cast her way. She snugged her hat and raised the collar of the coat.

"What you have, young fellow?"

The question turned her around. A portly man with an apron much like the barber's stood on the opposite side of the counter. She realized he was a bartender, but she didn't know what to tell him. "You mean to drink?"

"Why else are you here?"

Not wanting to inspire more curious questions, she answered with her first desire. "How 'bout some milk?"

The bartender cracked a grin. When she realized how silly her reply was, she darted her eyes to the side to see if any others had heard it. The loud voices shielded her from more laughter.

"You see any cows in here?" He laughed aloud. "If you want that, you have to find one in the stock pens up the street. Or go find your ma's bosom."

"Just give me a whiskey," she said to shut him up, but the order only curled his eyebrow.

"How old are you? I don't cotton to serving children."

With her gut churning from the fear of being revealed a girl, she thought of just what answer would be given by the meanest man she knew. Smith's words rattled off her tongue faster than she thought them out. "Mister, I just rode three weeks from Abilene, Kansas, over the worst ground God has ever made. I didn't come in here for your lip. So, sew it shut and give what I asked you for."

Her sharp tongue made the bartender step back, then reach under the counter to produce a bottle of whiskey. He took a shot glass from the shelf behind and poured it level. "Normally, I don't take no mouth from youngsters. But since you been on the trail, I'll let this one go. Don't think

I'll do it twice." He put the cork back in the bottle. "Four bits."

Unsure of the amount charged, she pulled out the five silver dollars given by Jody and put them on the counter. The bartender curled his lip, then stabbed his finger on one, slid it to the edge, and placed it in his pocket. When he drew his hand out again, he replaced the coin with a smaller one. Les swept the money from the counter and threw it in her pocket before more men noticed.

The bartender left. She eyed the amber liquor, never having tasted any in her life. Miss Maggie kept a single bottle, and only took a glass of it on the first day of the new year. A scolding and a strap awaited if Les were ever caught near it. The single time she'd dared touch the bottle was the day Sandy Wallace was hung. She took a quick deep breath and prepared to discover why all men desired it so.

She sipped at the edge of the glass. Like liquid sand, it dried her mouth and stung her tongue. She swallowed quickly to rid herself of the horrible taste, but the gulp made her gag. She coughed, heaving in air. A laugh from in front made her peek at the bartender. His sly grin was the same as before, but he only turned away from her and shook his head.

Confused as to why anyone would want to drink this caustic liquid, worse than any medicine, she realized that men who did so had to be truly the fools that Miss Maggie said they were. Les swallowed spit as much as possible to wash away the scorching aftertaste. Like the chilied beans, it was a shame she'd spent money on it, but it was better to suffer that loss to learn a lesson.

While still regaining her breath, she noticed the men at the counter, including the bartender, were now huddled at the far end. As was her nature, she wanted to see what was so interesting. She went to the end, unable to see anything but the backs of the cowboys, until she stood on her tiptoes. Seated at the table were five men, and just when her toes began to ache in the oversize boots, forcing her back on her heels, she saw Hanks sitting with his back to the crowd.

The cowboys murmured their opinions on the play of the cards, many speculating what they would do if they were in the game. Perhaps it was because she felt she needed status among these men that she blurted out, "I know him. That's Josiah Hanks."

"You don't know your friends any better than you know your whiskey," said the bartender, who then pointed at Hanks. "That there is Rance Cash."

"Ain't so."

"Is too. And that man sitting across the table is Colton Schuyler, a gambler from the East who it's said has killed five men for cheating at cards. He is known all throughout the South as a gunman with a mean temper. Some are saying that they two already had words back on the Mississippi. If your friend has any sense, he'll leave the game."

Les stood with her mouth open but not taking in air. The bartender had spouted the news with such confidence, she took it as the truth. For nearly the whole trip she'd known he was a gambler, a man who used a welcome smile to sway people into doing what he wanted. She'd thought of him as a friend. However, friends didn't lie.

With two cards of different suits, Rance had limited options. The call of one hundred dollars wouldn't stand for long. As he glanced at Schuyler's calm jaw, he watched the turn of the first three cards in the center. Jack of spades, ten of hearts, five of hearts.

The pair of fives weren't much to back. If the remaining two cards were a nine and seven, then he'd hold a straight, but it was a lot to ask.

Schuyler thumbed out three more bills. "I'll raise."

In order to show strength for future hands, Rance needed to show it now despite having a meager play. "I'll call and raise one," he said, putting the last of his bills in the center. The dealer peeked at both men and matched the bet with double eagles.

The two remaining cards were turned. Four of hearts. Ace of diamonds. There would be no straight.

"Three hundred," Schuyler said, tossing in three bills.

Rance was out of cash in hand, and the pair wasn't worth risking more money. He tossed the fives to the table faceup. "Fold."

The dealer looked to his stack of coins. After picking them up to drop them back atop each other, he tossed in his cards. "Me too." Schuyler let his pair of deuces drop on the table while wiping the winnings toward him.

Rance forced a smile despite smoldering inside. He'd been bluffed with a worse hand. With no cigars, matches, or money, he wasn't about to surrender the contest. However, it was not the place to reveal where the rest of his capital was stashed. "Gentlemen, I need to retire outside for just a moment." Schuyler's right hand darted inside his coat as Rance rose. Deliberate with his movements, Rance flashed his bright smile. "Please deal me in. I won't be long."

Rance faced about and strode into the wall of spectators.

# 27

RANCE ANGLED HIS shoulders between those crowded around the table. He walked at a fast pace along the long counter on his way to the swinging doors. Les followed tight on his heels. When they both parted the doors, she quickened her step on the boardwalk to come alongside his shoulder. "I want to talk to you."

"I'm busy right now," he said in a dismissive tone.

She stopped and spoke in a firm voice. "I said, I want to talk to you, Mr. Rance Cash."

The name slowed his walk until he came to a full stop and faced about. "How'd you find out?"

"The bartender told me. Seems everyone in there knows who you are."

He winced while looking back at the saloon. "They do?"

"Yeah, and they know the fellow you're playing cards with. They say he's a gunman."

Rance cocked his head to the side and nodded. "They got that right. It appears word has spread further than I thought. Excuse me, Les. I have urgent business." He faced around and resumed his fast pace. She scurried to keep close.

"Why? So you can tell more lies?" The insult didn't

slow him. "First you say that you are a preacher, until Smith made you admit you weren't." He turned the corner of the building. The darkening skies made it difficult to see very far, but as she went she recognized the tall slim shape of an outhouse. "But you still kept lying about your name."

He opened the door. "In my profession, it's beneficial to keep as many names as possible. If one of those names earns a reputation for winning, it hurts business. Besides, what's the difference? You've known I was a gambler since the day I met you." When he opened the door to enter, she caught the edge and kept it open. "Do you mind?" he said, taking off his coat.

"I already seen one of what you got down there."

"Well, you haven't seen mine and I just as soon keep it that way."

She put her hand on her hip. "You seen mine."

"Not by choice."

"What're you saying?"

He took his eyes off his coat to look at her. "That was an accident. A happenstance."

Unsure of the word, she figured it was an insult. "Well, my happen—uh—thing is a heap more normal than what you men are toting in your trousers."

The gambler paused only a moment to raise an eyebrow at her. Then he tore the lining of his coat. "What's your point?"

She was already mad, and his inattention only turned her temper to a boil. "You lied. You said you were somebody that you weren't."

Her accusation made him turn to face her. "Just like you are now." His words acted like a bucket of water on a fire. He continued to rip fabric, sticking his hand inside as if he'd made a pocket. She didn't know what to say, and just stood there as he went on. "You are the one pretending to be a boy. I'd say that's greatly worse than me using another man's name. Especially since I doubt he knows I'm using it. But I'm not the one who deceived others to travel to Texas on a foolish whim, leaving behind what family you have that raised you. Now, if you excuse me, I do need some privacy." He closed the door.

Her stomach churned once again, but now it rolled taking all her breath. It was the first time she considered how much Miss Maggie must be worried. The woman was the closest thing she had to a mother. Les cringed recalling when the old woman had fretted over losing a stray kitten during a winter's storm. There was no sleep to be enjoyed in that house for three days. Images of Miss Maggie bent over in tears tore at Les's heart.

Rance the gambler came out of the outhouse with the same purposeful stride as before. Les didn't move as he passed her, but she heard his footsteps stop. "You all right?"

She nodded, still in a trance after the bitter reality of his words. She stood with her mouth open and a moment later, she heard his footsteps fade into the distance. With slumped shoulders, she faced about and headed back to the White Elephant.

When she got to the street, dusk had settled into night. The few lanterns propped near the doors of the buildings gave the town an unwelcome glow. She was about to take a step toward the saloon when the thundering pounding of horses at a gallop turned her attention to three trail hands riding at a gallop through the street. A blast of gunfire boomed, fire erupting into the darkness. The percussion pulsed through her spine. Another shot made her duck. Reflex made her scamper for the shelter of the saloon. While she was running on the boardwalk, a bullet splintered one of the planks. Laughter crested in her ears as she collapsed against the wall.

As fast as the attack came, it was over. The three kept riding further south, firing their pistols in the air. When she realized they'd been indulging in rowdy play, she noticed her hand tremble. She stretched her fingers and took a deep breath. Despite nearly being killed, she was still alive. A glance at the saloon doors showed no one coming out in anger or concern. Apparently, it all was part of being in the Acre.

Les entered through the doors again. The only source of light was the less-than-bright lamps. A bob of her head to the side to peer between the gaps in the crowd revealed Rance seated at the table. With nothing else to do, she went to the bar. The bartender was wiping glasses with a soiled cloth.

"Ready to give tequila a try?" he asked.

Les shook her head. There was another matter on her mind. "Do you have a piece of paper? Maybe a pencil?"

The bartender cracked another sly grin. "Why? You going to write a letter home to your ma?"

Without pause, Les nodded. "Yeah. I am. Do you have them or not?" The bartender arched his brow once more. However, after a moment, he put down the glass and went to the far end. When he returned, he brought back a leather-bound book and opened it. Numbers aligned one atop the other were written on the page. He licked his thumb and flipped to a blank page and tore it out. As if he was serving a drink, he slid the paper to her and removed the pencil from atop his right ear. "Here, this will do." When he gave her the pencil, he looked into her eyes. "I never did tell mine."

Les took the pencil and nodded her gratitude. When he left, she scribbled the first words on her mind.

*Miss Maggie,*
*Don't worry. I am fine.*

By folding cautiously, Rance had saved more than five hundred dollars, but he'd also lost some of his confidence. This Texas Hold-'Em was a peculiar game indeed. A shared pool with which all could complete their hands was novel, but costly. No sleight-of-hand tricks appeared possible without the likelihood of facing the point of Schuyler's pistol again, and maybe the pistols of the rest as well. Yet if he was to stay in the game, providence would need to shine his way. And very soon.

The absence of a good cigar to calm his nerves forced him to rely on the only ploy left. Engaging in banter had proved a handy distraction for past opponents. "So, Colton, you never said what brought you off the Mississippi and all this way to the dusty soil of Texas."

Schuyler's long glare wore into Rance's prolonged smile. The gunman's eyes never left Rance, even when the dealer finished the shuffle and waited for the deck to be cut. Finally, a corner of Schuyler's mouth turned up and he split the deck in two. "No," he quietly said. "As a matter of fact I did not."

As each player's pair was flipped out, Rance peeked at his. Nine of spades, nine of hearts. With a good beginning, he decided to afford himself a minor distraction, and perhaps even spread some to the other players. "It must have been a demanding offer for such a man of your interests."

From the eyes darting at him and Schuyler, Rance knew he'd stirred everyone's mind in an entirely new direction. The five middle cards were dealt facedown. The first player opened with one hundred dollars. Schuyler called it, as did the rest at the table, including Rance. Three cards were then revealed. Ten of spades, ace of hearts, four of diamonds.

Without much to build on, Rance sensed a change in stakes loomed close. The first player folded, exposing the four of hearts and three of diamonds. Schuyler was quick to raise the pot. "Three hundred." The next folded as well with only the deuce of diamonds and queen of clubs, but Rance called and so did the dealer. While awaiting the turn of the final two cards, Rance peered at Schuyler, whose eyes were glued to those cards. His own question, originally meant as minor agitation, now played on his mind. Certainly the amounts wagered in this game weren't the attraction. Pondering the actual reason plagued his concentration.

Two of clubs, ace of clubs.

Still in the game, Rance watched Schuyler. The gambler gunman peeked briefly at Rance, who tried not to notice.

"I'll raise five hundred."

The point was made. A bet as large as this was risky to lose. Having been bluffed before, Rance didn't want to walk away again and fall victim to another bluff. He was being tempted to slip a card into the mix. However, without one available that matched the deck, he was forced to play as an honorable gentleman. "I'll call," he said, tossing in the bills.

The dealer let out a long sigh. "Too much for me." He flipped up his king of diamonds and six of hearts. "But I'm going to have fun watching you two."

Schuyler placed his cards on the table with a sheepish grin. "Three aces."

Rance saw the spade ace and his heart went with it. Yet he kept his smile while flipping his cards to the table. "Two of a kind. Congratulations, Colton. You have fourteen hundred dollars of your money back." Schuyler shot a piercing stare at Rance, but a cool smile soon took over his face. Rance read the smugness as a sign that there was more at stake than just money.

"You talk too much, Mr. Cash."

Les wrote all the explanation she could squeeze on the paper.

> *And that is the reason I left. Do not be mad. I will come back soon.*
> *Les*

She folded the paper and yelled at the bartender to be heard over the boisterous crowd. When he stopped his tapping of a wooden keg, she shoved the note along the top of the counter. "Can you get this to Abilene, Kansas, for me?" she asked when he came closer.

It took a moment before he took the paper and tucked it in his pocket. "It will cost you at least a dollar to run it through the Wells Fargo line." He held out his palm. Les dug in her pocket and drew a single silver coin to slap in his hand. When he wiggled his fingers, she took another

moment to realize he wanted a fee. Realizing there was no
sense writing the letter if it didn't get to Miss Maggie, she
drew another dollar and placed it with the first. The bartender nodded. "I'll see it gets there."

Relieved of the burden in her mind placed there by
Rance, she turned to the tables. Some men stood, others
sat. Only those with money in front of them had smiles.
With a glance at the swinging doors, she saw Jody enter.
He stood in place for a moment wearing a new white shirt
with gray stripes and blue dungarees without chaps. Slowly
he pulled up the suspenders to his shoulders. As if in a stupor, he gazed blankly around the room until he saw Les.
His bright smile gleamed in an instant and he stumbled toward her.

"What are you doing in here, little friend?" he slurred.
Les had seen enough drunks in Abilene to recognize his
condition.

"I was looking to find you in here." She laced her tone
with a twinge of disgust. He raised his eyebrows, then
shook his head.

"I was over an hour ago." A wry grin creased his lips.
"But I found me a Mex woman." His brow rose up and
down rapidly. "Got me what I was looking for." While he
motioned for the bartender, Les tried to inhale away the
punch in the gut Jody's words had just delivered. He ordered two whiskeys, and the bartender quickly had them
poured. Jody lifted his glass as if in toast. "To Hell's Half
Acre." He swigged the liquor in one gulp. When Les didn't
pick up the other glass, he gave her a puzzled look. "Drink
up, boy."

"Nah," she replied with a shake of the head. "That stuff
tastes awful."

He slapped her back. "That's only at first. When you've
had two or three, the tastes goes away. And after the fifth
one, you can't taste nothing." He scooped the shot glass off
the bar and handed it to her. "Go ahead. Throw it down
your throat."

Out of excuses and not wanting to arouse further suspi-

cions as to why a boy in a cow town wouldn't want to get
drunk, she once more stared at the amber liquor as if it and
she were about to fight. With a deep breath, she opened her
mouth, propped her head back, and dumped the entire
glassful down her throat and swallowed. Like boiling water, the whiskey stung every nerve on its way down. She
blew hard, trying to put out the fire, but once she was out of
air, the burn continued.

Jody hooted, then lifted his finger to order another. She
grabbed the finger. "I'm not sure this one is going to stay
down there," she said. "Give me some time to be sure." He
chuckled at her honesty.

"Well, I know I'll have another."

While he was waiting to get the bartender's attention,
something caught her notice. "Where's Smith?" she shouted
over the clamor.

Jody shrugged. "Ain't seem him since we got in town.
Probably asleep in a bed. A man over forty years old like
him, that's 'bout all he's good for. Don't want no part of
the women and whiskey. It's a young man's game." When
he got another drink, Jody wasted no time drinking it
down. He slapped the shot glass on the wood top and threw
a coin next to it. An instant later he leaned closer to Les.
"Have you bedded a gal yet?"

The question made her catch her breath. At first she
thought to lie, but then surely she'd be asked about the experience and she wouldn't know what to say. However, her
lack of response didn't help her.

Jody pushed at her back. "Come on. Let's get your
pecker wet. And I know just the girl." She tried to keep her
feet firm to the floor in hopes he'd bounce off and be carried away by the crowd, but his persistent shove had her out
the doors and on the boardwalk.

"Where're you taking me?" When he pointed in the
night to shanties at the south end of town, she had her answer. "I don't know if I want to do this."

"Sure, you do. I know you are a mite scared, but that's

normal. Same for me the first time. But once you get some loving from a female, it will make you a man."

"I don't think so," she answered, shaking her head. Despite her objection, they kept marching toward the second shack. If she stopped, or fought him and ran, she wouldn't be able to lie herself out of it without Jody and the rest of the men suspecting something wasn't right with Les the boy. From all she'd learned, it was every man's desire to love on women. Even she admitted to some strange jitters in her gut when she looked at Jody, but somehow she didn't figure it was the same type as he held for any woman willing to be kissed.

When they arrived at the shack, Jody opened the ramshackle door. "Turn him into a man," he said, chuckling and tossing in a silver dollar. When Les hesitated, he shoved her inside and threw the door shut. The dark interior made it impossible to see.

A few moments passed before Les felt hands at her waist. Paralyzed except for shivering, she couldn't think how to leave. Surely Jody waited outside. The hands snaked inside the coat and up to her shoulders. She felt the coat pushed from her arms, then fingers raked down her throat, around her arms, and finally to her chest. They stopped. Without words, she knew a question was asked with the tender touch.

*"¿Una mujer?"*

Les grabbed the hands and firmly pushed them off her body. "I'm sorry," she said at the verge of tears. "I don't want to be here." The hands escaped her grasp, and for a very long moment, Les stood convinced that her secret had at last been found out. The scratch of a match broke the silence. The spark turned into a flame, which quickly grew once passed to a candle wick. The interior was illuminated, showing the four rickety walls, and it was not any bigger than a horse stall with a cot in the center. A Mexican girl not older than Les, with a long single braid extending down her back, blew out the match and faced her.

*"Tú eres una niña."* The girl, dressed in only a wrinkled shimmy that barely covered her thighs, looked at Les like some strange animal. Les did her best to calm her own breath so she could speak softly enough not to be heard outside the shanty.

"I don't understand no Mex. But please don't tell nobody."

The girl stood confused, but soon she shook her head. A frightened smile crept across her face. She pointed at herself. *"Me Teresa."*

"I'm Les. Nice to know you, Teresa," Les said, sensing her voice quiver. "I don't mean to waste your time. I just need to stay here long enough to make him outside believe we're done."

Teresa shrugged. *"No comprendo."*

"That's fine." Les held up her palm. "Don't say nothing." Figuring she had to wait at least another minute or two, she studied the tiny shack. Next to the cot was a wood stand with the candle and a figurine of the Mother Mary. An engraved pillbox next to the candle reflected the light and caught Les's eye. When Teresa saw Les notice the pillbox, she cowered in a corner. The reaction didn't seem normal, but standing inside the same room with a gal for sale wasn't normal either. Her curiosity piqued, she pointed at the pillbox, then at the Mexican girl. "These for you?"

When the girl appeared more frightened at the question, Les again held up her palm as a hopeful sign that she meant no harm. An idea came to mind and she reached for the pillbox. Teresa slumped onto the cot to avoid Les. Her eyes were wide like a cat that seen a dog. *"No me. No me!"*

Les put a finger to her own lips, then nodded, trying to smile to calm the girl. She opened the pillbox. Four tiny white pills no bigger than ladybugs were inside. Les took one, then shut the box. "If these are what I think, then we'll both have a better night."

Teresa again shook her head in ignorance of the words. Les winked at her, then picked up the coat from the dirt.

When she put it on, she again turned to the Mexican girl. "Thanks, Teresa. It was good to meet you."

Les left the shack cautiously. Jody was nowhere to be seen. Squinting to adjust her eyes to the darkness, she looked toward the White Elephant. She wasn't sure, but if her plan was right, she had found a way to keep her secret.

# 28

LES PARTED THE batwing doors. Almost at once, she matched eyes with Jody, who leaned against the bar. The need to show confidence and success had her arch her shoulders and cinch up the pants on her hips. Jody hooted and clapped his hands.

"I told you," he yelled across the room. She made her way through the crowd to the bar. "You don't feel the same as before you went, do you?"

She gave the question a moment's thought. "Not so much."

Jody hooted again and faced around. "We need two whiskeys to celebrate."

Les held her tongue. She wasn't anxious to drink the liquor, but it provided a great opportunity to go through with her plan. The bartender arrived with two shot glasses and the bottle. He filled the glasses and Jody paid him. With one shot glass in hand, the young drover gave the other to Les. She pointed into the crowd. "Is that Smith?"

Jody craned his neck to see. In an instant, Les pulled the pill from her pocket. However, Jody swung his head back to her too quick. "I don't see him."

Les shrugged. Before she could slip the pill into his

drink, he threw it down his throat. All she could do was
watch, and then she thought of the only other way. She
dropped the pill into her own glass. The pill bubbled, but
she swirled her finger in the liquor to dissolve it completely.

"Ah," she gasped. "This tastes worse than the stuff before." She put the glass back on the bar.

"What are you doing?"

"I can't drink that," she said, shaking her head.

Jody grinned at her weakness. "Here, watch me." He
took the glass and downed the whiskey in an instant. "We
don't waste that that's paid for," he said, wiping his lips
with his sleeve. "Although that does have a funny taste to
it." The concern on his face vanished and was replaced
with a happy smile. "Did that gal treat you special?"

Les nodded. "I think she treated me more special than
anybody she knew before."

Jody winked and nudged her with his elbow. "I knew
she was right for you. I haven't been with her yet, but her
ma said she was good but didn't speak a word. I'm planning on going to her next. Was she nice?" His question
came with raised eyebrows.

Les again thought how to answer, considering that
Teresa had been recommended by her mother. "She was
real nice to me."

"Good," said Jody, swaying in his stance. "I'll be nice to
her." His cheeks sagged on his face. The few times he
smiled appeared labored, as if his chin now weighed as
much as a sack of iron. The eyelids quivered as they
blinked, each time slower than before. "I feel a mite dizzy."

"Here," she said, pointing to a chair. "You ought to sit.
You don't look that good."

"Probably just all the whiskey." He took wobbly steps
toward an empty chair near the door. "If I get my second
wind, then I'll feel fresh as a daisy and can commence my
business with that little señorita." With Les's help, Jody got
to the chair and slumped into the seat. The jolt was as pow-
erful as any punch. His chin sagged to his chest and his
arms went limp.

If Les had played it right, there wouldn't be any business commenced by Jody for the rest of the night. She felt some satisfaction at her deed. Besides saving the young Mexican gal just a pinch more dignity, as well as the wear on her bottom, there was a minor pride in knowing that Jody wouldn't be sharing a bed with another female, especially one of a similar age as Les.

With another breath, she wondered why that should matter. She'd come to Texas for gold. However, there was that dream about a husband walking through a white gate. The loud laughter crept back into her ears and she faced around to it. As she watched the dirty, smelly, hairy crowd, she sighed away her daydreams of white fences. This was Texas. There probably wasn't a white fence in the whole state. As her eyes wandered, she recognized the familiar frame of the man she first knew as a preacher, then a gambler, and now as the famous Rance Cash.

Eighteen straight winless hands had lightened the weight of the coat considerably. After more than an hour in the chair, Rance had silently watched pots won by all those at the table except himself. Smaller pots were occasionally scooped up by the natives of the town, but the more attractive piles of money seemed to always go to Colton Schuyler. It was a clever practice, one meant to bleed the victims slowly while dangling fortunes so near their noses.

The single hapless loser, Rance still hadn't grasped the winning formula for this Texas Hold-'Em. It was a game of all bluff, and he soon found that he'd been bested by a man who presented a fearsome facade while actually holding little if any real threat. The nagging question of whether Schuyler was a threat outside the game wouldn't leave Rance's mind.

The dealer shuffled the cards.

"It appears luck is riding on your shoulder, Colton." Schuyler leaned back in his chair, only occasionally glancing at Rance. If there were an advantage to be gained by banter, the conversation should be distracting. "This reminds me of what I experienced on a train recently. I was in the company of a very attractive woman."

The majority of eyes glanced his way at that, but only for a moment. Then all attention returned to the pair of cards in front of each player. Rance peeked at a four of spades and jack of hearts. Without much to excite interest, he continued to divert the others' concentration from the play. "A lovely woman. Her entire body held the aroma of lilac. And I do mean her entire body. She claimed to bathe in its extract on a daily basis."

The first player threw in a one-hundred-dollar bill. Schuyler matched it, as did the next player. Rance had no affection for the four and jack, but he wanted to continue his diversion and it was good manners to keep playing. He called the hundred, as did the dealer. Finally he had a nibble.

"Why does some woman taking a bath remind you of playing cards?" asked the dealer while he flipped three center cards. At the sight of the jack of clubs, ace of diamonds, and seven of diamonds, Rance continued.

"Just that it's a challenge to read a woman's mind, much like a deck of cards. As soon as you count on it to keep its rational course, inevitably you'll get a jack following a deuce."

Two other players chuckled while the dealer appeared confused. Schuyler didn't flinch. The betting continued with everyone calling an additional three hundred. "I don't understand why that reminds you of playing cards," said the dealer.

"To hell with that," said the first player. "I want to know about this woman taking a bath."

With other eager eyes cast his way, Rance allowed himself a sly grin in the knowledge that he had them hooked but was yet to land the prize. "Perhaps she was the most beautiful woman I had ever had the pleasure of seeing in the flesh. Maybe even in the entire world."

"You saw this woman naked? Plumb down to her ankles?"

Rance shook his head. "Not wearing a stitch." The awe

of such a boast had every jaw dropped. Even Schuyler looked at him. "She stood not a foot in front of me," Rance went on. "Eager with carnal desires." Once the dealer closed his mouth, he turned over the last two cards. Jack of spades, ace of hearts. The first player hurriedly peeked at his hand, and threw in a hundred dollars. Schuyler was quick to raise to four hundred. The second player appeared cautious, but for only a moment, then called the bet seeming to want to pay admission for the rest of Rance's tale. It was time to reel in the catch.

Not wanting to scare away his fish, Rance simply called the bet in hopes that the distraction had worked. There was two pair already sitting on the table. However, the dealer folded, as did the first player, who had a question.

"So what did you do?"

The truth was the easiest he'd ever uttered and the sweetest. "I granted her desires." Among the hoots, Schuyler showed his hand of the jack of diamonds and seven of spades. "Full house. Jack high."

Rance swallowed hard at the upset. The second player looked at him, revealed the king of hearts and five of spades, then asked. "Did you stick it to her?"

Upon notice that he'd lost the hand, he eyed Schuyler, who watched every move. Without a cigar to light, without a drink to spill on his lap, and without even a spare ace hidden in his vest, Rance surrendered his losing hand. He had distracted everyone so well, he'd deceived himself. "You might say, it was me that it was stuck into. Three jacks," he lamented.

The remark took a moment before the three local players broke into laughter. Schuyler did not. Rance slumped in his chair. His cache was now down to a paltry five thousand dollars. If he were to stay in the game, he would need to return to the outhouse to rip open another seam in his coat.

"You look disappointed, Mr. Cash," Schuyler said while drawing the pot toward him. "Maybe you can revive your spirit if you were to finish telling of your experience with Mrs. Schaefer."

Suddenly, the loss of the hand and the money were of small concern. After an instant's paralysis, Rance did his best to react with his usual casual flair. "I don't recall mentioning her name. You know of the incident?"

As the dealer gathered the cards, Schuyler stared at Rance. A wry grin crept across his lips. "I do." Rance pondered the reply while the cards were shuffled.

Although he'd kept the tryst to himself, the legend of the encounter might have been spread by the woman herself. In fact, a bandit pair had nearly killed him just on the rumor of the reward. His heart pounded once he took into account that an actual reward might have been offered for all the reasons the would-be assassins claimed. He stared at Schuyler. Rance now knew the reason that the gambler gunman had made the long trip to Texas.

With a deep breath, he ran through his mind what plans might have been laid by Schuyler. The dealer dealt. When Rance's cards arrived, he peeked at them. Five of hearts, seven of spades. His fingers froze on the cards. He thumbed the five of hearts facedown and lifted the spade seven. The pattern on the edge of the design didn't match. With close observance, it was obvious this card wasn't from the same deck. He looked up from the seven of spades and found Schuyler staring only at him.

This was the card that had won the previous hand, the hand won by the gunman. Now with it part of his own hand, the evidence needed to accuse a cheat was at his fingers. He grinned, realizing the plan. If he said nothing, Schuyler certainly would, and if Rance exposed the planted card, it was the same as challenging Schuyler's honor. Either way led to conflict, which the riverboat gambler was adapt at settling. Rance was watching his own murder.

"Just when did you arrive in Fort Worth, Colton?"

When Schuyler didn't answer, the dealer appeared confused as to the reason for the question, then offered the truth. "He got here about a half hour before you did."

The gunman glanced at the dealer for only a moment, then turned his attention back to Rance, but said nothing.

"Quite an irony, don't you think? You and I meeting for the first time on the *Robert E. Lee* over a game of stud poker." Rance leaned forward in the chair, exchanging the seven of spades from his right hand to his left, then sinking the right hand into his coat pocket to grip the pepperbox. "That was after I took a large sum of your money. Now we meet again. In a dusty cow town, which I hadn't planned to visit until just recently. And you mentioning Mrs. Hiram Schaefer, a lady whose company I recently shared."

"What's your point?" Schuyler asked in a monotone.

Rance shrugged. "You're here to kill me. A man of your reputation wouldn't come all this way just for a poker game." He threw the spade seven faceup on the table. "You planted that seven. And won the hand." The other three players stared at the card for only a moment, then scooted their chairs on the wooden floor away from the table and out of the line of fire. "It was just luck that I would get the same card on the next deal. Maybe not. I'm sure you were willing to wait for me to use it."

He paused and swallowed hard. He'd never matched the draw of pistols with another man. Normally when faced with such disputes, he avoided bloodshed and left the game as he had on the *Robert E. Lee*. However, now he had no choice. Schuyler had seen to it. The die was cast. He smiled at the poor choice of words.

"Hiram Schaefer hired you to kill me, am I right? That's why you're here. You marked this card to have me accuse you of cheating, and if I didn't, then you would wait until I had the card so *you* could accuse *me*."

"Mr. Cash," Schuyler said, calmly opening his coat. "I don't know what you are talking about. But I resent such a charge. You are a cheat, and a coward. Either you retract your allegation, or I'll shoot you as the son of a bitch you are on the count of three."

Rance locked eyes with his adversary, intently watching for the slightest move. His sweaty right palm wrapped around the butt of the pepperbox.

"One."

His heart raced. His chest was so tight he couldn't breathe.

"Two."

If ever he wanted to die, he had just dealt himself a cold-handed way to do it. He watched Schuyler's lips for the final count, but a blur from the corner of his eye meant the gunman wouldn't say—

"Three," said Rance and he drew the pepperbox. Schuyler's pistol barrel cleared the shoulder holster. With the gunman in line with the sights, Rance pulled the trigger. The pepperbox hammer fell on the cap, but did not fire.

Schuyler's look of shock quickly changed to one of relieved delight. He leveled his six-shot revolver. Rance pulled the pepperbox trigger again. Still, no shot fired.

Schuyler aimed the revolver and fired. The bullet hit Rance in the left shoulder. He slumped from the chair to the floor. Throbbing agony seized every muscle, but he watched Schuyler stand and point the short-barreled revolver at him, while Rance kept the useless pepperbox aimed at the intended target.

"Good-bye, Mr. Cash. You should never have bet against me."

Rance squinted, preparing to receive a slug between the eyes. Schuyler cocked the hammer of the revolver. The pepperbox erupted. Rance's right hand was jolted by the recoil, his view clouded by white smoke. As it drifted to the ceiling, the figure of Colton Schuyler no longer stood over him.

Les was startled by the sound of the first shot. Seconds later, a loud blast turned her attention to the alcove. White smoke hung in the air. The room once full of cowboys was vacant. She glanced over her shoulder to see Jody still asleep in the chair. She got to her feet and saw one of the gamblers at Rance's table lying prone on the floor. She didn't see Rance.

Slowly, she crept to the alcove and peeked around the corner wall. Rance lay with his back propped against the wall. "Hi, Les," he said in good cheer. "Is he dead?"

She looked at the motionless man on the floor. It was the man the bartender claimed had come to shoot Rance. Three small bullet wounds dotted his neck. Other holes spewed blood from the left cheek, forehead, and the right bridge of the nose. She faced back to Rance, her voice shivering. "He sure looks dead." Then she saw the blood running down Rance's coat. "You're shot!" She ran to his side.

"Yes, I noticed," he said in a casual tone.

Muttering voices grew louder. The bartender and customers again filled the room like a flood. One of them bent over the dead man, then looked at the bartender and shook his head. "You killed him," the bartender announced while looking Rance's way. "You'll hang for it."

"There'll be no hanging."

The voice came from the doors. It was the most welcome sound Les could remember hearing, even if it did belong to Smith. As the crowd parted, there he stood, pistol drawn and pointed from the hip at the crowd. He walked through them with the same disdain a mean dog showed a mess of squawking chickens, and stopped once he reached the body. He then looked at Rance. "Did you know him?"

Rance nodded. "His name is Colton Schuyler. He's a hired gunman by trade, and a gambler by reputation." Rance winced.

"You're bleeding something awful," said Les. She looked at Smith. "We got to get him to a doctor."

Smith bent and picked up the gun next to the body, flipped open the chamber gate, slapped it shut, then cautiously came to kneel next to Rance. He gave the pistol to Les. "Here," he said loudly. "Any of them comes near, you shoot them." Never having held a pistol in her life, she was afraid to touch the iron. "Take it," he said. Reluctantly, she wrapped her fingers around the butt, but kept clear of the trigger knowing that was what set the thing off. She pointed the revolver at the crowd of men and did her best to show the courage to use it.

With the same touch he'd use branding a calf, Smith gripped Rance's coat and turned him to the side. Despite the anguished yelps from the gambler, Smith took a long enough look before setting Rance against the wall. "Looks like the bullet went clean through you. No broken bones are showing. You're lucky."

"Oh, I'm just giddy with laughter at the fortune of being shot."

"Could have been worse."

"How's that?"

Smith paused a moment and looked at the body. "You could have been dead like him." The old wrangler took the pistol from Rance's hand. "You used this?" Seized by pain, Rance could only nod. "By the looks of his face I'd say all six barrels went off together. I told you not to trust this fool weapon."

Rance smiled. "Can't part with it now. It saved my life." Smith grinned at the remark, then carefully lifted the gambler to his feet.

"You shot a man, mister. Some are saying that you drew first and killed him."

"He was going to shoot me," Rance said. "Just as the son of a bitch I am." Les looked puzzled at why Rance had insulted himself, as did Smith and a few others from the crowd. Their voices mixed together, some with shouts, but none of them could be understood.

Smith faced Les and whispered, "Go get Jody and you two take the remuda out of town before these rowdies find out about them. We won't have even the mules if they do."

"Why not get the sheriff?" she asked.

"There is no sheriff in Fort Worth. It's an open town. Now go on and get him."

"Are you taking him to the doctor?"

"There ain't no doctor neither. I'm going to break into the general store and get bandages."

"Do you know how?" asked Rance. "Not that I'm ungrateful for any help."

While supporting Rance's weight with his right arm, Smith took an easy step. "I've bandaged wounded before." He looked at Les again. "I told you to get."

"Wait," said Rance, craning his neck around. "The money." Smith nodded to Les, and she grabbed as many bills in one hand as she could hold and stuffed them in his coat pocket. "What about the silver coins?"

"Why not the cards while you're at it?" Smith sniped. "Forget the coins. We're leaving." He nodded again at Les. She held the pistol with both hands and swept it side to side like a broom.

"Only thing worse than a woman with a gun is a kid," was murmured from the crowd.

The comment hurried her steps to the sleeping Jody. "Wake up. Wake up." She kicked his boots, but still he didn't move. Remembering a trick from Miss Maggie, she pinched his nose shut. It took only a moment for him to come out of his slumber like a startled cat. "Jody, we got to go. Now."

Still blinking his eyes to focus, he peered at her through squinted eyelids. "What'd you do that for? What's going on?"

"Rance got shot."

"Who?"

"I mean, Hanks. His real name is Rance Cash, and that dead fellow over there shot him."

Jody shook his head while still in a daze. "How can a dead man shoot?" His eyes bulged when he noticed how Les carelessly held the barrel of the revolver in line with his chest. "Watch the aim of that gun!"

"Give me that." Smith snatched the weapon from her grasp. "Jody," he bellowed as he and Rance neared the door. "Take the boy and get the horses out of town. Now!"

# 29

DAWN BROKE BY the time Jody and Les got all the ponies from the pens and headed them south. As always, she held the mules' reins in her right hand with a firm grip. Not used to riding on the outer flank, she did her best to keep up with herd, despite the sluggish mules. However, her attention was split between watching horses and worrying about Rance and Smith in Fort Worth.

Jody appeared still under the effects of the chloral. His shoulders slumped forward and his chin hung near his chest. Occasionally, he shook his head in an attempt to stay awake, but his constant yawning showed he would battle the temptation to snooze in the saddle most of the day.

When the sun shined overhead, they reached the high grass prairie. The horses, like all animals, couldn't resist stopping to nibble on the tender stems. Jody didn't seem to mind. The slow pace provided more chances to shake his drowsy face awake without worrying about driving the herd. Les peeked again at the sun. Normally this time of day, she would have a fire started for the midday meal. She glanced behind once more, and an idea entered her head. She steered the paint toward Jody.

"What say we stop for dinner?"

He glanced at the sun, then at her, and nodded. "I guess we made our five miles. We'll stop here. Give me a chance to pour some coffee on this headache. How 'bout you? You feeling poorly?"

She acted casually as she shook her head. "No. I'm feeling like always."

He put his hand over his face. "I never had such a kick the next morning like this."

She sensed the moment was right to dismount and get about the business of setting a camp before more was asked about the previous night. She took the cooking irons from the packs. A fresh scent stirred her nose. "Looks like we got fresh coffee." She took out the new canvas sack full of the ground java, and saw even more sacks of supplies. "Must have been Smith. He got us bacon, biscuits—" She paused and sneered when she opened the last sack. "And more beans."

It took little time to find the spade, dig out a small pit, and gather enough brush as tinder to light a fire. Wood was needed. A cluster of trees lined a small creek less than a hundred feet away. While Jody sat with hat off, pointing his face into the sun, Les went to the trees. Cottonwood seed drifted in the air like snow. Locusts buzzed their mating calls. As expected, numerous twigs and small branches were strewn along the ground and near the bank of the creek. She collected an armful of firewood. Although more was needed to boil coffee, she faced about with plans to return. The locusts stopped buzzing.

A palm slapped across her mouth. She dropped the wood. The strong arm wrapped around her throat. Her breathing stopped. The firm grasp kept her from escape. The click of gun metal popped in her ear.

"Listen to me, boy. Just do what I say, and you'll live through this. Hear?"

The man's low evil voice sent her heart pounding through her chest. All she knew to do was nod.

"Now. We're going to go to your friend. Show him that

if he don't do what I want, then I'm going to kill you and
him. So, you don't try nothing foolish or I'll have to go
back on my promise."

A shove in the back forced her to walk from the cover
of the trees. With her eyes wide, she saw Jody still lying on
the ground, his hat propped over his face. The palm over
her mouth didn't allow for even a peep to warn him. Faced
with the threat of the unseen pistol, she didn't dare provoke
the man to use it. She was marched through the grass to the
cooking irons.

Jody stirred with his hat still over his face. "Hurry up
and get the coffee on the fire, Les."

"Sounds good," came from the voice behind her. Jody
popped off his hat. He reached for the revolver in his belt,
but he froze when the gun barrel was pointed at arm's
length at him. "Can I have some?" The voice paused.
"Hello, Jody Barnes." Les was pushed to the ground. She
faced around to see two men of similar build and both
wearing coats.

"What do you want?" Jody said with a lump in his
throat.

"Seems to me we have a score to settle with Mr. Jody
Barnes. Ain't that right, Eli?"

"You right, brother," said the other.

The man holding the pistol continued. "Where are your
friends? Particularly, that gambler worth all that money?"

Jody glowered at them with gritted teeth, but he didn't
speak. "He's dead," Les blurted out, turning all faces to
her. "Killed in a saloon in Fort Worth. A man called Colton
Schuyler shot him. They're both dead."

"Is that a fact," Eli said. "You wouldn't be lying to us,
would you, boy?"

"It ain't a lie," said Jody. Les faced him with surprise. "I
seen the bodies myself."

"You hush up, Jody Barnes," the gun-toter ordered. "You
stole from us, and I plan on teaching you a lesson for it."

"I wasn't going to let you kill a man."

"It weren't up to you." The man lurched forward, prod-

ding the muzzle at Jody's forehead while taking the revolver from Jody's belt. "We had a deal. And you broke it.
Now, it appears we're owed something for our trouble." He
stood straight and looked at the remuda. "Them horses will
do for a start."

Jody started to stand, but stopped once the pistol stared
him in the eye. "Them ain't our horses. They belong to Mr.
J.S. Cooper. You take them, and he'll send a hundred men
after you with a rope."

"I ain't fearing no Mr. J.S. Cooper. Not on this day." He
looked at his brother, then again aimed the pistol at Jody
and cocked the hammer. "You betrayed us, Jody Barnes.
The sentence is death."

Les's eyes widened as she watched the man's finger on
the trigger. "Wait!" All the men turned to her. "If I tell you
where a heap of gold is hid, you have to swear not to kill
him. Or me neither."

The brothers again looked at each other. Les expected
doubtful laughter, but instead they each arched a brow.
"What do you know about a heap of gold?"

She glanced at Jody, who also appeared bewildered.
Frightened, she realized the only story she had to tell was
the truth. "When I was in Abilene a man named Sandy
Wallace told me about gold that he hid. It belonged to the
South, and he told me he and some others hid it in a place
called the House of Ramon."

"You know of Sandy Wallace?" asked Eli.

"He was hung in Abilene. He told me this story for a
glass of whiskey on the day he got hung."

The brothers eyed each other once. "Sounds like something Sandy would do. He tell you about us? Or a man
named Marcus Broussard?"

She shook her head. "He never said no names. You knew
him?" Les asked, remembering Sandy's warning that other
men knew of the gold and might kill her if she knew of it
too. She closed her eyes thinking these might be those men.

"Everybody around here knows that tale. It ain't true.
Sandy Wallace is a liar."

Les opened her eyes in relief.

"He'd do anything for a drink. I'm surprised he didn't tell you he was President of the Confederacy for a whole bottle of rye." The man holding the gun again turned his attention to Jody. "Now it's time to settle up and be on our way."

"You promised not to shoot him. I told you about the gold."

"I made no such promise. And there ain't no gold. Not if Sandy Wallace swore to it. It'd be like a preacher telling you there *weren't* gold there. You have to take it the other way."

"Then take the horses and leave us be." Jody appeared shocked she'd offered the remuda. "They ain't worth your life."

The brothers stood shoulder to shoulder, the one holding the pistol continuing to tighten and loosen his grip on the butt, as if he was deciding whether to shoot.

"We can't just leave you here," said Eli. "You'd run off and tell the law. Ain't that right, Levi?"

Levi paused, then looked at his brother. "No. There is a way." He waved the pistol at Les and Jody. "Shed them clothes."

"What?" Jody asked.

"You heard me. Get down to your bare skin. I'd think it'd take you quite a time before any folks around here would trust a couple of naked trail hands near their house."

Eli hooted. "At least long enough to tell them about us."

"I ain't doing it," Jody said defiantly. "I just bought this shirt."

Levi aimed the gun at Jody's nose. "You ain't got no choice. Not one that lets you live."

Reluctantly, Jody unbuttoned his shirt. Levi turned the gun at Les. "You too."

She shook worse from the threat of revealing her secret than from the gun aimed at her. The long journey came to mind. All the days of hiding her shape from prying eyes would end. She had come too far. She peeked at Jody. He

had his shirt off and had unbuckled his pants. Her breath
was choked. Tears welled in her eyes. It wasn't fear. It was
the loss of pride. "I can't do it."

"The hell you can't, boy. Get them off."

"No."

Eli lunged at her. "Don't sass me, you sniveling kid."
His hands pawed at her coat. She slapped them away, then
slapped his face. Eli backhanded her chin. The blow
knocked off the hat and put her on her back. Eli, crazed by
her defiance, quickly threaded the coat buttons free. Still
dazed, Les couldn't stop him. He stripped the coat from
her arms, then paused.

"I'll be damned." He ripped open her shirt. "This one's
got tits!"

Les lay huddled on her side. She closed her eyes, sob-
bing at the terror of the attack, the humiliation of the brothers' laughter, and the knowledge that now everyone knew.

"Hell, Mr. Jody Barnes," she heard Levi say. "You've
been traveling with a damn split-tail."

The loud guffaws pounded her ears. She peeked at Jody.
There he sat, arms on bare knees staring at her with mouth
open, eyes wide, and brow raised. She closed her eyes
again. Now, she wished she had let Levi shoot her.

"Come on. Let's have a look at the rest of you." Eli slid
the oversize boots from her feet and tugged at the trousers.
Les grabbed the waist, but Eli's strength and excited fury
was greater. More laughter had her curl her legs and fold
her arms. The sun's heat and slight breeze reached every
part of her body.

"Leave him alone," Jody shouted. "I mean her—it."

His words stabbed her worse than the brothers' chortles.

"Quit your crying."

Les wiped away the tears from her eyes. Eli leered at
her and unbuckled his belt. "She don't look like she's ever
been poked. I might need to show her what makes a man
and dip into some fresh honey while I'm at it."

Jody rose, even with Levi's gun jabbed at his chest.
"You touch her and I'll kill you."

"I might just kill you now," Levi growled.

"Then do it. If you got the guts to force yourself on women—a girl, then you should have the guts to shoot me. I ain't wearing a gun. Hell, I ain't even wearing pants. Should be easy for you."

Levi scowled. Les shivered and choked back more tears, terrified that the next instant she'd watch Jody's murder. Levi took a step back while Eli dropped his trousers, showing the red long handles.

"Pull up your drawers," said Levi.

"But what about her?"

"We ain't got the time. Now, pull up your drawers and let's get these ponies out of here." Slowly, Eli complied. The brothers scooped up the loose clothing and started walking to their horses. Then Levi took three steps back. "I'm going to let you live. This time. I see either one of you again, or hear of you bringing any law down on us, and I'll cut your throat while you're sleeping. Hear?" With slow steps at first, he soon ran to join his brother and mount his horse. Whistles and hollers scampered the remuda, including the paint and mules, to the southwest.

Jody fell back to the ground, staring at her, taking heavy breaths, his brow furrowed. "Who are you?"

Les swallowed hard so she could steady her quivering chin and answer. "I'm Les, Jody."

"No, you're not. Les is a know-nothing kid. A boy. A boy who wanted to come to Texas to be a drover."

She shook her head. "It's still me, Jody. Only I never came here to be a drover. At least not at first."

"What? You mean for this gold you've told them about? Or was that just another lie? Or were you lying to me and Smith all this time?" He said, his voice growing louder and angry. "Like you lied about being a boy!"

His tone yanked at her heart, pulled her breath, squeezing her tears, but she was determined not to cry. She didn't let herself cry when everyone thought she was a boy. "Jody, please don't be mad—mad at me. It was something I thought I could do. I didn't mean to hurt anybody. No one thought I'd come this far. And maybe I didn't neither. I didn't do it just to fool people. I did it because I thought it would get me what I want."

"And what that be?"

She calmed her chest enough to speak. "A girl always dreams about living in pretty places—"

"Don't call yourself that," he yelled, then turned his head. "Cover yourself up. I can't even look at you."

She crawled backward in the high grass and sank her head to the ground so he couldn't see her. It was all she could do to muffle her breath. Many times during the trip she'd wished for a hole to crawl into and find her way back into her bed. Now she prayed for one.

The breeze kept waving the weeds. It was the only sound she heard for the minutes that dragged into hours.

Ear to the ground, she stirred to the pounding beat of hooves. Her heart skipped at the thought that the brothers had returned to kill them after all. Gradually, she raised her head above the swaying stems. Two riders approached over the rise. When she saw who they were, she was able to breathe deeply, until a second thought reminded her that Smith would learn her secret.

Both he and Rance, his left arm in a sling, rode in a direct line with the still-standing cooking spit. They reined in and looked about. Les didn't have the courage to yell to them. She thought Jody would, but it took Smith's cautious call and the drawing of his revolver to get Jody to reveal himself.

"Don't shoot, Smith," Jody said, but he did not stand.

"What are you doing in the grass?"

A long pause followed. "I ain't got my clothes."

"So? Put them on. Where are the horses?"

"I'm trying to tell you that. They were stole. Two rustlers bushwhacked us. Stole the horses and our clothes in a deal not to leave us dead. A gunshot might bring them back."

"Well, come on out of there. I don't want to be talking to a bunch of weeds." Smith's irritated tone brought Jody in

view with his hands crossed below his waist. "Where's
Les?"

Another long pause followed. She needed to make her
whereabouts known, but she wasn't going to stand. She had
more to cover than Jody. "I'm over here."

"Well, stand up, son. I don't have time for shyness."

"He ain't no boy, Smith," said Jody with twinge of
disgust.

"What are you talking about?"

Rance cracked a smile at Smith's confusion and turned
his head.

"He's a girl. I mean he ain't—Les is a girl."

The pause became strained silence. Between the tall
yellowing stalks, Les watched the old wrangler drop his
jaw with the same disbelief as Jody before. His head appeared as a lidded pot on the boil about to burst. "I'm sorry,
Smith. I meant no harm," she said hoping to ease that pot
off the fire. Yet she shivered on the ground and waited for
his tirade.

However, his voice spoke in a calm tone. "I knew there
was something wrong with that boy." He chuckled once.
"Damn, I must be getting old. You ain't got no clothes, do
you?"

"No, sir."

Smith untied his bedroll and let it unfurl to the ground.
"There's a slicker in there. I suppose that will cover most
of your nakedness. Jody, once Les has his—*her* pick, there
are a pair of britches I ain't worn yet." He turned his horse
about. It took Rance, now with a saddle and bit on the red
dun, more than a moment to copy the move, and they both
rode to the other side of the rise.

# 30

STRADDLED ACROSS THE dun's rump as it walked through the grassy prairie, wearing Rance's coat and Smith's slicker belted around her hips, Les steadied her balance with a hold of Rance's waist. "Remember, you promised not to turn around."

"I'm a man of my word."

"Since when?" Surprised at her own remark, she was suddenly worried by his lack of response. "I'm sorry. I ain't myself."

"No harm done. I can understand what you must have went through. I can't say how I would have dealt with that. I admire your courage, Les."

Now she was really surprised, and a bit embarrassed at the praise. "Thanks. I guess."

"From what I observed, Jody didn't take the discovery well?"

She scoffed. "No. He didn't. He hates me."

"I think that's a strong assumption. Only natural for a man, or woman, to take certain things for granted. Speaking only as a man, I admit that when men share a long enough time together, a bond emerges, even when they don't realize it."

Normally bored by Rance's long-winded words, she found herself hanging on each one the more sense he made. He angled his head to the side.

"I think Jody thought of you as a younger brother in a way. And when he found out he had a sister instead, well, I believe it must have hit him hard. Only in the fact that he felt a fool for not noticing. I have to say, you hid your, well, the, your . . . *identity* very well. I think his pride is a little hurt, that's all. I don't think he hates you. But it might take some time for him to realize that himself."

"Is that why he and Smith rode on ahead and haven't been seen for an hour?" She didn't expect an answer. She knew the reason.

"Smith's horse is a little stouter than this one. I suspect it carries two men better and faster."

"There ain't two *men* on this one, remember?"

He paused and huffed a single chuckle. "Why, Les, do I sense a hint of shame? Do you wish you were really a man?"

The question stuck in her mind. It wasn't a matter she'd ever thought about, yet if she had been one, all the troubles she now faced would disappear. Upon more pondering, she shook the fool notion out of her head.

Despite not ever being concerned with how curled her hair was for Sunday service, the unique pattern to her dress, or how many beaus were asking to sit on the swing with her after the noon dinner, she was a girl, a female, a young woman. One that had traveled over five hundred miles of *the worst ground God ever made*. For nearly three weeks, she slept on the ground, rode her rear raw in a saddle, tended to stubborn mules, built fires, and ate the same rotten beans every night. A boy would have had to do the same, but not with a heavy coat buttoned to the top, much less having to find his way in the woods, alone, day or night to tend to nature's call and not be noticed.

"No. That ain't what I meant. I just wish we had a stouter, faster horse is all." When he laughed aloud, she did too. The hole in the pit of her gut wasn't as deep. It turned her mind in a different direction. "Hey, why did you shoot that fellow back in Fort Worth?"

"Oh," Rance said with a casual tone. "He was trying to kill me."

"Kill you? For what?"

"Well, see, there was this woman." He stopped as if the truth were stuck in his throat.

"Ah-huh."

"Well," he continued, "she and I found ourselves in the midst of intimate relations. I really shouldn't be telling a young girl about this."

"And she had a man, didn't she?"

"Worse. She had a husband. An old husband. An old rich husband. So, he took it personally, even though it was his dear wife's desire for . . . attention."

"And that was the husband you shot?"

"Him? No. He was an assassin. A hired gun, sent to kill me and be paid by that rich old husband. Be glad you aren't a man, Les. Their sense of pride often leads them to villainous conclusions."

She recalled some of the girls at the church socials. "Oh, I know some females who'd do the same." Again, his laughter stirred hers.

"We better hush. If some of the fine folks in this county saw me with a near-naked girl, I'm sure the local morality would put me at the end of a rope." With his attention turned to the west, he pulled the dun to a stop. "I hope my eyes aren't deceiving me, but that appears to be Smith and Jody riding this way."

She focused on the single horse with two riders. The distant figures soon became those of her friends. Rance steered the dun in their direction, and they met under the shade of a tall cottonwood. "I was beginning to think we may have lost you," Rance said, to Les's surprise. She held her tongue.

Jody, wearing a white shirt and better-fitting trousers without suspenders, slid off the mount. Smith soon followed. "We found a farm about five miles south. The wife was willing to sell us some clothes." He paused to peek at

Les. "She felt it her Christian duty once I told her we'd found a lost girl."

His softer-than-usual voice amazed her more than the gesture of finding her clothes. He held out the folded bundle, and turned his head. "Here. I thought the dress would fit you. The woman sent the things for you that you're to wear under it." Les took the folded bundle and grunted to direct all the men's attention in the opposite direction. When she didn't see any eyes her way, she slid off the dun's rump and went to the other side of the thick tree trunk. One last glance showed them looking to the east.

She unbuckled the belt to let the slicker fall to the dirt. Quickly, she threaded Rance's coat button free. Faster than at any time, she stepped into the pantaloons, tied them to her waist, and pulled the chemise over her top. The deep blue dress with white spots easily fit her small shoulders. She straightened the lace collar. Once sure all her areas were covered, she stepped around the trunk, presenting herself as a lady for the first time in three weeks.

Rance removed his hat at the sight of her. Smith tipped his. Jody, without a hat, still wore a wary expression. "Les," Rance said while eyeing her head to bare feet, "you make a much better-looking girl than boy." Too embarrassed to thank him, she noticed a different gleam in Smith's eye. It seemed he also was caught in need of words that didn't come naturally.

Finally, the silence boiled up from her chest into her throat. "I'm still the same person."

"You try to remember that," said Smith, facing about and heading to his horse. "We'll see how well you ride with that dress when we catch up to those horses."

"You're going after them?"

Smith cocked his head to the side with a mild snicker. "Well, I don't reckon Mr. Cooper is going to think much of us showing up without them with a story they were stole by a pair of rustlers. Likely is, he'll reckon we had a hand in it."

Les stood amazed, and her feeling was shared by

Rance. Jody appeared aware of the plan. "So, you know where they went," she said.

Smith faced her. "Jody was telling me you told them something about some gold hid somewhere?"

She sank her head for an instant. "I don't take no pride in it. But yeah. I told them about some."

"Gold?" Rance blurted out. Smith gave him a sign to be quiet, then motioned at Les to continue.

She inhaled a deep breath and recounted the story. "I snuck into the jail the day Sandy Wallace hanged. He told me he would tell me about some hidden gold in Texas for a sip of whiskey. So, I got him some and he told me."

Rance scoffed. "Texas gold? I've been hearing about gold deposits in every corner of the West except here. Most of the people with knowledge of such things tell me the state is barren of the precious ore."

"It weren't mined gold." She looked at Smith. "It was gold snuck here for the Confederacy. To start a new government in Mexico. Is only they got caught, and Sandy Wallace said there were others that knew. I thought them pair of brothers might be those others, but they said it was a lie."

"So you believed them?" asked Smith. "The same pair that said they'd kill you?" He shook his head. "So, where did you tell them it was hid?"

Les swallowed hard. "A place Sandy called the House of Ramon." Smith nodded. "Do you know where it is?"

"There's an old Spanish mission probably not more than fifty miles from here. Mission San Ramon de Bosque, it sits about a mile off the Bosque River. The legend is it was a Spanish mission built over a hundred years ago to reinforce the trade routes east. It was abandoned after everyone in it were wiped out by Comanches. It's just a sod and clay building that ain't all crumpled to the ground yet."

"So now you believe them?" asked Rance. "That Rebels hid treasure in the place?"

Smith shrugged. "There's a lot of stories like that around. Can't say any of them are true." He gazed at the open prairie.

"Since the war, it's hard to know what's true. A lot of folks in this state have lost near everything. Reconstruction duties on cotton have forced most people off their land. Ain't nothing else to farm to pay the taxes on the land, much less raise their kids." He grinned at Jody. "When I got home, there weren't no jobs, except those to drive cattle. And there was plenty of beeves to drive. I heard it said there were more longhorns scattered in the hills of South Texas than there were prairie dogs on the northern plains." He then looked at Rance. "That's what brought money back in this state. That's the real Texas gold."

Again, he stared blankly out to the field. After a moment, he took the reins of his horse. "It'll take the rest of the day and most of the night to get there riding double." He climbed into the saddle. He held a hand out for Jody, who hesitated only a moment, then took the hand to mount the back of the horse.

"I can't expect you to come along," Smith said to Rance. "There'll likely be shooting. Don't know how it'll come out." He pointed at the dun. "I wouldn't let you keep the horse for your own business. But if you get her to a safe place, then I'd say you earned the right to keep it."

Rance peeked at Les, then nodded at Smith. "I'll do it."

Les stood confused. "I thought I was going with you," she told Smith.

"I was just funning. I can't have no female around where there's likely to be shooting."

Smith's tone burned in her gut. After only a moment's thought, the fire in her burned from her tongue. "To hell with that. I was a female when you had me hold that pistol on those fellows in the White Elephant. And I've been one for every dirty job you sent me to do. I'm going with you, Smith." Smith looked at Rance, who then looked at Les. He slumped his shoulders, relenting.

"All right. Get on the horse."

# 31

THE LONG NIGHT on the dun's rump kept rocking Les to sleep. Frequently during the trip, she leaned her sweaty head against Rance's back, readjusting her position to find a dry spot and stay on the animal.

"There it is."

Smith's words brought Les to her senses quicker than a water splash to the face. She popped her head up. A half mile away past rolling hills, a small building stood in the center of a clutch of trees. She squinted to focus on her surroundings. The sun was perched well into the eastern sky, shining brightly on the grassy plain. Jody stood next to Smith's horse just a few feet ahead of the dun. The old wrangler drew the repeating rifle from the scabbard.

"This is as close as we can get on horseback." He removed from his belt the short-barreled revolver he'd taken from the dead gambler and gave it to Jody. "You use this. I'll take the yellow boy and we'll flank them to the north and west."

"What is our part?" asked Rance.

Smith angled his scowl over his shoulder. "You load that peashooter?"

Rance glanced at the sling on his arm. "I'm sorry. I was distracted when I last fired it."

"No matter. That damn thing couldn't hit anything beyond ten feet." Smith drew the revolver from his hip holster. "One shot from this .44 will feel like all six from that pepperbox."

Rance took the pistol. "I'm used to it. Remember?"

"Yeah. But after the first one, you got five more just like it with this weapon. Try to stay on your feet." He turned back to Jody.

"What about me?" asked Les.

He faced about slowly. "You stay out of the line of fire. Just hold the horses."

"That's all? I can't do more?"

"Like get shot?" Smith shook his head and pointed at the ground. "You stay here."

"And what are you going to do?" she asked defiantly.

Smith glared, but replaced it with a smirk. "I'm fixing to settle a feud I should have settled a long time before."

Rance slid off the dun, easing his arm from the sling to slide his right arm through the coat sleeve and hike the other side over his shoulder. Once the left arm was suspended by the sling again, all three men marched toward the mission.

Les slid off the dun and took the reins of both mounts. As she watched, she couldn't help feeling the urge to follow. As before with Jody chasing gunshots, she figured that after allowing them a few minutes' start, she could trail just enough behind to watch and maybe help.

Convinced her plan was sound, she started forward when the men entered the surrounding woods. In a short time, she found a small mesquite bush and tethered the reins to its snarled limbs. Like a child on Christmas morning, she lifted the hem on the dress and scampered closer to the trees, stopping to crouch every ten feet. Once confident she'd not been noticed, she crept nearer.

At the edge of the cluster, she bobbed her head to see

Smith, rifle in one hand, sidestep to the cover of several trunks. She couldn't see Rance, but Jody nestled behind a long log to face the arched front of the dilapidated structure. The crumbling white walls stood at jagged levels like a broken bottle. Old wooden double doors sat off the metal hinges to lean against the opposite sides of the arch, leaving a foot-wide gap between them. Since there was no glint of sunlight inside, the roof must have been in place.

Muffled shouts forced her to the next tree so she could hear.

"That you, Jody Barnes?"

Jody glanced at Smith, who nodded.

"I come for what you stole."

"That's the thanks I get to let you live? Now, I have to kill you for sure. Who is out there with you?"

As Jody again looked at Smith, he saw Les and waved her back. "Just me and that fool girl."

She put her shoulder to the small trunk, but couldn't keep from watching, and edged her head enough to see.

"You want them horses? Come and get them and be on your way."

Jody once more looked to his right, but when Les peered the same way, she didn't see Smith. A long silence made her think that since the brothers had kept their word about not killing them, he might be sincere about allowing the horses to be taken.

Wood splintered above her. Pulp splattered her face. The ripple of a gunshot echoed through the trees. A plume of smoke drifted through the gap in the doors.

She slammed her back against the small trunk, but it wasn't wide enough to hide her body. In panic, she fell onto her belly and crawled next to Jody. "What are you doing here?" he asked with hushed excitement. "Get back to where Smith told you."

"I can't. I almost got shot where I was. If I go further back, I'll be shot for sure."

"Well, keep your head down." He raised up enough to shoot a single shot at the doors, then returned behind the log.

"Where's Smith?"

"I don't know. He's probably gone around back to sneak up behind them."

"What about Rance?"

"How should I know? He likely turned tail with that shot."

She looked to the left and right, and neither Smith nor Rance were in sight. Then another absence piqued her attention. "Where's the remuda?"

After a pause with a confused face, Jody looked at her. "I don't know. They got to be on the other side."

Sensing a need, she crawled backward. "I'm going to find them. Maybe I can get them without anyone getting killed."

Jody stuck his head up in surprise. "You stay away from there before *you* get killed."

A blast tore a chunk out of the log. Jody shrank behind it. Les hurried her crawl even more, like a turtle seeking the shelter of water. She passed the trunk with the bullet hole, and continued until she got beyond the last tree. Still cautious, she darted from tree to tree, circling to the west of the mission. Slowly she came to its side.

Shattered blocks of masonry littered the length from the front to the rear. No windows were cut into the walls, so the further she got, the faster she scurried. Another volley of shots shook the air, forcing her to stumble. Fear of bullets flying near got Les to her feet and around the rear edge of the old church.

Between the trees, she spotted the horses corralled by two parallel ropes bound from tree to tree to form a square. More gunshot blasts made them jittery. All that was needed was to cut the ropes and the whole herd would run free. She was sure of it.

Gradually, Les neared the horses and by doing so, also walked near the back of the mission. The urge to be quick overwhelmed her caution, and she ran to the ropes. Without a knife, she had to untie the knot looped around a massive tree trunk. Her fingers fumbled with the taut-wound hemp, frustrating her and making her groan. Unable to budge the knot, she pulled at it, only increasing the tension on the rope and her nerves. Finally, she stepped on the bottom rope and pushed up on the top one. The width was only barely enough for herself to squeeze through. She looked to the far end of the rope, about to run to there, when her head snapped back with a yank of her hair. A muzzle prodded her ear.

"What are you trying, girl?" She saw Eli from the corner of her eye. "Come back 'cause you missed me? Want me to finish my business with you? I will when all this over." He pulled her by the hair into the mission. Every attempt to escape his grasp only intensified his tug. Although she knew worse pain waited inside, as before she couldn't overcome his strength. He shoved her through the rear doorless archway. She tumbled onto the broken floor planks, barely avoiding a pit dug in the center. Twisting around, she met his eyes as he stood in the sunlight. Distracted to the east, Eli's face fell to one of disbelief.

"You?"

Eli's chest exploded. Blood spewed out his chest and his back. The next instant he collapsed to the ground. Les scrambled to her feet, but another arm wrapped around her throat and dragged her further to the front.

"Did you kill my brother?"

Unable to speak, she shook her head while trying to keep her feet, but Levi pulled her to the floor. A gun barrel poked at her temple.

"I've got the girl! If you want the horses, take them now! Anyone I see come in here, I put a bullet in her brain!"

Les looked to the rear entrance. Only Eli's body and the horses were in view. The long silence outside made her afraid she'd been abandoned. She closed her eyes, assuring herself that Jody, Smith, even Rance would not leave her behind.

"Sons of bitches are trying to rush me!" Levi shouted. The barrel's prod vanished. A gunshot rang in her ears. The stench of gunpowder stung her nose. She craned her neck to see to the right. A bullet pierced one front door as another shot outside echoed. Levi returned fire. So near the percussion, she covered her ears. Her motion brought the gun muzzle back her way. She pushed it aside, putting it inches off the floor when Levi squeezed the trigger.

Sparks and smoke covered the planks. She turned her head in order to breathe. Levi coughed. The white plume rose, but didn't fade. Another glance through the thick smoke showed the bullet hole and the glowing embers on the rotted wood.

Levi shoved her away and stood. On her back, she stared at him while the barrel was aimed at her. She screamed and squinted her eyes shut. A loud click of the hammer falling on a spent cartridge opened them. He stood staring at the pistol. Les jumped to her feet, but a punch to the jaw spilled her again.

Dazed, she watched a small flame pop up from the embers, growing larger every second, igniting dead brush like tinder, spreading to another plank. Levi ejected the empty shells and shoved three bullets into the cylinder. The flame behind licked at his trousers.

Instantly, he jumped and shook his legs with his trousers ablaze. The more he kicked, the more the flames climbed up his clothes. The floor flared up, sending flames to the ceiling. With cries of agony, Levi charged through the double doors. Smoke choked Les's throat. While coughing, she heard one gunshot followed by another, then five more in rapid succession.

Her eyes teared. She inhaled the hot smoke, then coughed and convulsed, strangled by the gray cloud. Her mind swirled, dizzied by the lack of air. The hem of her dress ignited, but she had no strength to fight it. Wood shattering brought her attention toward the front. Rance leaped through the flames, his coat covering his head. He bent on one knee and smothered her hem with the coat. As if he was fighting a monster, he then swung it side to side, swatting the fire back until the coat also began burning. When he began coughing, he released the coat and with his one good arm, clutched her next to his ribs and stampeded through the flames and out the front archway.

They both collapsed, hacking out smoke and sucking in life. After several heavy breaths, she was able to regain her senses. Jody knelt by her side with a canteen. He poured water to douse small embers on the dress, and splashed it on her face and mouth. She gladly gulped it down, cooling her insides.

"You all right?" he asked in a panicked voice.

Les only nodded, unable to speak. She peeked at Rance, who lay on his back, spitting out the last of the smoke. A loud aching groan brought all attention to the fire-engulfed mission. Black smoke clouds billowed into the sky. A dense haze hung overhead and the radiance heated her face, but she was alive. She closed her eyes for a small simple prayer.

Through the swirl, she saw Levi's corpse facedown in the dirt. A few yards away, Smith lay propped against one of the masonry blocks. "Oh, no."

Her alarm turned Jody's attention. Rance looked in the same direction. Despite having been nearly roasted alive, she rose to her feet, as did the men, and all three ran to their friend.

Blood seeped through the fingers of Smith's right hand, which covered his belly. His eyes were glassy and a smile creased his lips. "I see you made it."

Jody knelt by his side. "I didn't know you got shot."

"Didn't know myself until I saw them come out of there."

"Let me have a look." Gradually lifting the hand, Jody saw that the red hole oozed blood over the checkered shirt. "Les, find something to make a bandage." She lifted the hem to rip the seam from her pantaloons and handed the cloth to Jody.

Smith shook his head. "Won't help." He closed his eyes. Pain seized his face. His clenched jaw eased to a slight smile of delight as he muttered, "Deborah." He blinked twice, finally opening his eyes.

"Be quiet, Smith." Jody stuffed the cloth in the bloody hole.

The old wrangler stared into Les's eyes. A fond smile creased his quivering lips before he pointed at Rance. "See to her. She's just a kid." His voice was breathy and strained. "Not a bad cowboy. For a girl."

"I will, old man," Rance answered. "Now, you take it easy and you'll be good as new."

"Who are you calling old, you snake." He grinned only a moment, then coughed blood. A red trickle trailed down his trembling chin. When he was able to take breath, he pointed in a direction behind Rance. "She's over there." He sucked in another breath. "Find her. Put me next to her."

Only taking a glance at the spot, Jody leaned closer to him. "Who is, Smith? Tell me. I don't understand. Who's there?"

He shook his head. "I don't have enough wind." The blood flow from his mouth increased. His throat choked as he took the revolver from Rance's hand, cocked the hammer, and fired where he'd first pointed. The bullet popped dirt under the shade of trees. He fired once more, striking what Les saw as a headstone.

"What are you telling us, Smith?"

He didn't answer. Instead, he gazed at Jody with the same fond expression. His eyes darted to Les, still with the smile. The pain forced him to wince, but when it passed, he swallowed hard, and winked. His jaw relaxed, his eyelids slid half closed. A hiss came through his lips.

"Smith?" Jody asked. "Smith!"

Rance exhaled long and loud. "He's gone."

Jody's shoulders sagged and he bowed his head, his jaw sunk to his chest. Tears welled in Les's eyes. Her chin quivered. The old man she'd first thought the meanest cuss in the world was the only man in her life to show her true affection.

"What do we do now?"

Upon Jody's question, Rance faced about. "I think he was trying to tell us something."

Jody and Rance slowly approached the grave. The first shot had dug a small hole in the grass with the dirt peppered on top. Both men looked to each other, then at the name on the marker. "Are you thinking what I'm thinking?"

Rance nodded. "Well, better get busy digging."

"Just like that? We ain't going to even take the time to pray over the dead?"

Rance rolled his brow. "You want to pray over him before we get him in the ground? You think that would be the right thing to do?"

Jody hesitated. "Well, I think it would be the Christian thing to do."

"The Christian thing is to honor what that man died for and to get him next to his maker as quick as we can. What that includes is digging a grave where he was showing us to dig." He looked to the sun. "We don't have long to do just that."

After Les and Jody found the mules among the scattered remuda, they retrieved the spade from the pack. Jody went to his saddled horse and opened his saddlebag. He palmed an object from it, stuffed it in his pocket, then he and Les returned to the graveside.

With Rance's arm still in a sling, it was Jody who dug at the grave. "I still ain't sure this is the right thing to do."

Les wasn't sure as to the reason, but she knew the grave meant something to the old wrangler. "I think this is what he wanted."

While Jody dug, Rance kicked and pulled the thick growth a few feet to the side of the grave. "I think I found something here." Les joined him. They both stared at another headstone emerging from the weeds. They all read the marker in silence.

"Maybe that's why?"

"Do you think she belonged to him?" Les asked.

Rance looked to her. "I suspect so." He took the spade from the sweaty Jody and dug some of the hole himself.

The afternoon passed, Rance slapping at the dirt with one hand, and Jody complaining that more dirt was falling in the hole than was coming out. Almost two hours after they started, a hollow boom thudded with one of Jody's thrusts. All of them stood stunned for a moment, then all clawed with bare hands. With most of the dirt on top removed, they recognized a wooden coffin.

Rance again peered at her. "Do you think that's it? Or are we about to disturb the dead?"

She shrugged, her heart pounding as it had so many times during the trip. The story she'd chased for hundreds of miles seemed true, and with a few hard tugs, was unearthed and at her feet.

Jody looked to the sky. "Lord, forgive us for what we're about to do."

They jabbed the shovel under the lid and pried until it creaked open. She took a deep breath and closed her eyes.

"I can't look. Tell me what you find."

She heard more fumbling with the lid, but soon she heard the crackling snap of the lid being fully raised. Neither of them said a word for almost a minute. Then Rance laughed. "It's money!"

Les squinted open one eye. "Money?"

He grabbed a stack of wrapped bills. "Confederate money. Worthless Rebel script."

She opened both eyes. "What?"

Jody spoke in disbelief. "This must have been what they hid."

"Worthless money?" she asked.

Despite his chuckles, Rance found breath to speak. "They must have brought it all this way thinking they were transporting real gold. But all that they had was gold certificates backed by nothing but the honor of the South. And nothing else."

Les's heart slowed. She sighed. All her expectations

about this trip had been off the mark, so it was only fitting that this too would end up disappointing her. She looked at Smith's body. "You suppose he knew?"

"I think so," answered Rance. "After all, didn't he say the only real gold in Texas was cattle?" He smirked. "Then again, maybe he returned here to bury his wife, and take what was really in there?" They all stared at the woman's grave, then back at each other. All of them shook their heads.

It was several minutes before Jody jumped back in the hole. Daylight ebbed into dusk by the time the grave was fully dug. With solemn grace, the three took the old man they knew as Smith to the spot where he'd pointed as a last request. After removing the gun belt, hat, and boots, they lowered the body into the now-empty coffin and then it into the ground. All three filled in the dirt. Les fought back tears once more.

"Something ought be said." Jody peered at Rance. "You claimed to be a preacher."

Rance removed his hat, grunted his throat clear, and inhaled a deep wind. "Lord, we give you the soul of Captain Marcus Andrew Broussard, Second Dragoons, Fourth Texas Brigade. May he join his lost comrades and his wife, Deborah. We hope you'll accept our friend in your heavenly bounds. And forgive him all the sins he may and likely did commit during his time on Earth. He's not such a bad gentleman once you get to know him. Amen."

Jody drew the harmonica from his pocket and blew the tune that the gruff old man liked to hear during the trip to Texas.

Once he finished his serenade salute, Jody faced about.

Rance put on his hat and turned to Les. She smiled at him. "You're not a bad preacher for a no-account gambler." They all grinned as they walked to the remuda. "So, where are you headed, now?"

Rance glanced at the smoldering mission. "Well, since I let a fortune in greenbacks go up in smoke with my coat while saving your scrawny life, I guess I need to find me another place to ply my trade and seek my success. Maybe open up my own establishment one day. How about you, Les? Going back to Abilene?"

"Maybe. One day." She avoided Levi Curry's body. "What about him and his brother?"

Rance casually suggested, "We'll tell the local county sheriff two bandits attempted to rob us here while we buried our friend." He glanced back at Smith's grave. "They don't ever have to know." He paused only a moment. "Where is it you said you were from, Jody?"

"My folks, they have a small spread in the hill country."

"Didn't you say you joined the cattle drive there?"

"Yup. It's where I first met Mr. Frank J. Pearl. And it's where I met Smith. I think he had a place of his own down there."

Rance hesitated before taking his next step. "Really? And just where might this place be?"

"Just west of San Antone."

The gambler stopped walking completely and rubbed his chin. "San Antone, you say?" He glanced back one more time at Smith's grave, faced about, and nodded. His bright smile flashed once more across his mouth. "You mind if I come along?"

Spur Award-Winning Author

# Jory Sherman

## Sunset Rider

After Johnny Stagg shoots down the men
who killed his father, he must ride into
the setting sun to escape the angry
outlaws who want revenge.

"JORY SHERMAN IS A NATIONAL TREASURE."
—LOREN D. ESTLEMAN

"ONE OF THE PREMIERE STORYTELLERS
OF THE AMERICAN WEST."
—DON COLDSMITH

0-425-18552-4

Available wherever books are sold or at
www.penguin.com

EDITED BY
## ROBERT J. RANDISI

# WHITE HATS

BUFFALO BILL CODY, BAT MASTERSON,
AND OTHER LEGENDARY HEROIC FIGURES OF
AMERICA'S OLD WEST GET THE ROYAL
TREATMENT IN 16 STORIES FROM ESTEEMED
WESTERN AUTHORS.

0-425-18426-9

# BLACK HATS

A WESTERN ANTHOLOGY THAT INCLUDES TALES
OF BUTCH CASSIDY, NED CHRISTIE, SAM BASS
AND OTHER HISTORICAL VILLAINS FROM
THE WILD WEST.

0-425-18708-X

AVAILABLE WHEREVER BOOKS ARE SOLD OR AT
WWW.PENGUIN.COM

ATTACKED. OUTRAGED. AVENEGED.

# LYNCHED

A NOVEL OF WESTERN JUSTICE BY
## ED GORMAN

WHEN MARSHALL BEN TULLY CAME RIDING BACK INTO
TOWN, THERE WASN'T A SOUL STIRRING.
NOT THE SPRAWLED, BLOODY MAN OUTSIDE HIS DOOR.
NOT THE STRANGER STRUNG UP OUT BACK.
NOT HIS RAVAGED WIFE.

A DIRTY KIND OF JUSTICE TOOK OVER WHILE HE WAS
AWAY, BUT NOW THAT HE'S BACK, NOT A SOUL
RESPONSIBLE WILL STIR FOR MUCH LONGER.

**"Ed Gorman writes like a dream."**
—Dean Koontz

**"One of the best Western
writers of our time."**
—*Rocky Mountain News*

Available wherever books are sold or at
www.penguin.com

"MAKE ROOM ON YOUR SHELF OF FAVORITES
FOR PETER BRANVOLD."
—FRANK RODERUS

# THE DEVIL GETS HIS DUE
A LOU PROPHET NOVEL BY
# PETER BRANVOLD

On the trail with Louisa Bonaventure, "The
Vengeance Queen," bounty hunter Lou Prophet is
caught in a bloody crossfire of hatred between
an outlaw who would shoot a man dead for fun
and Louisa, who has sworn to kill him—even
if she dies trying.

"THE NEXT LOUIS L'AMOUR."
—ROSEANNE BITTNER

0-425-19454-X

B248

THE EPIC WESTERN FROM THE AUTHOR OF
*THE GUN*

# JUSTICE GUN
## LIVE BY IT. DIE BY IT.

### BY LYLE BRANDT

GUNMAN MATTHEW PRICE DID NOT THINK
HE WAS GOING TO MAKE IT OUT OF
REDEMPTION, TEXAS, ALIVE.
BUT AS HE STUMBLES OUT OF TOWN
GUT-SHOT AND DYING, HE IS RESCUED BY A
BLACK FAMILY PIONEERING THEIR WAY TO
FREEDOM. NOW, MATT MUST RETURN THE
FAVOR AND HELP THEM WHEN
TROUBLEMAKERS IN THEIR NEW SETTLEMENT
OFFER UP A NOT-SO-WARM WELCOME.

0-425-19094-3